Thank you, Michael for your love, patience and support. I could not have done this without you.

Thank you, Susie for your time and excellent advice.

F. A. ISBELL

authorHOUSE®

AuthorHouse™
1663 Liberty Drive
Bloomington, IN 47403
www.authorhouse.com
Phone: 1-800-839-8640

Published by AuthorHouse 3/1/2013

ISBN: 978-1-4817-1885-1 (sc)
ISBN: 978-1-4817-1886-8 (hc)
ISBN: 978-1-4817-1887-5 (e)

Library of Congress Control Number: 2013903160

In the time before time,
Evil darkness undefined
Ruled the world God left behind.
Now the prophecy refined,
Our destiny entwined,
With motives carefully enshrined
In destiny's future now aligned.

TABLE OF CONTENTS

Sydney Gazette, Saturday, June 16, 1986:

PIRATES OVERTAKE AND SINK THE HMAS HAWK

Previously known as the HMAS Vigilant and famous for its involvement in WWII Darwin Harbor the HMAS Hawk was attacked and sunk yesterday apparently by pirates near the Amundsen Sea off the coast of Southern Australia. The pirates took control of the famous warship 140 miles off the coast. Distress calls were made and recorded, providing evidence of the horrifying event. Just after dawn, a group of heavily armed Japanese pirates boarded the ship and began firing automatic weapons. All members of the crew, including the captain, were gunned down and thrown into the icy ocean. The small ship was looted and sunk. The pirates have not yet been apprehended.

A fine crew of sixteen brave men died yesterday trying to defend their famous ship. This ship was part of a small fleet of ships commissioned by the Australian Navy to patrol the waters around Australia.

This ship was commissioned to locate and deter illegal whaling activity, but it had a remarkable history. It is well known in this area that the HMAS Vigilant was the ship that rescued eighteen drowning soldiers in the waters off Darwin Harbor in February 1942. The brave rescue took place during the Bombing of the town of Darwin. The ship was also involved in the Battle of Timor in May of 1942 and was used to carry supplies to various ports during the end of World War II.

Chapter 1
ATTACK AND RESCUE

The ancient floating tin can of a war ship, which had been so highly honored in its prime, waited helplessly and hopelessly in the open sea, west of Australia. The usually active, noisy engine on the vintage war ship, the previous day, had given its final effort. It creaked and moaned as the near empty vessel rocked between the ocean swells in the pitch black darkness of the night. It was scheduled to be scuttled as soon as the crew could be evacuated. The Australian Navy had decided weeks before that no further repairs would be made on the refurbished whale patrol vessel after the expense of its last costly repairs.

The captain and crew had enjoyed a late evening of drinking, smoking and card playing. They referred to their little party as a wake, honoring the illustrious life of the HMAS Hawk. The old ship should have been retired in 1966 when the Australian Navy redesigned and updated it to be an axillary whale patrol vessel. The proud ship had received glory and honor in the Royal Australian Navy during The Second World War. Back then it was named the HMAS Vigilant. The ship had helped achieve an important victory in the famous battle in Darwin Harbor on February 19, 1942. In 1943 and 1944 the war ship had been used as an emergency vehicle in the Timor Sea and was credited with the rescue of countless Australian sailors and soldiers. Afterwards, and for more than forty years, the sturdy old boat had championed the cause of protecting the whales of the open seas around Australia. It had been one of the first ships requisitioned by the Australian Navy for that purpose.

The crew was sleeping peacefully in the wee hours of the morning on June 13th 1986. They were unaware of the approaching renegade Japanese pirate ship. Shortly before dawn, the ship crept up and paralleled the rusty side of the HMAS Hawk.

When a large ocean swell forced the wooden fishing vessel to bounce along the steel riveted panels a few of the sailors were startled into consciousness. The men stumbled from their tight bunks and struggled to hurriedly put on their boots and multilayered uniforms. At the time the temperature on the surface was hovering just above zero. The boat rocked from side to side and unfamiliar noises on the starboard side continued to alarm the sailors.

"Where is the Captain?" asked one of the sailors as he pulled on his thick rubber waders.

"I dunno'," another answered.

When they opened the creaking steel doorway and stepped out onto the outer deck they began to hear loud voices on the bow of the ship. They heard their captain hollering, "No, no! You can't do that! I am the captain here. This is a patrol vessel. What do you want with us?"

The angry unintelligible voices that responded were shouting in Japanese. The sailors on the starboard side of the Hawk looked at each other and froze against the icy cold steel wall. Before they could speak, a small man carrying a black machine gun rounded the corner and approached them. He pointed his weapon at the three men and shouted angry obscenities at them in Japanese. He motioned with his machine gun for the men to go forward and join their Captain.

The nervous, wild-eyed, heavily armed Japanese pirates barked their orders in harsh loud voices. They moved their hostages to the cable railing on the port side of the ship and without warning the terrible carnage began. The creeps lifted their firearms in unison and released a barrage of bullets at their captain's head! The three sailors watched as the officer's head shattered in all directions. His limp headless body then fell with a bloody splash into the freezing ocean below.

Immediately realizing his own likely fate, one of the American sailors reached quickly into the deep pocket of his jumpsuit and pulled out a small revolver. Without hesitation he pointed the gun straight

2

at the pirate with the red knitted cap and began firing. Three, four, then five bullets struck the Japanese pirate in his chest squirting blood through his thick, padded coat. He squeezed the trigger of his machine gun spraying a line of bullets across the deck as he collapsed dead on the deck. The American was hit in his shoulder and stomach. He looked down and saw blood gushing from his side, and then he fell, head first into the icy ocean still gripping his revolver tightly in his hand.

The pirates began screaming and shouting wildly. The other two Australian sailors, who had also been shot but were still alive, were then unceremoniously pushed and kicked overboard into the freezing water below. For a few moments the pirates argued among themselves. Apparently the man who was lying dead on the deck had been their leader. Suddenly an agreement was made and they scrambled to return to their own wooden craft.

Meanwhile the crew members of the HMAS Hawk who were still below deck had become aware of the attack above. They frantically contacted the command base to alert them of their distress as the ruthless pirates viciously slaughtered the sailors above.

The last Japanese pirate on the deck of the dying war ship clumsily and hurriedly pulled a package from his black zippered back pack. He quickly tossed the wrapped bundle into an open porthole on the Australian ship. Then he jumped onto the wooden ship with his comrades. As they shoved away from the larger vessel, one of the Japanese pirates pressed a red button on a small black box. A deafening explosion burst through the thick hull of the ship. Tremendous fire and smoke poured through the hole on the side and brought the heavy steel vessel down through the icy black waves.

The explosion destroyed the venerable ship and killed all of the remaining sailors onboard when it sank to the bottom of the freezing ocean. Afterward the pirate ship puttered away across the open sea and disappeared over the horizon.

When the rescue vessel arrived a few hours later at the designated coordinates they could see only floating rubble from the famous old ship. No bodies were recovered from that terrible marine tragedy.

News of the awful attack was published a few days later after most of the next-of-kin had been notified.

The Australian Navy then canceled the scuttling of the HMAS Hawk. The job had been done for them by a group of renegade Japanese whalers. The pirates were never found and punished for their crime.

As he emerged from the blank hollow emptiness of his coma, Michael Ellsworth could not move his limbs. He wriggled inside the warm, soft cocoon. He was unable to see but he could hear as the aids shuffled around the room. Consciousness gradually seeped back into his head through a fog of recollections. The constant whir from the fan and the gentle breeze reassured him that he was still alive. When he heard the attendant's steps close to his bedside he tried to clear the knot from his throat, but he couldn't speak. Someone entered and began a quiet conversation with another person in the room. Michael could not understand their jumbled syllables and assumed that he had been saved from the Antarctic Ocean by foreigners, angels, for he was sure that he should not be alive.

Gradually he organized his memories, often forcing the jigsaw puzzle pieces into positions that somehow didn't seem to fit. He remembered the attack on the HMAS Hawk by pirates off the West coast of Australia. He remembered, with horror, the vicious and terrifying murder and shooting spree by three thin, Japanese men wearing hooded camo-jackets and carrying machine guns. The memories began to flow-- more rapidly than he cared to remember. He tried not to think about it. He tried to convince himself it was all a horrible nightmare and soon he would open his eyes and emerge into the light. But the dream was too real. Suddenly he remembered that he had been shot. He remembered a bullet had entered his abdomen, and another one hit him in his shoulder. Then, he had fallen into the freezing ocean. He remembered the stabbing pain of the icy water, but after that he remembered nothing. How could he have been saved? He should not be alive, and yet he was. And where was he? Clearly he was in a hospital somewhere, but where? And were there any other survivors?

When Michael tried again to open his eyes a blanket of gray enveloped him tighter than the wrappings around him. Footsteps entered the room again and again. He tried to speak, but only managed to produce a guttural moan. However, that was enough to create quite a stir around him, and the attendants began to move in and out and talk among themselves in a strange language using quiet voices. He felt warm feminine hands on his cheeks, and saw a shadow move across his face. He tried to focus his eyes on the shadow and the voice as it hovered above him. As she came into view, he briefly considered that he had indeed died and gone to heaven because the image that unfolded in front of him was like none he had ever seen. It was the face of an angel. She radiated an aura of blue, and to Michael, as he adjusted to consciousness it was like seeing the aurora borealis within the whiter-than-white hospital room. Her pleasant face calmed him, and he drank in the comforting image and dove into the beautiful green eyes of his savior.

As the next few minutes passed the fuzzy shadow gradually grew clearer and an uncomfortable apprehension grew in Michael's rattled brain. Something was wrong. The image of a drop-dead-gorgeous, tall, Amazon woman appeared. Her thin hands and sharply carved features, her tiny nose and enormous eyes seemed unreal to the handsome sailor. Then as he looked around the room and focused on the instruments, the bed and the walls, he had a strange feeling that he *"wasn't in Kansas anymore."* Something was seriously strange about this room and about this woman. Michael used all his strength to rise up at his waist but his arms did not cooperate with his intentions. The brilliant white bed sheets were tightly wrapped around him. He struggled inside his cocoon. Instantly his world went blank again. The room began to spin, and darkness folded in around him.

When Michael emerged again from his slumber his arms were free to move and the beautiful nurse he had seen earlier was washing him with warm soft sponges. His eyes, now clear, began to examine her face, inch by inch. This woman was unreal, like one of those perfect computer generated images in a video game, a super-hero type. Her long wavy mahogany hair was pulled back tightly into a lumpy bun at the back of her neck. Her triangular face was uniquely framed by the sharp point of her hairline in the center of her forehead. She gently dried him from the waist up with a small white towel and offered a slight smile as she finished. Her large jade green eyes blinked in what seemed to Michael to be a strange, exaggerated way. Then she asked him in English, but with an odd accent, "Are you hungry? Would you like something to eat?"

Michael nodded, still unable to speak clearly. Soon another gorgeous, tall, female attendant pushed in a tray of odd looking food. He tested his own ability and reached to pick up a fork which seemed to be made of some kind of large fish bone. He stabbed at the food on his tray with the fork and brought his nose down close to the purple blob and the white wrinkled mound and found the odors to be strangely inviting. His stomach growled and encouraged him to give it a try. The warm gooey dishes soothed the tightness in his throat. He consumed the unusual food and drank the dark sweet beverage gratefully. But as he ate he realized that his feet were still bound and strapped to the bed. Cautiously he finished most of his meal. He cleared his throat and managed to speak to the gorgeous warden. "I have to go to the bathroom" he asked politely. "May I get up and go to the bathroom...please?"

Without a word she reached for a vessel on a nearby table and handed it to him. Clearly she expected him to empty his bladder into the bed-pan. Apparently Michael didn't really have to go to the bathroom, or if he did he forgot about it momentarily, as he was blanketed with an overwhelming feeling of dread. His heart sank to his belly and then to his feet. He grabbed the opalescent urinal object and threw it against the wall! When he did, it made a strange plastic thump and bounced across the room, but it did not shatter.

"Where am I?" He demanded to know. "What is this place? Who are you and where did you come from?' The questions poured forth from his clenched teeth as he struggled to free himself from the soft woven ties at his angles.

The tall brunette straightened herself and grasped her hands together in front of her apron and she waited for the man's tantrum to cease. She responded patiently, "Calm yourself, Sir. All your questions will be answered."

"Answer me this question, lady...am I your prisoner here?' His eyes narrowed.

"I am not free to answer any of your questions at this time. You will have the answers soon. First you must get well." Then she waved her arm, infusing an odd aroma into the room, and promptly left the room. Her calm, reassuring voice sedated the young man for a few moments, but soon he began huffing and talking like a crazy man demanding answers from himself. That was short lived, however. In a matter of minutes he was sleeping like a baby.

When Michael woke again, his clothing had been changed into the same uniform he had worn when he was shot and abandoned to die in the freezing ocean. But now it was clean, dry and mended to perfection, a gray pair of pleated pants and gray button down shirt. He had also been wearing a heavy wool sweater and a waterproof jump suit when he fell into the icy water, but those things were not necessary here. He was also alone and in a different room. This room had some of the same strange features as his hospital room. The floor of course, was flat, but the walls were irregular with rounded edges. They were strangely transparent like thick ice or like being inside a huge crystal. And though the room was warm, the walls were cool and dry.

Michael was surprised at the speed of his recovery. After just a little more than a week he had only small scars on his side and on his neck to show for his injuries. He did not realize that he had been in a coma as he convalesced. Michael quickly noticed he was no longer attached to his hospital bed. He was able to move freely around the small room. He examined all the wires and plumbing, strange writing on geometric surfaces with rows of blinking lights in assorted colors. He climbed out from under the satiny sheets and looked around the room, no doubt contemplating his escape, but he could not find the *door*! Upset and confused he sat back on the edge of his bed which seemed to be bolted firmly to the floor. He stumbled and as he righted himself. He turned and did not believe, at first, the scene in front of him. In the center of the blank wall, a huge arched doorway suddenly liquefied and instantly drained into a long rectangular slot at its base.

That whole section of the wall disappeared and through it walked an odd-looking man in a long white asymmetrical robe. The man was very tall and slim. The white, thinning hair on his head was cut short and seemed to be plastered to his irregular scalp with some kind of hair dressing. The man spoke slowly with a strange accent "Mr. Ellsworth, I come to give answers to your questions." Michael did not know where to begin. The man spoke again. His English suffered in translation. "You come. Follow me. We go to another place." He gestured for Michael to follow him as he turned to walk down a cavernous hallway.

They followed the gradual curves of the unusual hallways until they came to a large opening and faced an empty white wall. The doctor (at least Michael thought he was a doctor) touched a faintly glowing light on the wall and another rounded section of the wall liquefied and drained into the floor with a gurgling sound. The man stepped through the opening and Michael promptly followed him into a large oval shaped room with rounded corners. Strange organic veins and colorful pipes clung to the curved alabaster walls of the enormous room. A bright almost blinding light illuminated the entire space. The central chandelier hung down from the apex of the huge bubble room in a twisted, tangled wreath of unrecognizable organic forms. Ahead was a table which looked like some sort of ancient Greek column, but it was horizontal, about three feet tall. Behind it three men were seated. There was a lone chair on Michael's side of the column and his escort motioned for him to be seated.

Michael stared at the men in awe. He had never seen people like these men before. They were human, but they were different. Michael couldn't quite put his finger on it, but he was beginning to understand that there was something strange and unearthly about this place and these people. Yet he knew too, that his life had been saved by them, so he assumed they meant him no harm. He sat in the chair, which was molded to the floor and composed of the same crystalline-plastic material as the walls and practically everything else. He turned and watched in amazement as his escort exited through the liquid door. After he had passed through, a sheet of water flowed from the top of the doorway and instantly solidified. The round doorway then

8

disappeared entirely and the wall became smooth as a round glass fish tank. He turned and asked the council members seated across from the huge column "What kind of place is this? Where am I?"

The three men wore similar, tan and maroon uniforms, made from what appeared to be organically grown fabric sheets. Unusual, oblong silver ornaments on satiny cords hung around their necks. The gentleman on the left stood and responded first. "Greetings Mister Ellsworth and welcome to our colony. We call this place New Mene'ah. You are in a village that exists deep within the solid ice shelf in what your people call the Southern-most part of earth." The man spoke slowly and clearly, enunciating each syllable flawlessly.

Unsettled by the first answer and not quite believing what he had just heard, Michael continued. "Who are you guys? Where did you come from?"

The large gentleman in the middle calmly rose to answer the next question. His composure never changed and he answered Michael's question in simple, straight-forward responses. He turned to the man on his right. "This is Naha'ran de Lunon. He is our spiritual leader. I am Nah'reem, and this is Josi'ah. We are from a solar system that is approximately fourty-three light years away. We are three of the twelve council members of the New Mene'ahn council. Our people have been here observing your planet for very long time".

"You are from another planet? You guys are aliens! Yea, right!" he said in apparent disbelief. Then upon looking around and reviewing this strange environment, he began to entertain the idea more seriously. "You look human, a little strange, but human."

"We are indeed human, sir; perhaps we are even more human than you," the older gentleman responded sternly, as if speaking to a child.

Before he could contemplate that answer he threw out another question, "Who saved me? ...and why?"

Two men turned to face the man on the left as if to say this is YOUR question. The tall, thin man, Naha'ran answered the question. He looked to be much older than the other two men. He was the principal spiritual leader in New Mene'ah. He rose and faced Michael with a stern expression and began slowly. "My granddaughter witnessed the attack on your ship remotely...Against our advice she and her sister fished you and your friend out of the freezing water and brought you here. They then nursed you through your trauma."

"My friend... Oh My God, Who? You have one of my crew-mates here too?

Who is it?" Michael was obviously relieved to know that another member of his team had been saved.

"I believe your fellow ship-mate is called McKay, James Arley McKay."

Michael beamed. "That's great! I want to see him. Is he OK?... Oh man... I saw him get shot. I saw him go into the water. I was sure he was a goner."

"You will certainly be allowed to see him. He is recovering, though not as rapidly as you have. You may see him when you choose."

"I choose. I choose to see him right now. This is incredible!" In his enthusiasm Michael jumped up and stood in front of the wall where he had seen the doorway appear and disappear.

Puzzled the three gentlemen asked in unison, "You have no additional questions for us?"

"Later! Hey thank you guys so much. I owe you my life, and you saved James too." Michael rambled on as he extended his hand to shake the hand of each council member individually. "I want to see James. He is a good buddy o' mine! And he's alive! I gotta' see him! You guys are awesome. Thank you so much!"

"You may go and speak with your friend now. Hickok will come and escort you to his room. Please wait." In a few moments the doorway melted into liquid again and Michael was escorted into the tubular hallway. *Hickok, huh?* Michael wondered how he would remember that name. He tried to associate names with something familiar about the person, but there was nothing familiar about the man escorting him through the hollow hallways. After another moment of thought he considered the word "hiccup" and that stuck. "So, Hickock, how far is his room?"

"It's just through here, sir." And as another doorway sloshed and drained into the floor, Hickock pointed with his upturned hand to the young man whose leg was strung up awkwardly in a white hospital-type bed.

Michael rushed up to his buddy's bedside and James's face lit up like a birthday cake. "Oh my God, I don't believe it! You look great for a dead man," his buddy joked.

"Can you believe this place? Isn't it amazing?"

James McKay was a rough-looking young man. His long straggly black hair nearly touched his shoulders. He kept it tucked behind his ears as it obstructed his view. The dark shadow on his face showed more than just a day or two of stubble. He was overjoyed to know that both he and Michael had survived the awful ordeal of being shot and left to drown in the icy ocean. The two talked for a while. There was plenty to talk about.

James was shot in the neck and the right leg. Another bullet skimmed his rib cage. His recovery would take longer than Michael's, and he had feared he would never be able to walk again without a limp. The bullet had shattered the bone in his leg. He had no way of knowing about the miraculous healing powers of the Mene'ahns.. Their conversation took a more somber turn when Michael began to talk about getting in touch with his family. He made statements like "when we get home...and can't wait to see so-and-so." James knitted his brow every time Michael spoke of those things.

Finally Michael said, "OK, what's the matter? You don't think they're going to try to keep us here permanently, do you?"

James looked down at his hands, with his fingers folded across his chest. "Well, if what they are telling us is the truth, they can't let us go. Michael, think about it!" They have kept this place a secret for, I guess hundreds of years. They can't let us go and spill the beans!"

"Come on man, that's bullshit! You mean they patched us up just to keep us here as what... their slaves?! You really think we are prisoners here?"

"Yes, I do" James answered calmly.

"We'll just see about that!" Michael peered out of the round doorway looking for Mr. Hiccup to take him back to the question and answer dudes.

WELCOME TO NEW MENE'AH

With balls as big as church bells Michael stormed down the tube-like hallways of the city inside the ice glacier. Unable to find any doorways or openings, into adjacent rooms, he soon found his quest to be a frustrating experience. Before, when he roamed the world's oceans, policing illegal whaling activities, he had been an American Marine. To say he was a tough-guy was putting it lightly. He began to yell, quite loudly, but politely at first "HELLO...er... EXCUSE ME...SOMEBODY open a door somewhere. I need to talk with somebody!"

Down the narrow hall Michael could hear the familiar sloshing sound of a doorway and he turned and dashed toward it. It was the opening to his own familiar hospital room. "No sir, I don't want to go back in there. I am afraid you'll close that door on me and trap me inside." He spoke, loudly, to the empty air around him; then he listened for a response. "I wanna' talk to somebody!.. PLEASE... LET ME OUT 'A HERE!" Another round opening gurgled nearby and his beautiful nurse stepped calmly out and walked toward him.

"How can I be of service to you Mr. Ellsworth?" To Michael the lady seemed to be seven feet tall. Actually he was not too far off. Lune'ah was 6feet, 3 inches tall. She stood arrow straight, only slightly taller than Michael, with long fingers tightly knotted in front of her slender frame.

"Answer me straight, I'm real grateful that you saved me n' all, but you gotta' tell me the truth. Am I your prisoner here? You *are* gonna' let me leave, right? Don't lie to me."

"Mr. Ellsworth, you are not a prisoner, you are our guest, for as long as you wish to stay." she answered with a forced smile. Then with a blank expression and a hint of sternness she added, "Mene'ahns seldom lie sir. Although we can lie, it is quite awkward for us." Her voice was silky smooth, like a melody.

"No kidding. Wow," he said skeptically. "That's cool." He was relieved to know that he was not a prisoner, where-ever this actually was!?

"I have been assigned to help you assimilate and to answer any additional questions." Michael's mouth was hanging open, just a few feet from her ample breasts. "Would you like to begin now?" she asked politely.

"Sure." As he followed her down the hall he admired the firm shapeliness of her bottom. She pretended not to notice.

"Through here you will find one of our six large dining halls. Look...do you see this little bubble. This must be activated in order to open any doorway." She continued her instructions without looking at her handsome charge. "Do you see where the doorway is marked?" she asked with her long finger pointing to the row of green lights overhead. Lune'ah waved her hand across a bubble on the crystalline wall and an image of a tangled maze of lighted tubes crisscrossed on a panel of air. "Here is a map of this level, you can see that we are here" She pointed to the green lines, and she moved her finger to show where the dining hall lay just beyond the wall. They moved on down the hall. Lune'ah's slender finger gently touched the bubble, and the large door quickly liquefied and slurped into the floor revealing a huge colorful dining hall.

Michael's head did a 180 as he passed through the doorway, "I'll never get used to that." A few steps into the room he asked, "Say, what is your name? You know mine?"

"I am called Lune'ah."

Michael thought, as he followed his gorgeous tour guide" *Luneah...kinda sounds like it means moonbeam or moonlight.*" This is how he would remember her name, he thought to himself,.. his lunar lady. He smiled as he eyed her all over and pursed his lips in a mock-whistle. He figured she was *way* out of his league but he could not ignore his magnetic attraction to the stunning Mene'ahn who had saved him from certain death.

"This dining hall serves a variety of Mene'ahn food and is supplemented with nearby ocean–caught delicacies," she continued her lesson as they passed through the restaurant. "We have been able to cultivate a wide variety of produce and marine life that is native to our planets. Many of the dishes are quite delicious, though some I do not care for." Her English was better than perfect, and to Michael she almost sounded British. As she spoke Michael stopped hearing her words and dove head first into her emerald green eyes. He watched her lips forming the words but he could not hear anything except his own heartbeat. From that moment he thought of nothing except Lune'ah.

"We have a dining hall on level four, which serves primarily food from your oceans. Everything served there is delicious, especially if you like spicy food. You may try any of our restaurants. The food, of course is complementary."

She stopped and faced him resuming her instructions, like a teacher in a formal private school. "You will want to keep occupied in a constructive way. We have many opportunities; agriculture, construction, art, music, entertainment, research, janitorial, health. We all use our time constructively as it pleases Mene'ah." Michael was a bit confused but he didn't ask about it. *Who the heck is Mene'ah? I thought that was where they come from?"* He thought to himself.

The impromptu tour continued for half an hour or more. Then Lune'ah mentioned he had only been out of his hospital bed for one day after being severely wounded and being frozen and even in a coma, and that perhaps he was tired. Michael admitted he was tired but he did not want to leave Lune'ah. She left him just outside his room. He admired her figure and held his breath as she walked away. Then he passed his hand over the bubble and watched, amazed again, as the water wall liquefied and drained into the floor.

Michael was tired, for sure, but he could not sleep for several hours. His mind was spinning. He had fallen hopelessly in love with Lune'ah and he was pretty sure that she did not feel the same about him. Minutes turned into hours as he contemplated his strategy to win her love. Eventually, he succumbed to the weight of his eyelids and he reclined on his small white bed. The lights automatically dimmed and his thoughts faded into dreams.

Lune'ah and her sister Luci'ah made reports to their grandfather the next day. Naha'ran de Lunon was an old and prominent citizen of New Mene'ah. He had completed three hundred and nine earth years. On his planet Lunon, he was eighty two. He was the head of a prominent family in the colony of New Mene'ah. Two of his three offspring and most of his grandchildren chose to return to Mene'ah on the eighth expedition returning from Earth. Lune'ah and Luci'ah chose to remain to help their grandfather with his important work here on earth. Naha'ran was many things in the colony. He was a religious leader as well as a doctor, a teacher and a politician of sorts. He was an elder in the colony and a member of the council which made all the decisions of importance to the colony. He was a powerful and respected servant of Mene'ah. (footnote) *The Meneahn's system orbits around a large star which they call Mene'ah. It is also their name for God.*

Of course, Naha'ran was aware of the rescue of the two American citizens, and he already knew that his granddaughters were caring for them as they convalesced. The two stunning women stood before their grandfather respectfully waiting for him to speak. "Lune'ah and Luci'ah, have you a report concerning the two men."

"The man Michael Ellsworth is recovering rapidly, Grandfather, Ah'men Mene'ah" (*may God's will be done.*) Lune'ah's eyes were focused on the floor in front of him as a sign of respect. "I am already showing him the functions of the colony and making him aware of his many options. He seems to believe that he will be allowed to leave the colony. Of course, I explained his choice. I don't think that he fully understands."

"He will soon enough" The old man's voice was low and rough. In that moment the younger sister Luci'ah, chimed in. She gently touched her Grandfather's hand and stood in front of him looking at the floor. "I have good news to report on the patient James McKay. He improves daily. Ah'men Mene'ah."

The two women acknowledged each other with smiles, but neither

15

spoke again until Naha'ran continued. "I must tell you how proud I am of both of you. You have succeeded in your determination to save those two men. I'm glad your hearts are as beautiful as your faces. You have pleased Mene'ah and your grandfather with your heroic efforts." Naha'ran embraced his granddaughters and added, "Have either of you experienced any signs of illness?'

"None, Sir," they responded in unison.

"Are you monitoring your health symptoms regularly? Do you think it is safe to take the men out of quarantine?" asked the concerned grandfather.

"We are well Sir. Yes, we have administered many tests, and the men are free of any harmful bacteria, as are we. Lune'ah added, "Michael Ellsworth is doing quite well, sir. He seems accepting of his circumstances."

"Good, and the other man, Mr. McKay?" Naha'ran asked Luci'ah

"He is still unable to walk, but he is eating and asking many questions" she responded. "His leg will heal satisfactorily and I predict he will be walking soon."

"Mr. Ellsworth and Mr. McKay have not asked the important questions. Keep in mind that these are very primitive people. Answer their questions carefully. They do not need to know everything all at once. They would be confused." He held out his hands and the three Mene'an's formed a circle and focused on the floor in the center. "Ah'men Mene'ah Orah Mene'ah e sha Mene'ah, mon sah ha wa lah sheha Mene'ah, Ahmen." they said synchronizing their voices. (*God be praised, and His will be done.*) The two women departed together and walked down the hall in the same direction. As they walked they excitedly continued their conversation about their two handsome American patients like two schoolgirls with a new project.

Luci'ah had a motherly attitude toward her charge. She admired his strength in overcoming such damaging physical trauma so rapidly. She believed him to be exceptional in many ways. She thought he was surely much more intelligent that most of the earth citizens.

Lune'ah felt differently about Michael Ellsworth. She considered the man to be very primitive, somewhat childish and immature. She would not admit, even to herself that she was strangely attracted to his rugged appearance and impulsive mannerisms.

Michael ventured out of his small room as soon as he felt well rested. Right away he found his way to his friend's room. He promptly found the "bubble" swiped it and the doorway immediately liquefied and flowed into the floor. He stepped into the room and grinned at his friend still immobilized in his bed. "You are not going to believe this place! Lune'ah has been showing me around, it's amazing...and the dames. Oh my GOD! They are gorgeous."

"And tall!" his buddy answered back with a grin.

"Yeah, and a bit stiff and snooty too, but definitely eye candy. I plan on getting a little o' that before I leave this place," said Michael. "When you gonna' be able to get outta this bed?"

"I think I'm ready to give it a try." McKay sat up in his bed and turned to twist his legs over the edge. He cautiously slid down until his feet touched the cold floor. His right leg was encased in a clear plastic form with a soft elastic stocking beneath. He grimaced and motioned for Michael to hand him the crutch that was leaning against the wall to his left. He awkwardly placed it under his arm and forced his center of gravity forward. After making a few steps around the room he settled back on the edge of his bed. "I am so ready to get out of this room."

Luci'ah appeared in the doorway at that very moment. She was effortlessly guiding a streamlined floating chair. "Mr. McKay would you and your friend like to go to one of our dining halls to have a meal?" the beauty asked, with a pleasant smile.

"Hell, yeah!" Michael responded. And the three headed down the tubular hallway.

Luci'ah wore a gorgeous dark green dress, made from multi-textured hashi'ah sheets cinched together in all the right places. She escorted the men to a nearby dining hall and shared a few pointers on etiquette and Mene'ahn procedures.

The two men dined on a feast of crab and sea cabbage, seasoned with dried sardines and red seaweed called cherry grass. Luci'ah had suggested they might like it and they certainly did. A lemony beverage was served in tall irregular shaped glasses like sea shells that had been ground flat on the bottom so they stood upright. Here the men saw dozens of Mene'ahns dining and enjoying the company of their friends and family. Michael and James could not help but notice that there were also a few earth-type humans, apparently content to share their existence with the Mene'ahns. They stood out. They were shorter and hairier than the citizens below the horizon.

The Mene'ahn men were all quite tall, some nearing eight feet. Each one had a distinct appearance. Generally the men chose to dress in darker colors with earth tones. Some wore long wide pants with tunic type jackets that were uniquely a-symmetrical. Each costume had irregular edges, no buttons and no bling.

Most of the older men cut their hair short. Some chose to allow their thin facial hair to grow quite long. Michael noticed one older Mene'ahn man who had grown his reddish beard so long that he parted it in the center at his chin and braided the two parts almost to his mid-section.

The females were much more elaborately and colorfully dressed. Fabulous costumes and long dresses or wide pants exhibited style and creativity that astounded the two American men. The tall graceful ladies enjoyed long, flowing dresses adorned with organic shapes and accents plucked directly from the ocean floor. The two men were awestruck by so many gorgeous women, so stunningly and elaborately attired. A few of the women wore costumes that were simple with subtle organic decorations, but the majority donned almost outlandishly colorful and creative outfits. There were no straight lines in any of these outfits. All the clothing for the men and the women was made from organic *"hashi'ah"* sheets, grown in huge deep sea caverns near the Great Barrier Reef of Australia. Fabric of every possible texture, color and pattern, from fur to scales, was harvested directly from aquatic plants. The Mene'ahn people proudly designed and created their own costumes. The two men noticed that the physical appearances of Mene'ahn men and women were every bit as diverse as in earth humans. Their skin color ranged from pale cream white to very dark mahogany. Likewise their hair color and texture was wildly different. Also, the men could see that Mene'ahns grow old and wrinkle and their hair grows thin and turns white just like earth humans. They were in fact, quite human.

The only real difference that Michael and James noticed, other than the fact that they were so tall, was that the Mene'ahn people had straight eyebrows that pointed to their temples, unlike the native, earth people whose eyebrows curved down.

To Michael and James this world was vastly different from the harsh atmosphere above. They were rough seafaring adventurers now stuck in this unsettling sterilized maze of temperature controlled hallways. The beautiful cavernous architecture defied anything the two young men had ever experienced. The rooms, some of which were enormous, were carved (or melted) out of solid ice. The surfaces were polymerized and solidified into an incredibly hard plastic-like substance and could be shaped and molded into virtually any shape using just plain sea water. The temperature was always the same and gentle breezes and strange aromas filled the hallways.

The two men were temporarily resigned to accept the hospitality of the beautiful and friendly aliens and to make the best of their current situation. They enjoyed their abundant meal and even toasted their good fortune with a clink of their beverage vessels. They had invited their lovely escort to join them for their meal, but she declined. "Perhaps another time," she had responded politely. "My sister and I are going for a swim in Lake Mene'ah."

The men continued their feast and delighted in the wonderful variety of new foods. As they ate they noticed that the Mene'ahn's at some of the other tables were drinking a dark green liquid which Michael and James suspected might contain alcohol (or something similar). When the server came to their table the two men requested a sample of that drink. Soon two tubular shell goblets filled with the icy green liquid were placed in front of the unsuspecting guests. The two men clinked their glasses together, "to New Mene'ah," They made the toast and turned up the ends of their glasses chugging the liquid down their gullets before they really even tasted it. Their ears began to ring and their stomachs churned in revolt at this obtrusive foreign substance, but they found the after-taste to be quite delicious so they took another long swig.

A wave of silliness came over Michael and he suddenly stood up and announced to the patrons of the entire restaurant. "Greetings, I am very proud and honored to be your guest here in this amazing place. I want to thank you for your gracious hospitality." With that, he gave an exaggerated bow. James was embarrassed by this behavior and asked him to sit down. The other patrons of the dining hall acknowledged his toast with nods and smiles. Some even lifted their goblets and offered the gesture of a toast.

Michael requested another drink despite the advice of his friend. The server even suggested he had had enough, but Michael insisted. "What is that green stuff called anyway?" He asked.

"It is called Motling ale, Sir. May I suggest some Cherry Grass tea or a nice hot cup of sweet Sapro, it is a coffee-like drink, sir? I am sure you will like it." The lovely server looked at James instead of Michael as she spoke.

James responded for his friend. "Yes, please bring us a couple o' cups of that, and thanks." The shapely waitress smiled and left the table. But before she returned, a strange and worried look came over Michael's face and he suddenly stood up and unexpectedly walked out of the dining hall. James called to him, "Where do you think you are goin'? Take me with you!"

"I gotta find Lune'ah," he answered as he hurried back to his friend and grabbed the handles of his hover chair, "I gotta' ask her something" Of course, Michael had no idea where he was going. Also he was not accustomed to the stimulating effects of the Motling Ale. As he and his friend approached the union of several hallways, they stopped and looked helplessly around. They passed a few Mene'ahns and Michael asked them "Do you know Lune'ah? Have you seen her? I need to find her." The tall strangers just shrugged their shoulders and went on their way.

"Michael, what are you doing?" James turned and grabbed Michael by his shirttail and stopped him in his tracks. "First of all, you are acting crazy. Second, Luci'ah said that she and her sister were going for a swim in the lake, Lake New Mene'ah, remember?"

"Yeah, right, thanks. Come on man. I gotta see her. I gotta talk to her. It's important." And then he spun his handicapped friend around in his hover chair.

"OK, buddy, let's go an' find 'em," said James as he held on tightly to the soft arms of his floating chair.

Chapter 3

THE SISTERS

The two friends headed down the, cavernous and confusing hallways, questioning several Mene'an citizens along the way. One helpful Mene'an pointed to a mapping panel like the one Lune'ah had used, and Michael passed his hand over it as she had done. The illuminated lights immediately showed an image of intricate tangled lights and hallways with large and small colored spaces. The diagrams of each level looked like multi-armed amoebas stretching out in all directions with veins and organs depicting the inner functions of the system. He waved his hand over the monitor again and another illuminated illustration showed several levels below them. "Holy cow! Take a look at this! I can't believe this place. It's huge!"

"Can you make it out? What does it mean?" James asked.

The diagram, of course, was not in English; but Michael was sure he could decipher it, at least in part.

"Look here, this looks like a huge lake at the end of a wide entrance on the second level. This is amazing!"

Just then an older Mene'an lady stepped up and asked, "Is there something I can help you with?" The tall slender female had an abundance of white hair piled artfully up on her head, making her appear quite tall. She wore a long, flowing, opalescent skirt of many thin, irregular layers, a tight-fitting corset which accentuated her thin waist, and a cape that seemed to be made of a limp, pink sea fan. The two men were genuinely grateful for her help and kind smile and graciously accepted her assistance. "Where would you like to go?" she asked.

"We want to go to Lake Mene'ah." Michael quickly responded,

"Lune'ah and Luci'ah said they were going there, for a swim." He pointed to the colorfully lit monitor. "Is that it? And how do we get there from here?"

"Yes, that is Lake Mene'ah. It is quite lovely. Not only do our citizens use it for recreation, it is also used to cultivate a variety of foods and useful and decorative items. You must go down one level in order to reach the entrance to the lake." She pointed to the green arrow on the monitor. "You see, you are here. And over here, is the central terminal, where you may access any level. Lake Mene'ah is down just one level," she repeated. "There are seven levels in all. Welcome to New Mene'ah." She smiled as she turned and glided down the hallway.

Michael touched the monitor on the level of the lake, and immediately the floor plan of the entire colony appeared. They could see the central terminal from where they stood. They were astounded at the complexity of the colony, and they took a few moments to explore the diagrams on the colorful monitor. A small city was revealed to the men as they touched on each level. They could make out what they thought were businesses, farms, libraries, schools and unusual spaces that confused them entirely. But instead of straight edges and sharp corners, the entire colony was made of organic shapes with tubular, curving hallways. They thought the diagram of each level looked like spider webs. All the webs and veins and arteries converged at the huge water elevator in the center of each level. Michael touched the screen again on the level of the lake and renewed his determination to find Lune'ah and her sister. Then he shuffled off in the direction of the central terminal, pushing James effortlessly in front of him.

An enormous, round, spiral staircase seven levels deep, appeared in front of the two men, as they approached the central terminal. A curved, brass-looking banister encircled the steep edges of the staircase. The steps and walls of the staircase were made of the same polymerized ice that made up every other wall and surface in the colony. The staircase curved around a central, round elevator which was propelled by water rising and falling under it. As the men looked down, in amazement, a clear-walled, cylindrical tube with three Mene'ahn citizens inside, was lifted by a column of water. It rose quickly to the level just below the two men. The glassy tube gurgled open and deposited the inhabitants onto a platform below. They watched as three Mene'ahn women and two small children stepped into the same clear tube. The tube closed quickly, and they were lowered steadily down through the center of the stairway which spiraled around it until it disappeared past the view of the two men.

Opting in their haste to take the stairway instead of the water-elevator, Michael whirled James around backward, grasped the handles securely, and guided his chair awkwardly down the staircase, to the level below. James grimaced with each and every shift of the floating apparatus. The stabbing pain in Michael's side as he struggled awkwardly with the strange floating chair, reminded him that his own wounds had not fully healed. Unsure of which direction to take upon arrival at that lower level Michael waved his hand over another directional monitor. He determined to go down a large hallway which opened near the elevator. After what seemed like a very long distance down the curving hallway, they finally reached what they assumed was, Lake Mene'ah.

At the end of the cavernous hallway, an irregular alabaster wall seemed to go on for a hundred yards or so. All along it was a huge, clear, glass-like panel which made the sea life visible through it. The gradually rising ramp on either side of the main hallway seemed to stretch upwards toward the light. Michael and James continued in awe, like children witnessing a huge aquarium for the first time. Sea turtles, crabs, lobster, and hundreds of fish were all swimming among a huge variety of colorful coral and plant life. The bright light from the upward-sloping hallway beckoned them. They moved up, quickly, without taking their eyes off the underwater scene. When they reached the top of the incline they found themselves on a sandy beach overlooking a huge crystal-clear and icy-blue lake. And they were not alone. Several tall Mene'an men and boys were knee deep in the water, skillfully casting out circular, weighted nets and pulling in lively, fighting silver fish. Scantily clad Mothers with their babies and small children were relaxing on the sparkling beach, enjoying the sunshine. Only it wasn't the sun. It looked like the sun. A huge blinding ball of warm light hung suspended from the center of the icy dome giving the illusion of an infinite sky above them and a bright noon day sun. The artificial Mene'ahn Sun provided enough light to actually grow palm trees and other vegetation on the dunes by the beautiful lake.

The two adventurers paused and basked in the light and the warmth of the Mene'an sun for a while and momentarily forgot the object of their quest. The scene before them seemed so natural and earth-like. The men stood watching the fishermen and admiring the charming scene until James mentioned "the girls," he said, "We still gonna' try to find the girls?" Michael did not answer as he swirled his friend's hover chair around and started back down the ramp.

As the men headed down the hallway James turned for one last look at the Mene'an Sea aquarium. "Holy shit, Michael, wait up!" he shouted as he twisted his body awkwardly in the chair to look behind him. "Look at that!"

"Woah!...What the...?" Michael's mouth hung open for a few seconds as he looked at in the image in the aquarium glass. "It's them, isn't it?" he said.

"I think it is, man," his friend responded.

Michael turned the floating chair, and the men approached the concave glass panel more closely. The two Mene'an sisters were dancing in a surreal water ballet in the lake before them. Their colorful lacy teddies swirled around them as they held hands and twisted and dove deeply into the crystal clear water. Their long unbound hair curled around them and followed each erotic movement through the water. The men stood motionless, jaws open, as they watched the girls suddenly shoot up to the surface to catch a breath, only to dive down again to resume their dance. Lune'ah and her sister twisted around each other, moving unhurriedly through the water in a dance as if to music. After a few minutes the girls could see that they were being watched. They seemed to enjoy this fact, as they swam closer to the glass to give the men a better view. They continued and even exaggerated their movements. The men did not move or speak as they watched the sisters perform their intoxicating ballet. When one of the girls pointed to the surface in the direction of the beach, the men just looked at each other, grinned and dashed back up the ramp to meet the girls in the Mene'ahn sunshine.

The two men watched as the women rose up out of the water through the rippling waves of the Mene'ahn lake. Their skimpy thin garments barely covered their ten-plus bodies. The girls did not bother to dry off and the pale fabric clung ever-so-closely. The men could see that the two Mene'ahn women were indeed, 100% human, anatomically correct in every way. The girls walked up so boldly that the men actually stepped back. Lune'ah spoke first. "Isn't our Mene'ahn lake beautiful?" she questioned.

James answered, craning his neck to look up from his floating chair but he wasn't looking at the lake. "It is awesome, amazing! I can't believe it."

Michael was speechless for a moment, flustered by the beautiful, wet, nearly naked women, standing so close to him. The statuesque girls stood barefoot in the soft sand so that Michael and Lune'ah were almost eye-to-eye.

"Would you like to go for a swim?" Lune'ah asked Michael.

"No, thank you," Michael gulped. For the moment he had completely forgotten why he had been searching for the ladies in the first place. By this time, the effects of the Mene'ahn liquor had almost completely worn off. It was testosterone that was now addling his brain.

"My sister and I come here often." She continued in her teacher voice. "This is our salt-water lake. It is quite large, and it is where we harvest much of our fish and crustaceans for consumption. We have a fresh water lake on the other side of the city on this same level, but it is a much smaller and colder lake." After a short pause she continued, "I am sure you have many questions."

At that, Michael remembered why he wanted to find Lune'ah. He had many questions to ask, but one important question had to come first. "Yes, yes, he stammered, the main question I had to ask is..." Michael stopped because he was afraid he was not going to like the answer. For a moment he just stood there staring into her enormous, emerald eyes. He looked down at her stunning figure and then looked away toward the horizon across the lake and finally asked his question. "Why? Why did you come here?

Puzzled, she answered "You saw for yourself, sir, to swim."

"No," Michael clarified. "I mean, why did your people come here, to Earth? What do you want from us?"

"Oh" Lune'ah considered her response quite carefully before she continued. "We want nothing from you, sir. We are here to help mankind. In doing so, we are also able to help ourselves. We have been coming here for a very long time." She reached for her robe which was lying in a clump near a green cactus-like plant. "Ours is a very old civilization and we want to share what we know with our friends here." She shook the clinging sand from her robe as she continued her lesson. "We have an exceptional library here where you can learn everything you wish to know about us and where we came from. It will be my pleasure to show you where it is and how to access any information." Lune'ah did not lie, neither did she tell the entire truth.

After the girls threw on their wrap-around robes the four began to move slowly toward the entrance of the lake continuing their conversation. The salty breeze off the surface of the water and the consistent sound of the waves seemed very familiar to the men as they stumbled through the deep sugary sand. Michael stopped briefly at the top of the ramp to stomp the sand off his boots. As he did, he paused for one last look at the breathtaking Mene'ahn salt lake. Across the lake he could see the sandy beaches of the opposite shore, crowded with children and young mothers enjoying the warm salt breeze and healing sunshine. His mind drifted off to some distant memory of another beach and another time, when he would watch the sun setting beyond the horizon as he shared the company of any number of lovely ladies from his past. In New Mene'ah however, the sun never sets. It remains suspended in the icy blue sky above the Mene'ahn salt sea where it burns brightly for three days out of every six when it gradually dims to total darkness. The Mene'ahn salt lake sun is on Mene'ahn time.

"Preparations are being made for your apartments," Lune'ah stated flatly as they walked.

"Apartments?" Michael responded. "What apartments?"

"Each of you will have your own apartment, where you will live… unless you prefer to live together?" She responded matter-of-factly.

Michael and James locked eyes and simultaneously said "cool," and then they added, in unison, "No, we don't want to live together."

"How long will it take to finish our apartments?" James asked.

"It will require only a few hours, once you have decided on the location, the size, and the amenities that you would like to have.

"That is awesome, brother." said James. "Can you believe it? Our own apartments, poof! Just like that! No down payment, no closing costs, no RENT!" How large would you like it sir? Would you like cable with that sir? Would you like ceiling fans in all the rooms?"

Then Michael smiled and added, "This is great."

"There are many spaces available for your apartments on levels two or on level seven," continued Lune'ah. "If you wish to live on a different level, you must get approval from the council."

"So, if *you* were choosing the location for *your* apartment, would you choose the second, or the seventh floor? What else besides the lakes, is on the second floor? James inquired.

"I would choose the second level," she responded. "The second level, of course is where the lakes are. There is also a very nice diner with a good variety of western foods. It is close to everything," she continued. "There are only apartments on the seventh level, except for a small pizza type diner." "My sister and I live on the second level because, as you know, we love to swim," she added as if she thought it really wouldn't make any difference to the men.

"Well, then, we wanna' be on the second floor," James grinned.

They continued to talk as they walked down the long smooth corridors. There was an opening on the right. As they passed they could see that it was some kind of prayer room. Looking down the brightly lit tunnel, they noticed it curved to the left, and the edge of the central elevator became visible. "We can show you some spaces that are available on this level now, if you wish," said Lune'ah.

Lune'ah and Luci'ah escorted the men down the first hallway on their left after they passed the central terminal. As they walked, Lune'ah used her familiar teacher voice to describe the process that was used to create all the useable spaces in the colony. The men tried to imagine the huge rooms and tunnels being melted out of the ice by a heating element and the water being sucked out with a vacuum hose. They learned the entire city was carved out in this way, deep within the polar ice sheet. The Mene'ahn people were able to transform and manipulate water and they used this ability for a variety of additional purposes, like opening and shutting doorways and raising and lowering the central elevator.

"There are several spaces available in this area," their gorgeous tour guide said as she pointed down a curved hallway. "It is quickly accessible to both the diner and the sports arena. The diner on this level serves outstanding crusted rockfish and delicious, sweet, pickled turtle eggs,"

Lune'ah continued her lesson to describe how the colony obtains its heat and energy. "Power cables are forced deep into the earth's mantle, and the heat and energy is transformed to supply all of the heat and power for the entire colony." The two men listened in amazement as the shapely Mene'ahn ladies led them on the guided tour. They became more and more astounded by the sights at every turn. Luci'ah took over Michael's job and began pushing James's hover chair through the cavernous hallways of the colony. The girls showed them a huge sports arena on the same level, a flat round space with a black gravel surface surrounded by steps and seats carved out of ice. On the far side of the arena was the fresh water lake. The fresh water lake also had its own faux sun suspended from an icy blue dome above. It was every bit as beautiful as the salt lake. Literally everything was excavated from the Antarctic glacier, but the temperature everywhere remained a comfortable 72 degrees.

"You are both familiar with the upper level, where the infirmary is," "Were you able to get a look at our beautiful cathedral there?" Then she added, "Our mother designed it." The four walked slowly back to the central terminal and they continued their tour. As they approached the gurgling water-elevator Luci'ah asked, "'We have a bit more time, would you like to go up to see our cathedral and our transport system, or would you like to go down to see our school and our farms. There is so much to see. We have theaters and beautiful chapels on almost every level. And our congressional hall is quite impressive. It is where all the important decisions are made by our Counsel."

"Let's go down to see the farms and stuff," said James. Then Luci'ah pushed James's hover chair up to the entrance of the water elevator where they waited for the concave glass to liquefy and disappear into the floor of the elevator. The four stepped into the glassy tube and the doorway gurgled back up from the floor and solidified instantly. Lune'ah waved her hand over a panel on the curved wall, and they could feel the water level below them as it dropped rapidly. The round elevator room had a soft tan woven carpet with a pattern that looked like fish swimming in a circle. The walls were panels of clear glass and brass.

That day the men walked or floated from one end of New Mene'ah to the other. By the end of the day their heads were spinning with the images they had seen. They talked on for hours after their tour, especially about the children's playground. It was an ever-changing carnival/water park. And they were blown away by the art. Everywhere they encountered art, fabulous traditional sculpture, colorful paintings, crazy, unusual electric art, moving art, glowing art, functional art, even bizarre erotic looking art. New Mene'ah was indeed a splendid prison.

The girls had advised them to compose lists of their various needs. So the men fell asleep that night preparing their "wish lists" in their heads. They were to provide a list of personal items, a list of the types of clothing they wanted to wear, a list of electronic and kitchen equipment they wanted, and a list of the types of foods they would like to have in their apartments. They were instructed to be very specific. How many rooms? How big? What type of furniture, rugs, storage units and a number of other specific details. The items they requested would be provided as quickly as possible. They were warned, though, that many items were unavailable in the city, and some might have to be substituted for similar, equally functional items.

Even though they actually liked the idea of having their own spaces and getting to choose all those things, they remained a little skeptical. They wondered if they would ever really be allowed to leave the colony.

Chapter 4
SETTLING IN

Thirteen days after Michael and James were saved from the icy waters of the South Antarctic Sea, James was busy watching and directing the construction of his apartment on the second level in New Mene'ah. He was recovering rapidly from his injuries. He was even walking, with a little help from a bamboo cane, and both men were adjusting very well to their new environment, all things considered.

James usually spent most of his time in the Library. What he learned in the Library both fascinated and scared him. James read whole sections of the Meno'ah, which is similar to the Bible. Parts of it were written fourteen thousand years ago, that is, Earth years. He learned that the Mene'ahn civilizations began thousands of years before. He learned that they have been exploring our planet and began visiting here long before Christ was born. He learned all about the Mene'ahn government and how it was first established when the twelve districts on the nine planets that orbit the Mene'ahn sun, united. He learned about their religion. On Mene'ah there is only one God. He watched and learned from the Mene'ahn colonists as well. He envied them their blind and unwavering faith. There are no independent factions of the Mene'ahn religion. There is no apparent controversy about this. In many ways the Mene'ahn faith mirrors Christianity. The only thing James found strange about their religion was that they don't believe in an after-life. For the Mene'ahn people THIS life is IT-- no heaven, no hell. And they are, quite frankly baffled and disturbed by Earths many religions and our obsession with paradise after death.

The Mene'ahn people generally do not live above the horizon

because they are susceptible to viruses and bacteria. Many who have tried to live on the earth's surface, in the past, did not live long. They originally came to our planet over ten-thousand years ago, because their own civilizations in the solar system of Mene'ah were becoming overpopulated. At first they were sure that the Earth would be an ideal planet to colonize, because the atmosphere and temperature was almost identical to the Mene'ahn planet Siano. However, the deadly strains of bacteria and viruses on earth made colonizing our planet right away, impossible. But the Mene'ahns did not give up on our beautiful planet. They have been testing our atmosphere, experimenting and concocting immunities in their laboratories for more than two thousand years. And they have been breeding with the earthlings, too. They have found that the offspring of these unions, more often than not, are children that are healthy and immune to most of the viruses that plague the Mene'ahns.

James was a brilliant young man. His appetite for learning was insatiable and he absorbed everything he read like a sponge. He had been valedictorian at the high school he graduated from in 1976. He attended the University of Texas in Austin, but had some trouble during his junior year and never graduated. He had dreamed of becoming a doctor. Actually he had wanted to be a doctor and a lawyer. He wanted to be a lawyer who represented doctors in high-dollar malpractice cases. He wanted to earn, as he put it, "a shit load of money." He claimed that he was just taking a year off to be a whale boat cop, when he ended up trapped here in this strange place.

And James was married. Of course his wife Noreen, who lived in Sidney, believed that he had died on the HMAS Hawk. After a whirlwind romance she and James had married in secret over the last Christmas holidays. James didn't even tell Michael. He didn't tell Luci'ah either, and he should have.

Luci'ah had fallen for James in a big way. James was infatuated with her too. After all, she was drop-dead-gorgeous. Luci'ah made it her responsibility to oversee the handsome sailor's recovery and to educate him about Mene'ah.

Luci'ah taught James how to use the Library. The New Mene'ahn Library contained an enormous amount of information about every aspect of Earth and Mene'ahn life, condensed into a very small space. The data was stored in a unique filing system that was incredibly easy to access. James learned to simply wave his hand over a special panel and clearly speak his question or request. He had the knowledge of the Universe at his fingertips. The Library would come alive and within seconds, screens appeared like holograms, right in front of him. He would then touch the appropriate word or icon on the list of information sites. In this way he was able to learn everything he wanted to know about the Mene'ahns and about New Mene'ah. When he had questions that he could not find the answers to in the Library, Luci'ah was always there to fill in the blanks and satisfy James's insatiable curiosity.

Luci'ah had never known anyone with such an appetite to learn. She loved this about him. He was, without a doubt, physically attractive to her also. James was tall, dark and handsome. When his thick web of curly dark chest hair was exposed, even just a little, she began to stutter and look away. She could feel her heart beating faster and faster when he would come close to her. But she kept her distance because she was sure his feelings for her were purely physical.

Mene'ahn citizens are very intuitive and can sometimes see into the minds of others if they are able to look deeply into their eyes. Some have this ability more than others and some minds are more easily read. James was a difficult man to read. Luci'ah found that fascinating. She was glad James did not have this ability because then her lust for him could not be hidden.

James had scheduled a specific time to have his apartment excavated. He had his list of preferences and was looking forward to overseeing the process. He requested a large single room with a basic food preparation station and a relatively large bathroom. He arrived at the allotted time where his apartment was to be melted out of the ice. The technician was a very tall broad-shouldered young man. His thinning black hair was quite long and combed into a tight knot at the back of his head. He wore a utilitarian, one-piece blue toga and carried a huge case full of tubes and equipment.

"Good day Mr. McKay, I am called Foster" he said extending his gigantic hand. James smiled and shook it gladly. "So, this is where you want it? Shall we begin?"

"Absolutely" James responded enthusiastically.

Foster pulled a long, gun-looking device from his bag and said. "You'll want to step back." Then he aimed the tool at the wall of the hallway and a bright green and yellow fan of light began to melt the wall and then the ice behind it. The hole exposed a large black tube which the technician grabbed and pulled. He extended it out long enough to lay it on the floor nearby. Then he reached inside the hole in the wall and activated the suction hose. He pointed his portable ice melting machine at the section of the hallway where the entrance to James's apartment was to be. As the bizarre looking contraption melted the ice, the water ran onto the floor and was immediately sucked away, gurgling through the black vacuum hose. Obviously a skilled craftsman, Foster continued until he had excavated a large room. As he worked he would ask James how he wanted his apartment. He melted away the ice all around according to James's instructions. After all of the closets, cabinets and furniture were melted out of the white ice, he changed a few knobs and switches on his device and began to spray a rather smelly chemical, mixed with water, on all the surfaces. The floors, walls and ceiling of the apartment, absolutely everything was sprayed heavily with this milky liquid. Almost instantly the surfaces hardened into rock hard layers of warm ice. James watched with fascination as Foster executed his skillful craft on his new apartment on the same level where, just the week before, he had sculpted Michael's apartment.

The apartment that Foster had carved out of the ice for Michael, included several large rooms. Michael had envisioned Lune'ah, and possibly a family, one day living there with him. He was hopelessly in love with her. But social life in New Mene'ah was different in so many ways. For example, Mene'ahn women are chaste until they are married. They must have the approval of two or more of their closest relatives in order to marry. Michael ached for Lune'ah. He was tired of dating "old lady thumb and her four sisters." He had experienced dozens of women above the horizon, in his past, but he had never met a virgin who wasn't twelve years old. And Lune'ah was 76 years old.

Lune'ah was terribly attracted to Michael also, but she did not allow herself to show her weakness for that wicked smile of his. Often she would try to avoid contact with him because she was uncomfortable with his bolder and bolder advances.

One day, a short time before their apartments were constructed, Lune'ah asked Michael to come to her apartment. She mentioned she had a gift for him. His apprehension unnerved him and for once he arrived early, at her entranceway.

When the doorway swished open Lune'ah was standing square ahead and Michael could see that her lovely sister was also present, sitting on the overstuffed sofa. If she had been alone Lune'ah would not have allowed Michael to enter her apartment. He entered cautiously. Lune'ah stood straight and tall like a ballerina, draped with a jaw dropping shift made of a satiny green hashi'ah sheet gathered at her hip with colorful beads and fringe. A tiny white creature in Luci'ah's lap, looked up from its slumber and leapt to the floor barking and growling. The tiny mop of long feathery fur, with huge black eyes and a black nose decried the intrusion of the visitor with ear-piercing objections.

Lune'ah held her hand, with her fingers spread apart to the tiny canine's nose and spoke sharply to the animal. "Blanca, no! Blanca go to your room." She pointed to the room at the far end of the apartment, whereupon the dog cowered and began walking away, eyeing the intruder with each step. Before the fuzzy little guy exited the room she gave a growl and another bark or two just to say "I'm watching you buddy!"

Lune'ah smiled and invited Michael to come in and sit down after she apologized for the behavior of her dog.

"That was a dog?" chuckled Michael. "You sure it's not a creature from Who-ville?"

Lune'ah clearly did not understand the reference to Dr. Seuss. "Mr. Ellsworth, my sister and I have arranged for you and your friend to have your own confi'ahs."

"You mean one of those mood-ring bracelets that everyone wears?" Michael, at first, was less than thrilled. He was not the kind of man who wore jewelry. He scrunched his face up like a little boy about to take his medicine.

"It is quite necessary, Mr. Ellsworth." She used her British teacher voice again. "When you lived above the horizon did you not have a telephone?"

"A telephone? This, is a telephone?" Michael was baffled. "How do you dial the numbers?"

The sisters looked at each other and smiled. "Yes, it is a telephone and much more." "No numbers are necessary. Let me show you how to use it. I'll call my cousin Ziggy. I just have to think about him. I picture him in my head. It may help for you to close your eyes. You see how I touch the top of the stone with my finger. Now Ziggy, if he is wearing his confi'ah, he will experience a tingling feeling on his wrist and a sensation of urgency. He will then touch his bracelet in the same way I am doing and...ah' here he is now...Zigmond, I am showing Michael how to use his confi'ah. Care to say hello?"

A clear, distinct, male voice radiated from the stone on Lune'ah's bracelet. "Hello Michael, I am looking forward to meeting you."

"That is so cool!" exclaimed Michael.

"We'll speak later, cousin, and thank you," said Lune'ah, as she turned to Michael. She carefully opened a large, silver lined, abalone shell box and removed his shiny new wrist phone and placed it on his arm. It immediately adjusted to fit his arm comfortably. "This wonderful little toy does more than just communicate, it translates also."

"No kidding. How does that work?"

"When someone is speaking a language you don't understand, simply concentrate. Think on the word "translate." You may have to repeat it in your head. Then hold your finger on the crest of the stone. It's really quite simple." Then she turned to her sister, "Luci'ah say something in Mene'ahn."

"Ha fue'ah zee mon ni'o yah zee, fue'ah sah rhina." Luci'ah grinned as she teased her sister who smiled and rolled her eyes.

"Now, touch the stone on your bracelet and concentrate. Think translate." Lune'ah instructed. "The English words will come from your confi'ah."

Michael followed her instructions, and Luci'ah repeated her sentence in Mene'ahn. "Ha fue'ah zee mon ni'o yah zee, fue'ah sah rhina." The words came from Luci'ah's lips then, half a second later a voice similar to hers transmitted from the bracelet on Michael's arm. "I think my sister thinks you are very handsome." They all chuckled and Lune'ah's face glowed pink.

Lune'ah then gleefully suggested, "Would you like to hear something really funny?"

"Sure," said Michael.

Lune'ah called her little white dog. "Blanca, sweetie, come here!" The animated little fur ball obeyed and immediately resumed her noisy objection to the male stranger in the room. "Now," Lune'ah instructed, "activate your confi'ah. Think *translate*," she said with a knowing smile.

Michael did as he was told, and in a few seconds, a low female voice coming from his bracelet, began to speak nervously, as the dog continued to bark. "Who are you?...What do you want"...I don't know you!...You scare me!...I'll bite you if I have to!...Don't hurt Lune'ah!...Stranger!...Stranger!...I don't know you...Who are you?...I don't like you." With every bark and growl Michael could hear the dogs meaning.

They began to laugh so hard they could no longer stand. Lune'ah sat on the long sofa by her sister and Michael fell to his knees on the thick furry rug. The more the dog barked and growled, the more hilarious the laughter became, as they listened to the words of the scared little dog, who was trying so hard to be brave. Blanca jumped up into the arms of her master and continued to complain. "Who is he?...Don't let him hurt me...I'm scared of him!" The laughter ceased when the little "who-dog" finally tired of barking.

Lune'ah was flattered when she first realized that Michael was smitten with her, but she held her guard up admirably. She tried to avoid looking directly into his eyes because she could see so clearly inside his head. When she did, her whole body seemed to fill up with light. She felt like she was glowing. And, at times, the magnetism, to kiss him on the mouth, was almost impossible to resist.

Michael wanted to be around Lune'ah every second and when he was, he could not take his eyes off of her. She was perfect, unbelievable, and eleven or even twelve, on a scale of ten. She was only an inch taller than Michael and to him, she seemed frail; but she was anything but!

Michael was late, as usual, on the afternoon of the Festival. He thought he would never be able to adjust to Mene'ahn time. Almost everyone in the city kept their time-pieces on Mene'ahn time, which meant 92 hour days. He showed up for the festival on that same beach where he had seen Lune'ah and her sister swimming. He arrived, looking a bit awkward in his home-made outfit. The Mene'ahn people usually all dress in what they make themselves.

He didn't really understand the significance of a "Fish Festival," except that the Mene'ahn people just love seafood. They have found so many wonderful foods from around the earth's oceans. They often send out small fleets of submarines to bring back exotic goodies from around the Southern Hemisphere. When the subs return, they all celebrate and eat! This time the fishermen brought back bushels and crates full of all manner of sea life: fish, lobster, crabs, sea limes (they look really strange, but they are delicious) and hundreds of other fine specimens from the salt waters of the world. Fire cooking pits up and down the beach began to emit amazing aromas of spicy roasted sea life and sweet hot beverages. Michael was happy to learn that Fish Festivals occur quite frequently.

That evening Lune'ah took Michael's hand. She gave him a knowing smile and began guiding him around the gentle curve of the beach to where the *real* party was. The Mene'ahn sun was growing dim, and clouds were forming at the apex of the enormous cavern beneath the horizon. Soon they were walking through a maze of flaming torches toward the titillating sounds of a lively band. Though many of the instruments sounded familiar, some made sounds that were quite unique to Michael's ears. But it was clearly dancing music. The rhythm of the music made Michael's feet begin to bounce and his shoulders begin to swing. Everyone was dancing, some with partners, some without, some with groups of people--just dancing, to the beat of that beautiful music. They all danced bare footed in the white, sugary sand.

They were also drinking that delightfully intoxicating Motling Ale, so it wasn't long before Michael was singing "Loui- loui" to the music of the alien colony. He and Lune'ah danced and laughed and talked on and on. Lune'ah even sipped a snifter or two full of ale and was looser than he had ever seen her.

Then without thinking Michael said the dumbest thing. It just fell out of his mouth. But afterwards, he honestly didn't regret it. "Lune'ah, will you marry me? Will you be my one and only, Babe?" He braced himself for a big sloppy kiss but ….

Lune'ah's expression changed, and not in a way Michael liked. "Mr. Ellsworth, you must be joking?" and, in typical Scarlet O'Hara fashion, she added. "Why would I want to marry YOU? You are too young. You have too much to learn. You have no useful skills. You do not know Mene'ah. NO. I apologize if I have given you the wrong impression Sir. Marriage between us is impossible."

"Why do you say that?…Hey, you love me! I know you do…Don't you?" He asked with uncomfortable uncertainty, his vulnerable ego resting in her lovely hands.

"Love? Love you?…Oh, no Sir. I cannot allow myself to love you! I can be your friend only, Sir. Marriage is not a consideration at this point. I don't think it would ever be permitted," she added as the distance between them grew. "You must understand. I am 76 years old, though we appear to be of similar ages I have lived much longer, and I know much more than you."

"Ouch," that was really a low blow to the man's cast-iron ego. "Hey, well, you know, never mind. Forget it! I didn't really mean it, you know. That Motling ale tends to make a person a little crazy," he added as she turned to walk away.

"I'm sorry Michael. I must go now," and she was gone.

Michael was left standing all alone looking quite foolish. He kicked the sand like a spoiled child and he left the party, grumbling. He passed his old friend James McKay on his way off the beach. James could tell right away that something was wrong and he jumped up and followed Michael down the sandy slope. "What's the matter, Bro'? Got woman problems?" James teased.

"Holy crap, James, I think I just asked Lune'ah to MARRY me!"

"Whoa, you really have lost it, haven't you?" said James. "Wha' did she say?"

"She said, NO!" Neither man spoke for a few seconds. "I must be out o' my head. She is 76 years old, you know. That is Earth years, not Mene'ahn years. I must be crazy" Michael rambled on. "But she is so gorgeous, and God, I just want her so bad!" ..."SHIT!"

Chapter 5
A QUESTION OF FAITH

For weeks Michael slumped into a pit of depression the likes of which he had never known. He occupied himself with projects around his apartment. He had access to the entire library, if only he were comfortable with the procedures for operating the computer. If he wanted to watch a movie, or see a documentary he would go to one of the media rooms, but he preferred to stay alone, in his apartment, away from everyone. He went to the food pantry every few days, where he obtained and consumed entirely too much Motling Ale. Lune'ah, apparently, was avoiding him also.

One day, after several hours of continuous drinking and mumbling to himself about his untenable situation. Specifically, he was in love with a gal from another planet! who was *way* too tall and *way* too smart for him, in other words -- she was *WAY* out of his league. He wasn't interested in any of the other women in the colony though, and they seemed to keep their distance from him as well. He decided to confront Lune'ah and ask her just what he needed to do in order for her to consider his proposal. But first, he had to find her. He had attempted to contact her many times via his handy wrist phone, but she was not responding. He strolled out of his apartment and casually moved around the series of winding hallways toward the chapel. And there she was, in the chapel, in the very first place he looked. He stood in the opening for a long while, just looking at the back of her head. He knew that it was Lune'ah because of the shape of her neck and the aura emanating from her silhouette. She had her mahogany hair pulled back away from her face and piled in loops atop her head, held there only by a sharp pearl studded bone. At times he could see the side of her face. It was flawless. She wore a sea-fan shawl which came to a point and was decorated at the apex and at the collar with black, baby sea biscuit buttons and white pearls. It was pale in color, and in the dim light it was hard for Michael to tell if it was green or blue.

He had no way of knowing that Lune'ah had spent many hours, on many days, in that same spot, praying for guidance from Mene'ah. She was confused by her attraction to Michael, and she feared that she had inadvertently encouraged his advances. Just being close to him made her feel uncomfortable.

"Lune'ah," Michael called to her, under his breath, just a whisper above the whirr of the fans moving air around the hallway. He knew she had heard him because she lowered her head, but she did not turn around. Michael stepped up and sat down in the narrow pew behind her. "Lune'ah, why are you avoiding me? Can't we at least be friends?" Of all the things he had practiced to say to her, that was not one of them. He intended to use his manly charms on her--charms that had won his way into the hearts and beds of many women. He had never really been a friend with any woman. But this woman was different. He actually wanted to be friends with her; and of course he needed her also. He felt lost without a guide. He hated that feeling of dependency.

Michael loved the open sea. He loved standing on a mountain top or floating in a hot air balloon across snow-capped mountains. It was downright claustrophobic in these icy caverns. He had always lived alone and enjoyed a life of independence and freedom-- able to go wherever he wanted and do whatever he wanted. He needed Lune'ah more than he cared to admit. He was alone in this strange world without her. And of course, he wanted Lune'ah in a physical way also.

"Michael, you should not be here. You are not prepared to meet Mene'ah," said Lune'ah as she tilted and turned her beautiful head.

"I am not here to meet Mene'ah, I am here to meet you." Michael said, matter-of-factly. "I have missed you, Lune'ah. I need you."

"And I care about you as well, Michael" she said, "but a relationship...a physical, or permanent relationship, between us is impossible, unless you are willing to comply with the restrictions of our Mene'ahn traditions. I could educate you about these traditions and laws, if you are open to this. There are tests you must pass in order to prove yourself to be worthy of... well, worthy of me" Then she added, "Do you think you can accept this challenge?" Lune'ah had her doubts.

"Yes, of course, Lune'ah. Just tell me what I need to know? What must I do to become a real Mene'ahn citizen so that I might win the hand of the lady I love?" Then he gave her that winning smile and picked up her delicate hand, whereupon she melted.

She smiled at him and rolled her eyes. *This man has no idea what this commitment involves,* she thought to herself. She took a deep breath and withdrew her hand.

"The most important first step in your journey is to accept Mene'ah as your only God." She spoke slowly and tried to look directly into Michael's eyes as she said the words. Michael had told Lune'ah that he was a Christian, at least that is what his parents raised him to be. He had always believed that Jesus Christ was the "One and Only" Son of God, and she knew he might have trouble with this requirement.

"Then, in order to enter into matrimony with a Mene'ahn you must have the approval and consent of your intended's two closest relatives, and you must have a council member who is willing to perform the ceremony. Then she added, "I know quite well those who live above the horizon are accustomed to having intimate relations before marriage. That is not acceptable here."

"How about kissing? Is kissing acceptable? I would very much like to kiss you." Michael said, as he tenderly took her hand. Their lips grew close. Then he released her hand and moved to sit beside her on the solid rock-like pew. He caressed her face and tilted it towards his. He looked deeply into her lovely green eyes and with his lips only inches away from his, he asked permission again. "May I kiss you?"

She fell into his eyes and surrendered herself to him, and said, "Yes." Then his mouth closed around hers and their faces melted into each other. Their kiss lasted more than just a few seconds. It ignited a passion within both of them, that neither could deny. Finally she pulled away and with short, heavy breaths she spoke his name, "Michael stop. Oh...Michael." Then she relaxed into his arms and they held each other for a long while, in the silence and darkness of the crystal walled chapel.

Luci'ah was confused by her feelings for James as well, but for very different reasons. She was always able to easily read the men in her past. She had known several men, though not in the Biblical sense, and she found them unimaginative and boring. James was different. He was so much more intelligent than any man she had ever known, above or below the horizon. When she looked deeply into his eyes, she saw a brilliant chain of ideas and memories, mixed with complex strategies for learning everything. She was sure that his interest in her was purely physical, but she knew he appreciated her helpful nature and she was always eager to assist him. She was not able to read James like she could the other men she had known and this produced a unique challenge to her. She tried hard to hide her obsession and her physical attraction for James. She succeeded with everyone except her sister and of course, James.

James did not have any intention of telling Luci'ah that he had a wife in Sydney, but she knew it already. She knew that his wife would never see him again and that she must presume that he is dead. James, the brilliant would-be doctor, was not aware, at the time, that the Mene'ahns had keen psychic abilities. It could be difficult to keep a secret from a Mene'ahn.

James had other thoughts that Luci'ah could read also. James wanted to escape from the colony. He wanted his wife and child to know that he was still alive. He also wanted the fame and fortune that knowledge of the New Mene'ahn colony would bring him. Everything he searched for in the library seemed to lead to that end. Luci'ah hoped she could keep that from happening. She chose the role of "guardian," and she took that job very seriously.

"So, how do your fishing submarines get out into the Antarctic Ocean? He asked one day, trying to sound casual.

"There are several vehicles which are used for fishing and exploration. They are all launched from one location on the first level. However," she added, "It is a restricted area. You will not be allowed entrance."

James quickly changed the subject, as if it really didn't make any difference to him, but Luci'ah knew the truth. There really was only one avenue of escape from the ice tunnels of Antarctica and that was by using one of the Mene'ahn submarines. He just had to figure out how to get his hands on one and how to operate the darn thing. At the time it didn't seem like such an unattainable goal. He found himself dreaming about life above the horizon. With what he knew, he was sure he could do great things and become very rich and powerful. *The world will want to know about New Mene'ah,* he told himself. *The world NEEDS to know about New Mene'ah.*

Meanwhile Michael contemplated the list of requirements that Lune'ah had described. He was not sure how he felt about denouncing Christianity. He wasn't a fanatic but he truly believed that Jesus Christ was the Son of God and he had accepted Him as his Savior when he was a boy of twelve in a country church just outside Bryan, Texas. Lune'ah had shown him on more than one occasion where the Library was, so one day he stepped aboard the water elevator, passed his hand over the operations panel and touched the button indicating the fifth level. The small round room steadily gurgled its way down to the library level. He calmly stepped out and went on to where he knew the library was, between the main food pantry and a small chapel.

The library consisted of two rooms. The room on the right, just off the elevator, was obviously some kind of media room. The rounded walls were studded with a variety of devices which projected images like holograms. There was a semi-circle of benches and stools around the curved walls. Four Mene'ahns were perched on the stools staring at the semi-transparent moving images and recordings. Michael paused at the entrance in awe of the advanced technology before him. The Mene'ahn citizens continued their work and did not seem to notice Michael staring in the doorway.

The entrance of the main Library was different from most other room entrances in the colony. It was completely open to the hallway and apparently was not made to close. A decorative, bas-relief time-line, of Mene'ahn history, was carved into the thick, semi-circular entrance of the main Library. It was a huge room with a round terminal in the center. Michael was fortunate his buddy James was in the library that day because Michael was unfamiliar with the operation of the intimidating panels.

"Well, long time, no see, Brother." said James, when he saw his friend appear from around the curved wall. James was sitting on a stool by a table with a bizarre and colorful centerpiece.

Michael knew James had been spending a great deal of time there, researching various things about New Mene'ah, so he asked, "Hey... what kind of research are you doing today?"

"Nuthin' too important. How you been?" He answered as he craned his head away from the image projected in front of him.

"Good, I've been good. I think I'm actually getting somewhere with Lune'ah. That is why I'm here. Maybe you can help me." said Michael.

"Sure, I'll try, what do you need to know?" said James confidently.

Their heads turned simultaneously toward the strangely beautiful, illuminated hologram between the men and the alabaster wall. A few moments of silence passed, as James passed his hand over a narrow, oddly shaped box. "This thing is pretty simple, once you get the hang of it," said James. "You see all these little pictures? Each one is like a little door to all the information behind it. See, here is a picture of a fish, if you touch it like this, you will be able to find out whatever you want to know, what restaurants are serving your favorite fish dishes, fish anatomy, fishing techniques or even fish breeding services—everything you could possibly want to know about fish." James went on to demonstrate the contraption to Michael as he extolled its amazing qualities. "It's like having the knowledge of the world at your fingertips. Now, what do you need to know?"

"I need to know about Mene'ah--you know-- their God. Apparently, I need to convert to their religion if I want to marry...one of 'em."

"Whoa—you're really gonna' try to marry Lune'ah?" James pretended to look shocked. "That's cool, man. I totally get it. She's amazing." He didn't wait for a response. He continued to tease, as he shifted his attention to the terminal. He began to touch the strange icons. "I'll try to access some of their Bible for you, they call it the

Meno'ah. It is amazingly similar to our Bible. Looks like it's going to transfer the *whole* thing."

"I'm goin' crazy Bro', just crazy, I don't know if I can fulfill all the requirements. It's not going to be easy. I was raised to be a Christian. It seems so wrong for me to denounce Christianity, just to be able to marry."

James touched the holographic screen of lights a few more times and a red light began to blink in the upper right-hand corner. "You know, you don't really have to denounce Christianity in order to embrace Mene'ahnism." said James.

Michael looked confused. "What do you mean?"

"Well, Mene'ah IS the God of Christ, and Mohammed and Buddha too. Mene'ah is the GOD of everything and therefore the GOD of all religions. Mene'ah is their name for THE God, the creator and life force of absolutely everything. It really is a beautiful religion. I think I am a Mene'ahn. It's beautiful because there is no controversy. No one questions the existence of God, and His Name is Mene'ah!"

"Looks like the Meno'ah is available to be sent now. Would you like me to send it to your apartment where you can read it there?" James asked.

"You'll have to show me how to do it." Michael felt dumb.

"Sure, no problem," said James as he rose.

As they proceeded out of the library Michael needed reassurance, "So I don't have to denounce Jesus Christ?" he questioned.

"Not at all." answered James confidently.

"Cool. Then maybe this won't be so difficult after all." said Michael as they headed toward his apartment.

As they walked, practically in lock-step, James added cautiously, "Oh, about Jesus Christ. I'm gonna' go ahead and tell you. You're going to find out eventually anyway; especially if you read the Meno'ah and if you intend to marry Lune'ah…"

Michael slowed his stride to hear what James was trying to say.

"You know that the Mene'ahn's have been coming here for thousands of years right?" James chose his words carefully.

"Right," Michael confirmed.

"Well,…hold your horses Bro'. Jesus…supposedly…was *fathered* by a Mene'ahn," said James. Then he paused, waiting to see Michael's reaction.

"What are you talking about? Michael pressed. "You're not kidding, are you?"

"Nope," said James raising his eyebrows and turning up one side of his mouth in a hint of a smile.

"That's crazy." countered Michael.

"Oh, it's true, I read all about it. It was actually part of a big experiment. And, Mary...actually was a virgin. She was artificially inseminated! You can read all about it yourself in the Chronicles of Gabril. Apparently this Gabril fellow was a Mene'ahn scientist who wanted to prove that breeding with earth humans could result in offspring that would be strong and have good immune systems. Apparently this experiment exceeded their expectations, because the offspring...Jesus...had superior abilities and wisdom. Unfortunately for him, he was a threat, both to the Roman empire and to the Jews."

"Wait a minute," Michael interrupted. "So you're telling me that the whole thing, all the Christian religions, everything, is based on a Mene'ahn experiment!" He shook his head in disbelief. "It's going to take me a while to wrap my brain around it. I was raised to be a Christian."

"Me too, but it's all documented in the Chronicles of Gabril, in the Meno'ah." James continued as they approached Michael's apartment.

"I have learned all I want, for today," said Michael as he shook his head.

They arrived at Michael's apartment and James showed him how to retrieve data from the terminal on an island in his apartment.

The information he had learned from James left Michael in an uncomfortable fog. Jesus Christ had been real to him. Now, poof! His faith was shattered. Just what was he supposed to believe...that Mene'ah is the ONE TRUE GOD of everything?! Michael just didn't understand. What he *did* understand made him angry! *Had he been lied to all his life, he wondered? Or maybe James was lying. Or maybe their Meno'ah book was just a bunch of hooey!*

After James left, Michael tried to sort through the English translation of the Meno'ah. He found it just confused him even more. All the words and phrases were similar to the ones he had memorized in Bible school in Texas. But something inside Michael told him he should believe what James had told him.

He fell asleep that night after hours of trying to close up the hole left in his spirit. In his silence, all alone in his warm bed he cried. He had only cried a few times before in his life: when his mother was killed in a horrible car accident and when his eighth grade girlfriend dumped him. But he cried for a long time that night. It was as if Jesus Christ had died and he was in mourning. He really loved Jesus and had grown to depend on his faith in Him in times of sadness or hopelessness.

Chapter 6
THE TRUTH

Michael and Lune'ah had agreed to meet by the lake to have a meal. Each had promised to bring a food item and a beverage. *In New Mene'ah they do not have breakfast or dinner, there are just meals, just food. They eat when they are hungry.*

To Michael it seemed very strange the way most Mene'ahns were like Mr. Spock in Star Trek, always calm, always logical. They never seemed to get angry or upset about anything. But that morning by the lake changed his view of the Mene'ahn people entirely.

Lune'ah was waiting for him when he arrived at the designated spot on the beach. The fake sun was glowing warmly under the infinite looking dome of ice.

Michael walked up carrying a container of Motling ale and a bag of deep fried, sweet sea biscuits; like a squash, but very sweet. Michael laid his offering down on the silver shark skin blanket that Lune'ah had spread out on the white sand. She had created a gorgeous salad with green lettuce and red clams. She sat gracefully and lifted her half-filled goblet to his. They tapped their goblets together and each poured a little of their drink into the other's glass. It was an ancient Mene'ahn tradition, a sign of complete trust. It was usually done with close family members and loved ones. Michael took this as a good sign.

They each took a small sip and then smiled. After they exchanged small talk and ate a few bites Michael wanted to talk about his conversation with James and what he had learned from him about Mene'ah. "I have to tell you that I'm having some trouble accepting the things I am learning about your religion."

"What do you mean?"

"Well, you know, it's hard. I can't just stop believing one thing, one day, and start believing in something else entirely different the next day." Michael didn't think he was doing a very good job of expressing his feelings.

"Why not?" she asked. "What more evidence do you need?"

"All my life I've had this concept of God. And now, I find out that this concept of God is completely wrong. I find out the "GOD" I have believed in all my life, was actually an eccentric Mene'ahn scientist who was conducting an experiment with mankind!" Michael watched the reaction in her face as he spoke. Her expression changed from pleasant to concerned, and then to aggravated.

"That's absurd." She straightened her spine.

"Excuse me." He was startled a bit by her cold stare.

"The scientist you speak of… Gabril, certainly was not God! Gabril was a brilliant and beloved Mene'ahn priest as well as a scientist. The experiment that he conducted two thousand earth years ago was extremely important and was well supported by the council at the time." Lune'ah began using her stern teacher voice. "No one could have anticipated that your people would fantasize him as a god or an angel. It really is such a primitive concept, Michael."

Michael stared at the sand. He was not accustomed to having his intelligence or his faith criticized and he didn't like it.

Lune'ah continued using a softer voice. She realized she had been too harsh. "Gabril hated the result of his efforts. It set a course of human history that no one in Mene'ah had considered." She paused. "He deeply regretted the suffering that Jesus endured. It tormented him until the day he died." Lun'eah did not look at Michael as she spoke.

"You sound like you knew him." Michael asked.

"No, I did not know him personally, but he is real to me, because I have seen historical videos throughout my life. He was a prominent citizen of Mene'ah. I have seen the face of Gabril and the anguish he felt over his son."

"His son?"

"Yes. Of course, Jesus was the biological son of Gabril, I thought you knew that." Michaels head was swimming with this new information. He tried to change the subject, but Lune'ah was not finished. He was afraid it was going to spoil their picnic.

"Michael," her voice softened, like she was speaking to a child. "Do you believe the evidence of your eyes, your senses? Do you believe that you are alive?"

He didn't answer.

"Do you believe what you see in front of you? Do you believe your life is important and that you have a purpose? If you believe in LIFE, then you believe in Mene'ah. Mene'ah is Life! It really is just that simple. For someone to say, 'I don't believe in Mene'ah,' it is like saying – 'I don't believe that the sun shines every day.'

I think even so-called atheists actually believe in Mene'ah."

"Would you like to try one of these little biscuits?" Michael shot her a prince charming smile, their eyes met and all the tensions evaporated. Moments later they were laughing and sharing food together like a couple of teenagers.

When they looked deeply into each other's eyes they could see past their own lives and into the lives of their children, their future. It was intoxicating to be around them.

Michael and Lune'ah continued to probe each other with questions about their lives and families. Lune'ah understood Michael's frustrations, knowing that he could never see his family or notify them of his survival. Michael understood and accepted that Lune'ah was a virgin and for him to even suggest that they consummate their relationship before marriage would jeopardize everything. When they were not eating or talking they simply looked at each other, memorizing features so that they could visualize their lovers face when they had to be apart.

Michael wondered what about Lune'ah's face was different from any other woman he had ever known. She had a long neck and a narrow face, perfect teeth and a small mouth with thick, luscious lips, huge green eyes with long black lashes. There was one dramatic difference. Lune'ah had let her dark eyebrows grow out thick and long. Instead of curving down to the cheekbones they arched upwards across the sides of her forehead. She combed them into place. Michael found this to be adorable. He was fascinated with everything about her.

Lune'ah told Michael she and her sister were born in the hidden city in the earth years 1911 and 1916. At the picnic Lune'ah tried to share her love of Mene'ah with him. She tried to live for Mene'ah in every aspect of her life and to fulfill His purpose for her. She explained, "He is the Host of our divine spirits. Without His love we would be primitive, like the animals."

"So you are saying I have this divine spirit as well?" Michael asked.

"Of course." she responded flatly and then she added, "There can be only ONE God, Michael, and we call Him Mene'ah. He has many names, on your planet; God, Jehova, Ahlah, but" she repeated, "there is only ONE God. For someone to think that there are several varieties of invisible gods floating around in the sky making trouble for each other is just, well...silly. Don't you think?" she said, going back to using her teacher voice again.

"Well, there certainly are a lot of people on this old earth who think that their God is the BEST God, and they actually kill each other because of it or Him or whatever." Michael really did not want to talk about God or Mene'ah. He wanted to talk about her and about when they could tie the knot.

"The diversity among your theologies, your ideologies, and your different cultures is remarkable." she said thoughtfully. 'Your wars and your power struggles have confounded us throughout the centuries." She looked away, out over the water, "So odd, so violent, so cruel. Why do your people act this way?"

"Yeah. When you think about it, it's really messed up. I always just accepted it as part of being human," said Michael.

"You might as well know this now---I'm sure you will discover this on your own, but..." Suddenly she became very serious. "There are two opposing schools of thought here in New Mene'ah and in old Mene'ah also.... "

"And?" Michael waited.

"One group over here," She held out her left hand far away from her body, "believes that earth humans are too primitive, too weak, too, pardon me for this, too stupid, and they should all be eliminated."

Michael stiffened.

She held out her other hand, "Then there is a group on this side that believes that earth humans are clearly human and that we should allow them to live and eventually incorporate ourselves here into your previously established civilizations."

"And where are you? Which side are you on?" Michael asked.

"I am somewhere in the middle. I admire so much about earth humans and many of them are quite brilliant and remarkable; but some of them have no value at all." She said it as if she were talking about an infestation of termites.

"Are your people planning something?" His eyes narrowed.

"Actually, yes, a large convoy of ships is on its way and will arrive in a few years," said Lune'ah. "They carry with them the ability to save or destroy your people without harming your beautiful planet. No one will be killed. Mene'ahns despise violence, but sterilization is one of the options they are considering. The Holy Council will decide the fate of your world."

"When is this supposed to happen?" Michael insisted.

"Convoy #9, under General Osaura will arrive during the Fall of 2016."

"Holy crap, Lune'ah, so what you are telling me, like it's nothing, is that the world as I know it could be ending soon. What am I supposed to think? What am I supposed to do with that information?" Michael stood up. "I'm sorry but I guess I'm done eating."

"Michael, I told you because I think you can help." she responded.

"Me? What can I do?" asked Michael.

"You can speak for your people. Michael, you can address the council." She picked up the serving plate and glasses from the shiny blanket.

"I'm not a speaker, or a politician. I can't influence anybody to do anything! I gotta' go talk to James about this." Michael said as he started to walk away.

Lune'ah's expression changed to her stern teacher face, and she calmly stood up also. "Fine, I'm going for a swim." Lune'ah folded everything up in the shark-skin throw and tossed it into the sand. Then she pulled a string on the side of her satiny shift. It immediately came undone and slid from her body. Her sleek athletic body in its skimpy organic bathing suit promptly dashed off into the shallow waves of the sub Antarctic lake. Michael watched as she slid into the water, and was disappointed when she didn't look back at him. He stood there for a moment as her perfect body disappeared into the dark waters. Then he went down the sandy incline where he could see her aquatic dancing beneath the waves. His face was glued to the thick clear pane as she moved and swirled beneath the water with the dolphins. She did not look in the direction of the viewing window.

Michael leaned against the uneven wall of the corridor and tried to clear his mind. He touched the stone on his confi'ah and concentrated on James. He tried to do like Lune'ah instructed. He closed his eyes and pictured an image of James in his head. With no response from his wrist-phone he left, dragging his feet. He proceeded in the direction of his friend's apartment. No one home there. His second guess for his friend's location was the library. The library was down on the fifth level, and Michael hopped on the aqua elevator which gurgled down steadily. In minutes he was searching for his friend in the library. No luck. He was not sure where to go next. As he exited the library he passed the central water elevator to check the diner on that level. That particular diner was one that served some traditional Italian dishes. Michael knew James particularly liked Italian food, and there he found his friend sitting at a small table enjoying the company of two lovely Mene'ahn girls.

"James, I've been looking all over for you." Michael said as he zig-zagged through the crowded restaurant toward the table. "How come you don't wear your wrist phone thing?"

"Hey, buddy, welcome. Come sit. Have some of this wonderful stuffed manicotti with marinara. It's stuffed with crab and sea bass, and it's delicious!" He introduced his friends, "This is Amar'ah and her friend Serina."

"Hi." Michael wasn't really interested in food or James's friends. "James, I *really* need to talk to you."

"Sure, OK," James smiled and remarked as he winked at his lady friends. "I'm beginning to like this place Michael."

Michael whispered into James's ear. "Lune'ah just told me some things that have scared the hell out of me. I *really* need to talk to you in private!"

"OK." James seemed to immediately understand the urgency. He very politely asked his lady friends to leave. "Thanks a heap, girls. D'ya-mind? My buddy needs to talk to me." As the two Mene'ahn girls left, James shot them the "call me" sign with his thumb and little finger, which, of course, they did not understand.

Michael sat down quickly on the stone bench beside James. His eyes darted around as if he were looking for spies listening in on his conversation. "James, did you know that there is a convoy of Mene'ahn ships on its way here, due to arrive in 2016?

"Of course, I knew that," said James as he took a swig of his ale, "Though I wasn't sure of the exact year."

"Did you know that the Mene'ahns may be planning to wipe out mankind when they arrive? Michael spoke quietly to avoid being heard by the other patrons of the restaurant.

James was silent. His expression spoke for him. His brow scrunched up and his lips pursed. He began to breathe forcefully through his nose, and his eyes darted around the room. In a few moments he looked like he was going to explode.

"Lune'ah thinks we can do something to help, that we can convince the council to change their minds."

"And if we can't change their minds? Then what? We just sit back and let this happen? What then? That is just crazy, Michael. Why do you think they want to do this?"

"Best I can tell, is they don't think we are doing a very good job taking care of our planet. They think they can do a better job." said Michael.

"But I thought they were not able to live above the horizon, you know, because of the germs," said James, obviously angry and confused.

"Apparently the ships that are arriving have solved that problem, and they plan to take over" said Michael.

"We have to warn the people, Michael. We have to get out of here, somehow. We have to make sure this doesn't happen. We have to stop them," said James.

"Lune'ah seems to think I can use diplomacy to change their minds, and I think I should try, but what if that doesn't work? James, this is huge!"

"The good news is that we have some time." James contemplated. "When did you say they were due to arrive?"

"In 2016," said Michael.

"Michael, you are saying that this big fleet of Mene'ahn ships is on its way. They have been traveling for over sixty years and they will be here in about 30 years?"

"It's really not that long if you are a Mene'ahn." Michael answered then added "They sleep for most of the trip."

James and Michael talked on into the night in James's apartment. The situation they found themselves in was overwhelming, but they had lots of time to stew on this new information, so they did what normal, red-blooded American men do. They got very, very drunk.

Michael ended up spending the entire evening on the sofa in James's apartment. And in New Mene'ah, those evenings are quite long. He wasn't sure what time it was when he woke. He was constantly confused by the Mene'ahn time system. James was not in the apartment and he didn't leave a note so Michael dragged himself to the door and returned to his own apartment. With his throbbing head, he lay on his ice-formed bed and he thought about Lune'ah. How could such a sweet looking, beautiful woman, talk so chillingly about eliminating millions of people? He decided he would talk more with her about it when he was not so hung over. He regretted the way he had left her on the beach. He hoped, as he drifted off to sleep, that he could make a difference -- that he could change the course of human/Mene'ahn destiny.

James had reacted to the information quite differently. He spent the following day in the New Mene'ahn Library researching "fishing excursion submarines" and watching virtual training videos.

TROUBLE IN PARADISE

Chapter 7

Michael appeared at Lune'ah's doorway later that evening. It seemed quite late to Michael because he was still trying to adjust to the ninety-two hour days, but Lune'ah was still up. He touched the bubble outside her apartment and the doorway sloshed open. He heard her voice but did not see her, at first. "Yes," she called from another room.

"Hey, it's me, Michael. May I come in?"

"No, it is not permitted," she said as she rounded the corner. Her little white dog began yapping and growling. She scolded her, sent her to her room, and returned to the door.

"May I talk to you? Michael softened his voice.

"About?" Lune'ah was not going to make this easy for him.

"Will you please come out into the hallway and talk to me. I promise I won't touch you. I just want to talk to you," said Michael as he waited patiently out in the hall.

After a few painful moments of silence Lune'ah answered. "Yes, give me a few moments." She went deep into her apartment and donned her wrap, a coral colored robe with long irregular fringe that seemed to float through the air. Moments later she returned. She glided through the doorway with one long stride. Michael breathed a sigh of relief, and their eyes locked together as they stood near each other in the narrow hallway.

"Lune'ah," Michael tried to speak, but he couldn't find the right words.

She placed her finger on his lips. "Michael, I understand what you must be feeling. I have told you too much, too soon. There is plenty of time to negotiate for your people. Nothing is permanently set. It's just that I do not want to keep anything from you. If you really are going to try to marry me, there is so much you don't know. Quite frankly there are a few things that may make you want to change your mind. You must understand," she continued, "I am in an unusual and vulnerable position, right now, and I'm not sure how I should proceed. This is quite unprecedented." She stood very close to him as she spoke. He could feel her warm breath on his face.

Michael tried hard to listen to her. He knew what she was saying was important, but he began to watch her mouth as she spoke, and the words lost their meaning.

"So, it's going to be, like thirty years before this convoy comes, right?"

"Of course," she answered.

"I just can't wrap my head around this right now Lune'ah," said Michael. "I just want to get married and settle down and have a family with my beautiful Mene'ahn lady. I can worry tomorrow about the world ending." Michael reached to touch her hand.

"You and I can make a difference, Michael. You can help me unite the Montagues and the Capulets." She was glad to see that Michael understood her reference to Romeo and Juliet. She drew her body even closer to his and they almost kissed, but didn't.

"Michael, you must become educated about Mene'ah." Lune'ah pulled away as she spoke.

"Become educated?" he questioned. He did not like the way she said it. He felt his intelligence being insulted again.

"You must learn about our planet and our government as well. There may be a test."

"A test? What kind of test?" This time it was Michael that stepped back. "Great! A test! Fabulous! Is there anything else I need to know?"

Suddenly an alarm went off, emanating from everyone's bracelets. It began as a high pitched whine and it grew louder and louder until it began to pulsate.

Lune'ah's expression changed to a look of urgency.

"What the heck is that!?" Michael asked as he looked curiously at his whining, vibrating wrist-phone bracelet.

"There is an emergency. We are being summoned to the main auditorium on the first level. You must come also." Michael could hear the urgency in her voice.

Michael did not question her orders. Hand in hand they hurried down the curving corridors toward the central elevator where a small crowd of citizens was already waiting. Rather than wait for the elevator, the two joined a growing group of citizens who were climbing the spiral staircase up to the level above.

As they walked through the crowd he continued to pressure Lune'ah. "What's going on?"

"I don't know Michael. We'll both find out when we get there. It could be any number of things. We could be in some kind of danger. Someone could have jeopardized our security. Just wait, be patient." Lune'ah spoke loudly over the growing crowd. The two squeezed into the huge auditorium and sat on the second to last row of benches. Within just a few moments several hundred more citizens, filed into the large semi-circular coliseum. All eyes were on the central stage, anxiously awaiting whatever urgent news they were summoned to hear.

The audience began to quiet down, in anticipation of the upcoming important announcement.

A tall elderly man in a flowing jade colored, hooded robe stepped out alone onto the central stage. When he did, the audience became dead silent waiting for him to speak. Michael could hear the English translation of the Mene'ahn language through his wrist band.

"Welcome citizens of New Mene'ah and guests." The old man spoke with his arms raised up to the audience as he moved around the stage. He spoke loudly and without the necessity of a microphone. "Let us begin with a prayer."

At that point absolutely everyone, closed their eyes and lifted their palms high in the air and repeated the following prayer in unison...

> Precious God, Giver of Light, Giver of Life
> We thank you for your many gifts, of love,

of strength, of family, of friends.
We ask you to lead us in a path that pleases you.

After the prayer everyone opened their eyes and lowered their arms and again focused on the central stage. The gentleman in green motioned for three other men to step up and they all came to the center of the platform.

The striking gentlemen were dressed in outrageous (Michael thought) costumes. One of the men even had, what looked like purple peacock feathers standing straight up on his collar. The three stood in the center of the stage and the one with the wild collar spoke first.

"Brothers and sisters of Mene'ah," he began. "I must inform you that we have successfully thwarted a vile effort to jeopardize the security of our colony." The audience hummed with chatter in various languages. "There has been an attempted escape by one of our guests," he continued. "In return for our kindness, this man tried to take one of our fishing vessels. In addition to the submarine he insulted Mene'ah by stealing one of our sacred ancient Meno'ah tablets.

Michael understood every word, and he immediately started looking around in the audience for his friend James. He was worried when he didn't see James. *Why would he have tried to escape, so soon?* His heart sank to his knees when a doorway near the stage sloshed open and James was led through it by two large, muscular, Mene'ahn guards. James's hands were bound behind his back. He was wearing the uniform he had worn on the whale patrol ship. James was scouring the audience looking for his only friend. Michael's brain was swimming as he tried to listen to the English translation. Apparently, James had been apprehended after he tried to escape in one of the fishing submarines. The colony used these vessels for retrieving food and decorative items from the Antarctic and Southern Pacific Oceans. Michael remembered that James was researching information about those submarines when he saw him at the library. Michael understood that James was being charged and apparently convicted right here, right now! He looked around the audience and spotted Luc'iah near the lower level. From her perfect profile, even at this distance he could see that she was crying, but her spine was straight as she faced the tribunal for the man with whom she had secretly contemplated marriage.

James was escorted to the center of the stage, and the three men faced the audience. Michael understood the English words he heard, but he really didn't understand what it all meant. *What was going to happen to James? Was there a prison, somewhere here in the colony?* He turned to Lune'ah and pressured her to fill in the blanks. "So, I don't understand... James's punishment has already been set?" he whispered.

"Quiet Michael, I must hear what is being said." Lune'ah snapped back and squinted to focus on the stage below. "Your friend has stolen a marine vessel, and he attempted to leave the colony. He also stole several hard documents from our library including an ancient Meno'ah." This is quite serious Michael. He will be forced to leave the colony.

"NO SHIT !" He spoke out quite loudly and several citizens nearby turned to scowl at the rude spectator.

The gentleman in the center of the stage announced to the audience, "This man is charged with attempted sabotage, theft of a utility submarine, and theft of irreplaceable historical documents. He was caught in the act of his treason. He was apprehended as he maneuvered the stolen vessel out of the subterranean harbor. Inside the submarine we found several stolen documents along with an ancient Meno'ah, and several other items that would be of interest to those above the horizon. This day, our council has unanimously voted to exile him from the colony, if no one will stand for him."

Michael whispered to Lune'ah, "So, they are going to exile him?"

"Yes," she answered.

"Well, that's not so bad. At least they aren't going to execute him. Where will they exile him to? And how are they going to keep him from blabbing about this place?"

"Michael, you really don't understand, do you?" Lune'ah looked down and rubbed her long fingers. "Your friend will be put out of the colony here and now, with nothing. He will not be escorted anywhere."

Michael's expression changed as he understood what Lune'ah was saying. James would be put out onto the surface of the South Polar ice cap, thousands of miles from civilization. James would be dead, frozen solid in just a few hours. He gulped.

"I'm so sorry." whispered Lune'ah as she reached for Michael's hand to comfort him, but Michael pulled away.

"What does it mean to stand for him?" His face distorted in his anger and confusion.

Some of the spectators nearby frowned again, at the couple.

"If we are going to talk, we will have to step outside." She stood up and held out her hand. He took her hand and they both walked around to the other side of the thick wall to continue their conversation.

"We do not have a penal system here. It is extremely rare that Mene'ahn citizens break our laws. Your friend has committed a despicable crime, that could have resulted in great harm to our colony. He is no longer welcome here." Lune'ah did not show any sympathy for James.

Michael repeated his previous question, ""What does it mean to stand for him?"

"In order to save your friend a Mene'ahn citizen must stand for, must accept responsibility for the condemned person," Lune'ah clarified. "If that person sins against the colony again, both could be exiled."

"Well then, by virtue of your having snatched me from the frozen ocean and imprisoned me here, I am a Mene'ahn citizen and I will stand for him." Michael

"No, Michael, please, you don't know what you are doing," she pleaded. But before she could warn Michael any further, he darted back into the coliseum.

He stormed boldly down the sloping steps toward the half-moon stage. "I will stand for him, the damned son-of-a-BITCH." He barked as he swiftly descended. He stopped briefly when a young man grasped him by his tunic sleeve and pulled him to the side. "Are you sure you want to do this, brother?"

Michael did not speak. His eyes pierced right through the well-meaning-Mene'ahn, and he was released immediately.

He charged up on the stage and insisted on "standing" for his undeserving friend James Arley McKay.

The stately Mene'ahn gentleman, with the outrageous peacock collared robe, stepped up to him with a look of horror on his face. "You are out of order sir. You must step down, immediately!" You cannot stand for this man. You are not a Mene'ahn citizen."

"Like hell I'm not. I live here don't I? Isn't Mene'ah the God of everyone and everything? Then you can bet your sweet life he is MY God too! You guys can't have HIM all to yourself. I am a Mene'ahn citizen and, as Mene'ah is my witness I will stand for this man!" he shouted out to the audience. "I won't let you put my friend out. I promise you. James McKay will never try to escape again. I will stand for him."

Michael stood before the audience in total silence for a few seconds. The three regal-looking gentlemen huddled together whispering their concerns as the burley guards stood by with their massive arms crossed across their barrel chests. The audience awoke with chatter and even some angry shouts. "Exile him, we don't need him here. We could never trust him again. He will bring dishonor and disgrace to our mission." But the sound that Michael heard was just noise. As the council members on stage conferred, the shouts from the audience gradually became one voice with a repeating message. "Exile, Exile, EXILE, EXILE!"

Michael impatiently waited as he stared out at the disquieted audience. A few citizens nearby, tried to convince him to abandon his position, but Michael was a boy-scout--a marine. He would never allow a friend to die if he could save him. He caught another glimpse of Luci'ah, sitting close to the stage. She faced forward with a blank expression but he could see the tracks of her tears. James showed no emotion as he stared down at the raised platform where they stood.

The three robed gentlemen stepped forward after their brief conference. The chief towered over Michael as he approached him. "We cannot make a decision on a thing of this degree of importance by ourselves. We must confer with the entire council."

"We have decided to allow you to have custody of your friend until a final decision is made. If you are in agreement, the prisoner must stay in your apartment and these two men will be assigned to be with him at all times."

"Sure. Whatever it takes," was Michael's irreverent response.

"Council members will be given all of the evidence and have the opportunity to hear testimony and a decision will be made in three days." Of course he meant Mene'ahn days or almost 300 hours earth time."

"Fine." Michael's expression revealed that he was clearly not happy with the circumstances.

"Very good, sir." The colorful gentleman turned to the prisoner. "Do you understand what is happening?"

"Have no idea." James responded. He was not wearing his bracelet so he did not have the advantage of a translator.

"Your friend has volunteered to stand for you. These two guards will accompany you to his apartment where you will be sequestered until the council makes a decision about your fate." As he spoke James's spine straightened and hope spread across his face. "One of these guards will be with you at all times."

After he spoke to James the tallest gentleman turned to the audience. "Thank you for coming. After a moment of silence and a show of gratitude for our maker you may return to your duties." This was followed by the requested brief silence and then a hearty "AH'MEN MENE'AH !"

The guard escorted James and his friend Michael off the stage and began walking, single file, up the shallow steps toward the main exit. As they walked, James turned to Michael and said simply, "Thank you."

Michael said nothing. He watched his feet as they ascended up the slick steps. As they approached the top level he grabbed James by the collar of his shirt and spun him around to face him. James was shocked to see the angry eyes of his friend and then, before he could blink, he saw his flying fist!

POW ! The audience hushed and looked on in astonishment. James fell to the floor. The two enormous guards just shook their heads and grabbed their prisoner by the ankles and wrists, jerked him up, and carried him out and to the elevator. James's head hung down and his dark hair swept the dusty floor as Michael followed in disgust, rubbing his fist.

Chapter 8
THE COUNCIL DECIDES

The following morning James woke up in Michael's apartment with a nice shiner. His good friend was sitting in front of him with his elbows on his knees and his head in his hands. After a few moments James sat up and faced him and tried to smile with half his mouth. "Michael, I'm so sorry, I really screwed things up, didn't I?

"You said it." Michael stared at the floor and did not look up for what seemed like a long time. "Lune'ah and I were going to get married, but now I have to baby sit my good buddy. What made you think that you could get away with stealing one of their submarines?" Michael turned to the somber faced guard and asked, "Would you mind standing just outside the door?"

The guard said nothing, but planted his feet firmly on the ground. His body language spoke for him. He would not leave the room. He obviously took his job seriously.

"Well I..." he stammered. "I figured out how to operate it. It seemed like a good idea at the time," said James as he shrugged his shoulders.

"Damn, James, to be such a smart man, you really are dumb! Don't you know that the Mene'ahn people are like, mind readers. They knew what you were up to. They were watching you."

"I had to try dude. I can't stay here," said James.

"Why not? It certainly is better than being dead, my friend. They saved us! We were dead! We owe them our lives." Michael continued. "This isn't such a bad place, hell-- it's paradise! The world up there, *that* is the fantasy for me now."

"You don't understand." James responded in a defeated tone.

"Explain it to me please," said Michael, sharply.

James gathered his thoughts and stood up to speak. Then, pacing back and forth he said "Remember, last Christmas when you went home to Texas and I stayed in Sydney to be with Noreen and her family? God I wish I had a cigarette right now."

Michael nodded.

"Well, Noreen and I got married over the holidays *and* she is pregnant" confided James.

"How come you never told me?"

"I dunno," James shook his head. "I really do love Noreen, and I want to see my child. She should have been born by now. I'm dying down here, Michael."

"What about Luci'ah?" Michael asked. "I thought you two would be getting together."

"Luci'ah. Yeah, I am attracted to her. She is so gorgeous, and when she looks at me, I become hypnotized." James's eyes widened and he hung his head in defeat. "Do you think they really can read our minds?"

"I don't *think* they can, Brother. They CAN!"

"Well she must think I'm a first class jerk." said James.

Luci'a didn't think James was a jerk. In fact, his attempted escape only increased her obsession for him. She knew how much James loved his wife and daughter. She had seen it every time she looked into his eyes. It hurt her to do so, because she wanted him for herself. Luci'ah had never known any man like James. He was so brilliant, so masculine and so inaccessible. She admired the way he soaked up knowledge and remembered details. She admired his tenacity and his passion to seek all the answers to all the questions of the universe. He was quickly learning their language and he knew his way around the colony as well as she did. She had studied tests on Earth dwellers, compiled by Mene'ahn researchers, but she never had her own specimen to observe. She was sure she was exceptional.

She had researched data from publications out of Sydney and she knew that James's wife Noreen had given birth to a baby girl and that she had married another man. Luci'ah did not tell James what she knew about his family. She didn't want James thinking about any other woman.

Luci'ah suspected that James might try to escape, but she did not tell anyone. It seemed to Luci'ah, that her life began the day he opened his grey-green eyes and she looked deeply into them. She could not escape her feelings for him anymore than she could betray her God. She could not let go of her hope, that someday he would love her.

As Michael and James were discussing their situation in Michael's apartment the sisters were in Lune'ah's apartment having a similar conversation. Luci'ah was quite distraught, and Lune'ah was doing what she could to comfort her. They had three very long days to prepare before they had to face the council, in order to try to save their friend.

Michael was the only one who did not seem concerned about the council's decision. He thought that it was a "done deal." He was wrong. Lune'ah was sure that the council would not allow Michael to stand for James and that the decision of the sub-council would stand.

Lune'ah convinced Michael that he must confront the council and give them additional reasons to save James. Michael asked Lune'ah to make an appointment for him to confront the council but he was completely unprepared. He went over in his mind the kinds of things he assumed they would want to know. Michael realized that he and James really had not been such great friends before they came to New Mene'ah. He remembered that James made him feel stupid sometimes. When they worked together patrolling the open seas for illegal whaling activities, James was a bit of a loner. When he wasn't out on the deck of the ship, he usually had his head in a book. Since they were comrades here in the colony, they had become close friends. Was it because they were stranded here and they needed each other? It didn't matter to Michael. His friend needed him now, and he was going to do what he could to keep him alive.

Lune'ah left her distraught sister alone for a short time. She came to Michael's apartment, just hours before the council meeting. Lune'ah asked Michael if he would like to begin a "lesson." She suggested they could study for his citizenship test, thereby using the time more efficiently. She could see that James, sitting in the corner, was well guarded by the stern-looking praetorian guards. She cautiously entered the room and sat extremely straight and tall on the soft cushioned sofa. She wore a multi-colored top that looked like it was made from a huge butterfly wing. It tied at the waist and then covered her opposite shoulder, down to the elbow. Tight fitting, bell bottom shark skin pants accentuated every curve. Michael could not help but admire her shapley figure as she entered the room.

"A lesson? About what?" asked Michael. "What kind of questions are going to be on this test? Will it be multiple choice?" Michael smiled that winning smile.

"No," she answered seriously. "The twelve council members will each prepare questions for you. They may have made their decision before any of the questions are even asked. I predict you will have a few, three or perhaps four questions only. They could ask you about anything. If the council agrees to grant your citizenship then you know you have passed the first test." Lune'ah thought for a few moments and then continued. "You will be asked questions about your character and your faith. You might also be asked very personal questions about your sex or hygiene. For example, they might ask if you are circumcised. They will want to know if you will honor Mene'ah. They will want to know if you will honor me. Some of them may question your knowledge of Mene'ahn history and philosophy. They will want to be sure that you will honor your commitments."

"Jeez!" Michael was beginning to feel the pressure. His eyes crept up and down her luscious body, and he became distracted, "So I guess we should start with some Mene'ahn history. Tell me what every Mene'ahn citizen needs to know about our homeland and its past."

"The Mene'ahn system is about 43 light years away at this time. Sometimes it is closer depending on its path along the trail in the Milky Way and its relation to your system. Mene'ah, the solar system, is made of twelve states residing on nine planets which orbit in one plane around our very large star, something like the rings around your planet Saturn." Drawing rings in the air, she used her hands to demonstrate. "Every 11,000 years our Mene'ahn system swings closer to your Sun and that distance is shortened by nearly five light years." Lune'ah spoke very clearly and slowly, using her teacher voice and pausing occasionally to allow her student to properly absorb the information.

"The earliest missions were unmanned exploratory missions, but from them we were able to obtain a great deal of important information and samples of various life forms. The earliest probes verified that the atmosphere was ideal. Our planets were becoming overpopulated and we began to consider Earth as a potential new colony. Since then our territories have succeeded in curbing the population growth." Lune'ah continued her lesson. "Our nine planets are quite diversified, and the citizens of each of the states, or territories, have developed their own traditions and even languages, just like on Earth. My sister and I were born here in the colony, but our family is originally from the planet Lunon. It is the planet farthest away from our Mene'ahn star. The surface of Lunon is made entirely of ice. Our colonies on Lunon were created just like our city here in New Mene'ah. Whole cities were created by melting out huge caverns in the rock-hard ice layers of Lunon. The people of Lunon perfected this process. And of course, we have used this same process to carve out our colony here." Lune'ah concluded her lesson by adding "Yours is a very turbulent planet. It is quite unique in that respect. Even your oceans flow in volatile, irregular patterns. I think this is because your planet is tilted on its axis. That is quite irregular you know."

"Do I need to be taking notes?" Michael smiled. "Would you like something to drink?"

"No, thank you," she lowered her eyes and returned his affectionate smile.

"Surely you have more questions for me." She paused. "It doesn't seem fair that I know just about everything there is to know about the Earth, and you know so little about Mene'ah."

"Well, let's see, where does the energy come from, to run a city like this one, here inside the ice?" Michael had been wondering about that from his first day.

"We use hydrogen and electric energy. We use the thermal energy from deep within your planet to convert water into Hydrogen and oxygen. Of course, you know that the center of this planet is molten matter, churning within your planet at extremely high temperatures. We simply drill very long cables deep down and draw up the tremendous heat. Then we use that energy to separate the water molecules into hydrogen and oxygen. Most of our technology requires hydrogen and then, of course, we breathe the oxygen. It is really a very simple and convenient process."

"If you say so," said Michael.

"What else would you like to know?

"Well, I've seen lots of Sci-Fi flicks. In the ones I have seen, the space travelers are put into some kind of hibernation. If it takes 90 years to get here from Mene'ah, do the passengers get frozen or what?" Michael asked.

Luneah smiled and said, "Actually, yes, travelers are able to sleep away much of the time during space travel, but they are not really frozen. A low temperature, concentrated oxygen, and a combination of drugs, induces a slow heart rate. This enables deep space travelers to sleep for very long periods of time, as long as ten or twelve years at a time. Those who travel such a distance, dedicate their entire lives in service to Mene'ah for this important mission."

"Tell me what strange lands you have explored, Michael. This planet is so beautiful…and terrible too. Have you seen exotic places? Where are did you grow up? Lune'ah wanted to know everything about him.

"I was born and raised in West Texas. Texas is a large state in our country…"

"I know what Texas is." she smiled.

"It's pretty boring there so I joined the Marines after high school. I saw a whole lot of the world while I was in the Marines. I've been to Japan, Germany, and some really beautiful parts of my own country. It really made me realize how much I love the U.S.A."

Lune'ah wanted to ask "*Why do you love The United States of America?*" but she decided to postpone that question for later. From Lune'ah's vantage point, she had watched, for seven decades as many of the decisions made by the American government, created and intensified world-wide conflict. Lune'ah believed that lust for money, gold, and oil in particular caused more wars and corruption above the horizon than anything else. She also believed that the United States of America was the wealthiest, most corrupt nation on the planet. She chose wisely, not to share her feelings with Michael at this point in their relationship. She was sure the government of The United States of America would be short lived.

"Do you still have a family in Texas?' she asked.

"I have a cousin I'd like to see again. Can I find out how he is doing?" Michael wondered. "I'd sure like to know if he is OK."

"I will be happy to show you how to access any information that has been published on Earth." Lune'ah added. "You understand why you cannot contact them, don't you?"

"Yeah. I get it." Michael didn't like the idea of being reminded that he was a prisoner so he changed the subject. "So how do you guys down here get along without money?" Michael asked.

"Each of us has a service to perform for Mene'ah. Some offer creative artistic services, some offer food service. When one of us, or a group of us, has a surplus or an idea that could benefit the colony we share it. We are all family members here--brothers and sisters. We simply work together to fulfill the future for Mene'ah."

"No one strives to be wealthy?" Michael didn't realize that he had about a hundred questions lined up to ask Lune'ah. There was so much he just didn't understand.

"Well, Michael, we are all wealthy." Lune'ah patiently responded. "We have everything we want. If we want a larger apartment, we simply request it, but then we have to keep that extra space clean and organized. We have jewelry made of diamonds which sparkle just as bright, even brighter than the little rocks your people value so much. And they cost us nothing. They are gifts from Mene'ah and we have them in abundance. Your people have placed value on materials instead of God."

"I want learn to play some of the sports games I have seen I the arena." Said Michael, eager to get on to another subject. "Will you teach me?

Lune'ah's face lit up. "One game I know you will love is a flying game in which your team tries to pop the most bubbles. You'll love it! Luci'ah and I are on a team. Sometimes participants put special prizes inside the bubbles. It gets quite exciting."

"Flying, for real?" Michael wanted to hear more about that game.

Just then Michael noticed that his wrist was tingling under his wrist band. He touched his finger on the oval stone, and an unfamiliar voice spoke. "The council is ready to convene. Please come to the main council chamber on the primary level. We will begin as soon as you arrive."

"Do you want me to go with you?" Lune'ah asked.

"No, thanks, I've got this." He gently pried his hand from hers and started down the hall with a hop.

The council meeting was held in the small conference room where Michael had first met Lune'ah's grandfather, Naha'ran. This time instead of three "answer dudes" there were twelve council members: a striking array of characters, two of whom were women. Each represented a district in "old" Mene'ah. They were elected by the citizens. One of the women appeared to be quite old. She walked and stood quite erect and carried herself like a ballerina. Anyone could see that in her youth she had been a beauty. The other woman was younger and much less attractive with masculine features and a sour expression on her face. Most Mene'ahn's are beautiful people. Unfortunately she was not. She was shorter than the others and her thin brown hair, slicked back, exaggerated the irregular shape of her skull. They entered the room in single file. All were dressed in similar uniforms; tunics gathered in front at the waist by huge shiny buckles. The costumes had ankle length wide pants, in various shades of coral, pink, maroon, cream and black, with crinkled, leafy edges. Michael's mouth hung open as they entered. All the council members sat in unison after they were in position at their seats behind the long table.

Michael sat facing them in the only stool opposite the long table. He waited respectfully, in silence, before the intimidating council. He noticed the beautiful matching necklaces each council member wore. Small, polished silver columns with decorative swirls and colorful stones, hung from long silver ropes around their necks. He wondered if the curious jewelry pieces might perform some special function.

Naha'ran stood and addressed Michael formally. "Mr. Ellsworth, we each represent one of the twelve districts in the solar system of Mene'ah. We understand that you wish to "stand for" your friend James McKay. Do you understand what this means?"

"Yes, I believe I do," said Michael.

Michael was prepared to hear a list of do's and don'ts about being James's guardian. He was not prepared to hear that the council had already decided not to allow Michael to save his friend from exile.

"We have deliberated on this issue and we are unanimous in our decision. We will NOT allow you to 'stand for' your friend".

"What!" He stood up suddenly.

"Unfortunately, sir," the elderly councilman continued." You may be able to trust your friend, but we are not convinced that your friend is trustworthy. This threatens our existence here. Perhaps if he had only tried to escape to above the horizon, we could be lenient, but your friend took one of our most precious artifacts. The only reason he would have taken our Meno'ah would be to gain wealth and power above the horizon. This would have risked the exposure of our colony. You must understand that our mission here is paramount. We simply must survive here in secret."

"So that's it! You guys are just going to put him out?" Michael voice grew very loud. "I can't let you do that. I'll watch him. I promise he has learned his lesson. He won't try to escape again."

"We understand how you feel about your friend, but our decision is unanimous and irreversible." Lune'ah's grandfather tried to console the young man. "Mr. Ellsworth, it is unreasonable to think you could watch your friend every minute of every day. You must think of the quality of your own life. Isn't it true that you would like to unite in marriage with my granddaughter?"

"I want to marry her. Yes Sir" he said, breathing hard. He tried to calm himself and he lowered his voice.

"Of course marriage, what a wonderful thing. I can give you some good news about that, if you are prepared to receive it." Naha'ran was glad to speak with Michael on a different, more pleasant subject.

"Well, hell yeah. I could use some good news right now." Then he shut his mouth and said, "Sorry."

"We know that you have requested an audience with us about another matter. You wish to be declared a citizen so that you will be qualified to marry Lune'ah. "Well apparently you have declared it for yourself sir, in the main auditorium three days ago. No council member here will question your faith in Mene'ah after the speech you made that day." Naha'ran was happy to be able to share this news with Miichael.

"So you mean I'm officially a Mene'ahn now?" asked Michael.

"Yes."

"So that means...?

"Yes, Michael, you have the council's permission to marry Lune'ah, and my permission also." said Naha'ran, smiling.

Michael was split in two as he mourned for his friend, knowing there was nothing he could do to save James from being exiled from the colony. But... at the same time, he rejoiced knowing that he would be able to marry his Menc'ahn sweetheart.

The council meeting ended and Michael immediately sought out Lune'ah to tell her the news. Luci'ah was with her. When she heard the news that the council had rejected Michael's offer to "stand for" James, she was devastated.

Luci'ah broke down in tears and left right away to try to find and talk with her grandfather.

As Michael and Lune'ah shared their concerns, the two guards were ordered to bring the prisoner back to face the council for the final determination of his fate.

It was an unhappy and desperate situation for James. Lune'ah was cold but cordial toward James, as the muscular guards whisked him out of the room.

They sat quietly for a few moments holding each other when suddenly Michael and Lune'ah found themselves alone, in Michael's apartment. Their eyes locked together. Now, they would be able to marry with the blessings of Mene'ah. They looked deeply into each other's eyes and then their lips merged. The magnetism of that kiss was electrifying. Their passion erupted like a volcano, and once a volcano, like this one, starts to erupt there is no way to stop it. Soon they were on the floor wrapped together, on a thick llama skin rug.

Michael, being unfamiliar with the unusual fasteners of her costume, began to fumble awkwardly along her side. This tickled and brought Lune'ah wriggling out of her passionate embrace.

Lune'ah giggled shyly, and rolled over exposing her backside to his embrace. Their knees tucked together as they held each other on the soft white fur. Without saying a word, Michael understood that Lune'ah was not ready to consummate their relationship. So he tried to change the focus of his attention to his friend who was, right now--as far as Michael knew--being put out onto the South Polar ice cap to die!

A SHOTGUN WEDDING

Chapter 9

The two guards escorted their prisoner to the chamber where the council members waited to pronounce sentence on James.. They seated him directly in front of the jury of twelve judges on the same stool that his friend Michael had just vacated. His guards stood one on each side. Naha'ran stood and began to address the prisoner.

"Mr. McKay," he said firmly "please stand." At that, the two muscular men helped him to his feet. "James McKay, we regret to inform you that our council cannot accept your friend's generous offer to stand for you. Do you understand what this means?"

Before he could answer, Luci'ah appeared in the doorway. She paused for a moment and then stepped boldly into the room and stood between James and the council members. "Please allow me to speak for this man." She waited respectfully for approval of her request.

"Luci'ah, we understand that you have an interest in this man, but your testimony in this case is futile." Her grandfather calmly suggested. "James McKay has been convicted of sabotage, theft, and treason. The punishment for his crimes is exile. Please go and accept our ruling"

"Please, I have information about this man that is relevant to his case. I am begging the council to hear me... Please allow me to share this information." Luci'ah bravely confronted the council as she wiped away her tears.

Without speaking, most of the council members nodded and none objected. Naha'ran made a motion with his hand, for her to step forward and said, "Very well, the council will hear your testimony. What do you have to share with us?"

Luci'ah gathered her thoughts and then spoke. "This man attempted to escape to be with his wife and child in Australia. I beg you respectfully, to have mercy on this man." James looked up dumbfounded. "Each and every one of you knows how important your families are, you must understand why he felt the need to escape. He wanted his wife and family to know that he is still alive. I understand why you would not allow his friend Michael to stand for him. Will you allow *me* to stand for him?"

"This is something our council will need to discuss. You understand that we must have a unanimous decision?"

"I understand. May I speak to the prisoner for a moment?" asked Luciah.

"You may," he answered.

Luci'ah turned around to speak to James and said. "James, I'm so sorry, I didn't tell you. I should have told you days ago. I don't know why I didn't. Your wife, Noreen, has remarried. I'm so sorry. You have a baby girl, they named her Grace." She quickly turned around again to face the council.

James said nothing. He just hung his head and looked at the floor.

"Luci'ah, we will have to convene in private to discuss your request. Please understand that your testimony here today may not bring about the result you desire." Naha'ran continued. "We have some important questions to ask you. Luci'ah, in order for you to *stand-for* this man, you must be in a position to be his guardian at all times. You understand what I am saying to you, what I am asking you? Are you willing to marry this man?"

"Yes I am. I love him." She did not hesitate to answer.

"In that case I have a question for Mr. McKay, and he turned to the prisoner. "Sir, this brave woman has offered herself to you in marriage, in order to save your life. According to her, you *were* married, but apparently your wife believes you are dead. She has remarried. Therefore you are now free to marry. Do you have feelings for Luci'ah?"

James was still digesting the information about Noreen, but he answered honestly. "Luci'ah is the most beautiful, most wonderful, most amazing woman I have ever known. My feelings for her are very strong. I would be incredibly honored to have her as my wife."

"Do you understand that this is the only way the council could consider suspending your exile from New Mene'ah. I cannot speak for the other council members."

"I understand," he responded.

Naha'ran then addressed the two guards. "You will take the prisoner to the holding cell on the second level. One of you must be at his side at all times. We will notify you when our council has made a decision in this matter." The guards acknowledged his order by crossing their hands across their chests and clicking their heels. Immediately they grabbed James by both arms and escorted him out of the council chamber.

"Thank you," Luci'ah whispered to her grandfather.

"Please join me and the other council members in a prayer for guidance from Mene'ah." They all bowed their heads, and raised their hands skyward and repeated their common prayer, ending it with, Ah'men, Mene'ah!"

Luci'ah floated out and down the snaking hallway and ended up at Michael's apartment. She touched the button outside the doorway and it sloshed open quickly startling our two lovers, who were awkwardly lying on the floor snuggling on the polar bear fur rug. They jumped up quickly, straightening their clothing, blushing and looking quite guilty.

Luci'ah rushed over to her sister and began overflowing with details about James and his predicament. She confessed she had approached the council shortly after Michael's petition had been denied. As she and her sister held hands and faced each other, tears rolled down their faces. Michael sat awkwardly on the cushioned sofa. The girls released their hands and sat down on each side of him. "Michael," said Lune'ah softly. "You are a Mene'ahn citizen now and you have professed faith in Him, will you pray with us. At times like these when we are helpless we need strength from God." Michael felt uncomfortable, but he agreed to pray with his intended and her sister for the life of his friend.

The words of the prayer seemed familiar. He had heard them

before, inside the auditorium at the end of the public forum. The prayer spoken in the Mene'ahn language flowed in a poetic and musical rhythm. He was able to remember most of the English translation. At the end of the prayer he joined the girls and said "Ahmen Mene'ah."

A unanimous decision concerning James's exile was not made in the council that day. Naha'ran requested and was granted another meeting the following day. Some of the council members were not convinced that James could be controlled. He was hoping, for his granddaughter's sake, that the council would agree to give the young American another chance. He knew that Luci'ah had never shown an interest in any Mene'ahn man the way she obviously cared about James. Naha'ran needed additional time to speak with the council members to overcome their objections.

During the waiting period Lune'ah suggested Michael learn to play a favorite sport of the New Mene'ahn colony called, Pongo. It is a delightful sport, much like soccer. In this game the teams try to air-push a balloon-like ball across a goal, thereby scoring a point for their team. However, all of the action takes place in mid-air! When Lune'ah explained the game to Michael he became very excited. He was going crazy waiting for information about James. He appreciated Lune'ah offering an activity which could help him get his mind off his friend.

"So the players actually fly in this game?" Michael questioned.

"*Yes*. Oh Michael, you must try it, you can be on our team!" Lune'ah's face glowed. "My sister and I are on a wonderful team. You will love it. It is so much fun." She bubbled with enthusiasm.

"I'm game." Michael countered.

Lune'ah advised Michael on the proper attire for the sport and helped him modify one of his costumes appropriately. Moments later they were headed down the hallway toward the sports arena which was nearby and on that same level.

The back-pack gear that Lune'ah handed him was a strange looking contraption. It had an organic shape like a snail shell. She demonstrated how to put it on and when he picked it up it suddenly inflated into a bulbous shape with a round luminescent ball inside, about the size of a bowling ball. It was worn securely with inflated, curved tubes over the shoulders. The tubes separated between the shoulders into two rubbery hoses that had control grips at the end of each one.

As the pair donned the equipment Lune'ah explained the object of the game. She described the way in which the captain or chosen member of a team would create the ball. The ball was like a big balloon, and a new ball was created for each play or point.

The tubes that came up over the shoulders were air hoses and were controlled by simple mechanisms on the handles. She demonstrated for Michael the proper way to hold the control device in order to operate the air pressure with the thumbs.

"So what is the back-pack thing for?" asked Michael, feeling quite awkward.

"That is your anti-gravity device." She answered matter-of-factly.

"How does it work?" He looked over the equipment for some sign of a switch or control buttons, but all the surfaces were smooth.

She looked at him and raised her eyebrows in a prideful way like a child showing off the workings of a new toy. "It is operated by your own brain patterns! You will have to align the bio-magnetic patterns of your brain with the unit in order for it to read your patterns successfully. As you put it on you must brush it across your head, it must come into contact with the magnetic field surrounding your head in order to program the device to respond to your thoughts." She smiled sweetly as she demonstrated this process with her own equipment. Michael followed her instructions. Then she adjusted and buckled the strap just below his waist. "It may take some practice at first."

"Right," he responded dubiously.

Once both of them had secured their equipment Lune'ah began her coaching with a hands on demonstration. Michael quickly mastered the use of the air tubes which were operated with a simple button and tab on the handles of each tube. Players were not allowed to touch the balloons with any part of their body. If they did, the balloon would burst! Only air could propel the balloons through the goals at each end of the arena.

Mastering the anti-gravity back pack was slightly more complicated. Lune'ah said it was simple...-just "think" yourself light. He watched her as she lifted herself up off the ground effortlessly. She showed him how easy it was to lean to the left or right to change direction. Still Michael's feet remained firmly glued to the ground. Lune'ah laughed at him and he became quite frustrated so she tried a diversion. She grabbed a handful of fabric on his chest, pulled him to her and seduced him with a passionate kiss. Their faces connected like a pair of magnets. Michael forgot his frustration and surrendered himself to the warm wet lips of his lover. Moments later, when the magnetism of that kiss released him, Michael opened his eyes to see his beautiful coach grinning from ear to ear. Then she raised her eyebrows and pointed down. Michael looked down to see that he was at least ten feet in the air.

"Oh my GOD!" He bellowed. "I'm flying!" And then he began to sink!

Lune'ah hoisted him up by the shoulder strap of his anti-gravity back-pack and literally threw him about twenty feet across the arena. "No, you have to stay up. Pretend you are Peter Pan. You can do it! Take a deep breath and hold it. Think to yourself...I am lighter than air!'"

Laughing, Michael began to flap his arms, and he floated upwards until he nearly came into contact with the domed ceiling. "This is amazing, I could get to like this!" he exclaimed. As he concentrated he floated gently down to Lune'ah's level where he leaned to the left and right to practice control of the anti-gravity device.

After several minutes of practice flying, Lune'ah reached up and pulled down a large round hoop which hung from the center of the upper dome. As she held on to the side of the shape it grew larger and larger. When she withdrew her hand it stopped increasing in size. It was like a giant soap bubble wand. Then she aimed her air hose at the center and a huge blue bubble, perhaps nine feet in diameter, emerged from the opposite side. As they watched the ball float across the field and finally pop on the ground, she explained that the balls could be made as big or as small as the team wanted. She proceeded to blow another enormous bubble-ball which wobbled as it floated out. Then the wand-hoop retreated back up to the ceiling. Lune'ah demonstrated the way the air hoses were used to propel the bubble-balls. Soon the second large bubble-ball that she had created touched the floor and immediately burst with a loud pop! "Are you ready to try it?" she shouted.

"Oh yeah, I'm ready," and he spread his legs and squared his shoulders like Captain America floating twelve feet off the ground.

Lune'ah floated effortlessly up to the ceiling to make another ball explaining that, generally the balls were smaller, like the size of a beach ball, so she made one about that size. As it floated toward Michael he pointed both his air tubes at the ball and squeezed, shooting the balloon rapidly toward the ceiling where it immediately popped. She laughed and made another ball with a similar result. But Michael soon improved his technique, and it wasn't long before he was flying around guiding and controlling those practice balloon-balls like a pro.

"Let's see if you can score a point! Try to blow the ball through these two posts over here. I'm going to try to blow the ball through the goal on your side of the court. "Ready?" Then she made another ball and took a central position on her side of the court.

Of course Lune'ah was a seasoned player and she made the first goal, but Michael gave her a run for her money. It wasn't long before she was breathing hard and racing to keep ahead of her worthy new opponent.

Naha'ran met with Luc'iah, and together they went to the room where James's was being held prisoner. The guard stood on the outside of the entrance with his arms folded across his chest. He whispered a few words to the guard and the pair was allowed to enter, followed by the burley guard who remained standing inside the room the entire time.

When Luci'ah and her grandfather entered James looked up from where he was seated at a small table and smiled but said nothing. Naha'ran began right away, "There are two members of the council who are not convinced that you can be trusted to stay here. My granddaughter has voiced her commitment to your salvation. I am here today to hear your words. If you can convince me, I believe I can convince all of the council members to grant a limited pardon for your crime against us."

James met Luci'ah's gaze with a slight smile. "Luci'ah, you are so amazing, thank you, thank you so much. I promise, you will not be sorry"

Naha'ran interrupted. "First of all, the council needs to hear your promise that you will not attempt to escape again. Do you understand why it is so important that you remain here?

"Yes, I understand sir." He answered.

"It is a matter of necessity. In a way we are all prisoners here. In a few years, when the next fleet of ships arrives we will all be free to leave this place."

"I understand." He repeated.

"Mr. McKay, will you be faithful to Mene'ah as well as Luci'ah?" Naha'ran continued with his interrogation. "It is very important that you share our faith. You will not be a good husband, friend, or citizen unless you follow the laws of our God. You will be asked questions about your faith during the wedding ceremony. Can you answer them honestly?"

"I have studied your religion. I have always believed in God, but I was confused by all of the many different faiths in our world. I've always known that there could only be one God. I believed that all those religions simply had different names for God. When I first began to study your religion, I knew right away that Mene'ah was and is the only God. Mene'ah is not only the God of the Mene'ahn system, but also the God of the Earth and the entire universe." James spoke without reservation. Naha'ran looked deeply into his eyes and could see that James truly meant the words he spoke. "I promise I will be faithful to Mene'ah and to my wife Luci'ah, if she will have me and if the council will give me the opportunity. I will not try to escape again. I swear." At the time James truly believed the words he spoke.

"These are the words I needed to hear." Then he turned to Luci'ah. "Granddaughter, you have made a difficult choice. Your husband is very young. You will have to teach him our ways. Also, many in New Mene'ah will not accept him because he is from above the horizon and because he tried to escape. Are you fully prepared to face these obstacles?"

"Yes grandfather, I understand that it will not be easy, but I don't think I can ever love another man the way I love James." Then she reached across the table and caressed James's hand. "Do you think you can learn to love me?"

"Of course, Luci'ah. I love you. I do love you already. How could I not love you. You are an angel, a beautiful, heavenly angel," he said sincerely.

Luci'ah smiled and asked her grandfather, "When may we be married?"

"First I must get a unanimous decision from the council. You must not make any plans until then." He reminded her that James would be guarded continuously until they were married.

Then Naha'ran motioned to the guard that it was time for them to leave. The guard escorted Luci'ah and her grandfather out of the doorway and he resumed his station outside James's apartment.

The council convened the following day and Naha'ran artfully convinced the two suspicious members that James could now be trusted. He made his case skillfully and assured the council that Luci'ah and James would be married as soon as preparations could be made.

The wedding took place only a few days later. Lune'ah, Michael and a handful of friends and family met at the appointed time in the small chapel on the second level. Lune'ah had decorated the altar with deep maroon and pink flowers that she had made from sea fans and anemones. She draped the ice-stone pews with rows of dark green sea grass knotted like a grass-skirt. Naha'ran, himself, performed the ceremony.

James was dressed in an elegant, borrowed tunic, a deep dark blue shiny marlin fabric over a soft pale cream undershirt. Around his waist he wore a braided rope with a brassy latch at his hip.

Luci'ah was stunning in her pink and gray ruffled gown with silver and black pearls accentuating the waist and shoulder decorations. The fabric draped to a V in the back exposing her perfect pale skin to her waist.

Luci'ah was just an inch or two taller than James as they stood at the altar facing the old man. They held hands as they repeated their vows. The Mene'ahn vows were almost identical to those of a typical Christian ceremony, except it was conducted in the Mene'ahn language. The elegant old gentleman asked the young couple several questions about their duties as a married couple and about their faith and commitment to Mene'ah. As James's confi'ah bracelet translated the words they responded positively to each question. He blessed the new couple and it was done!

The wedding and reception was attended by Naha'ran's wife, Tia'rah, the girl's grandmother, looking lovely but fragile in her floating chair, accompanied by her nurse. The elegantly attired old matriarch was slightly older than her husband and her health was rapidly fading. She did not want to miss her grandaughter's wedding. Tia'rah was dressed in a creamy yellow gown with a lacy shawl made of thousands of yellow pearls strung like a fishing net around her neck and shoulders. The two huge guards were also there along with several of the council members along with their wives. All of the guests were attired in their finest costumes. Uncle Josi'ah and his two sons were also in attendance but their stern faces revealed their disapproval.

At the end of the ceremony the entire group paraded down the long hallway toward the central water-elevator and then around the corner to the dining hall. There they were joined by a small crowd of Mene'ahns and everyone enjoyed a great feast. The joy of the occasion was mixed with a feeling of apprehension and distrust by many of the guests, but those feelings were ignored, for now. Marriage is a time of joy and celebration. All of the guests did their best to put aside their concerns for Luci'ah's and her new husband.

James seemed genuinely happy and often looked lovingly at his astonishingly beautiful bride. The young couple celebrated their union by sharing a variety of traditional Mene'ahn dishes and an inordinate amount of Motling ale.

One by one the guests grew tired and slipped out until finally the bride and groom were allowed to retire to Luci'ah's apartment to consummate their marriage.

Luci'ah was a virgin, but she was not unfamiliar with sex. She knew how beautiful and satisfying sex could be as evidenced by loving relationships she had observed. Luci'ah wanted children also. She could not remember a day in her life that she had not dreamed of having children of her own. It is unclear why, but unions between Mene'ahns and earth humans had historically yielded exceptionally beautiful, healthy children. Luci'ah was anxious, excited, scared, and happy, very happy. Her passion for her husband would be satisfied that night.

James watched as Luci'ah stood before a wall of warm blue light, slowly removing her jewelry. Her dress was tied beneath her arm and with a gentle pull on a satiny cord it revealed her bare skin in a narrow strip down to her ankles. She smiled seductively at her new spouse and asked. "Can you help me with this?"

James leapt to his feet and began to fiddle clumsily with the laces at her side. Soon it was loose enough so that she was able to slip boldly out of her stunning pink and gray costume. She kicked off her shoes and stood naked in front of her husband who gasped at the perfection he was lucky enough to now possess. Her photo-shopped physique was too perfect, like the centerfold in a Playboy magazine. At first James was reluctant to unmask his own imperfect body. His hairy torso had scars and there were pock marks all over his back. But the bulge in his pants soon became uncomfortable. It didn't take long for James to overcome his shyness and he quickly unbuckled his belt and removed his pants, shortly followed by his shirt.

Luci'ah dove her long fingers into James's hairy chest hair and smiled. "Most Mene'ahn men do not have this much body hair. I love it!" Then she pressed her slender body to his.

James gently embraced his bride and they kissed for the second time. The first kiss was at the end of the ceremony and it was little more than a peck. This kiss made their heads spin and their knees buckle beneath them. Soon they were on the floor devouring each other with their mouths and hands. His hands boldly roamed up and down her luscious body, caressing every inch.

Luci'ah did not want her new husband to be disappointed so she shocked herself by letting go of all her inhibitions. She began to seduce him boldly with her mouth and hands. She giggled and suggested that they move off the floor and into her bedroom where she had previously prepared seductive lighting and fine bed linens. Then they walked hand-in-hand into the adjacent room to consummate their marriage.

Chapter 10

THE BIG WEDDING

The newlyweds remained secluded in Luci'ah's apartment for nearly a week. When the two emerged they were both starry-eyed. Luci'ah practically glowed as she returned to her activities in the infirmary. Her sister had been busily planning her own wedding which promised to be much larger and more elaborate than her sister's rushed ceremony.

In a few weeks the entire colony would attend Lune'ah's wedding, and it seemed that half of the New Mene'ahn population was involved, planning games, refreshments, decorations and music. Two huge feasts were planned, one before the wedding ceremony and one after. The wedding itself was to take place in the main auditorium on the first level of the colony. A mountain of flowers would come from above and below the horizon. Music, food, and entertainment would commemorate the wedding celebration of Lune'ah--the beloved granddaughter of an important member of their own family, and the rugged American she had rescued from death at the hands of ruthless pirates in the icy waters of the South Antarctic Sea.

Luci'ah was at her duties in the hospital when a personal alarm was called for her and members of her immediate family, regarding her grandmother--Tia'rah. Luci'ah excused herself and contacted her sister, immediately, through her wrist communication device. "Lune'ah, did you receive the alarm? What is it about?" Her sister did not know, but she agreed to meet with her right away, on the primary level to find out.

Lune'ah was assisting in an important investigation in the main library but she excused herself, immediately, when she became aware of the family emergency at hand.

The two sisters met in the hallway outside their grandmother's apartment. They embraced and held hands. Lune'ah looked deeply into her sister's eyes and they instinctively knew why they had been summoned to their grandmother's suite that day. They gathered their courage, recited a quick prayer, and activated the bubble to enter the doorway.

Tia'rah, one of the loveliest most elegant matriarchs of the colony, lay reclined in her bed at the end of the large oval room, perched on a pile of colorfully embroidered pillows. She held out one of her slender hands to greet her granddaughters, but she did not speak.

No one spoke at first. The silence in the room was almost total. The girls floated in and stood beside her bed. They leaned in to kiss their grandmother on her soft wrinkled cheeks. The girls each took a hand, grasping them close to their hearts. They looked into the old woman's tired eyes and tried to understand the irreversible decision that Tia'rah was making.

"You still have so much life, my Ti-ra-rah." Lune'ah finally spoke as a tiny tear rolled down her face and dripped off her chin. She had called her grandmother by this name ever since she was a small child. "I cannot bear to see you go."

"No, mi-hi'tah. My life is over, my old body hurts, and I am so tired." She strained to force a smile as she spoke, her voice so soft that the girls had to lean in closer just to hear it. "I want you to know how very proud I am of both of you. You have given me so much joy." Then she looked directly at Lune'ah and said, "I'm so sorry that I will not witness your wedding, my dear. I'm just so very tired."

"We are so honored to have been loved and taught by you," said Luci'ah. "Thank you. Thank you, Tia'rah. We love you so much." At that, she broke down and began to sob, burying her face into the warm bony chest of her grandmother. Lune'ah sat up and poked her sister as if to say *get a grip.* Then Luci'ah wiped away her tears and tried to smile.

The girls had been raised by this beautiful lady when their parents decided to return to Lunon. Tia'rah and Naha'ran arrived on the earth in the year 1728. They had both been born on the ship "Courage" in convoy #7 as it raced to the earth at nearly half-light speed. They were small children when America was first formed. They married in the same year that the Declaration of Independence was signed. They had three children before Sam Houston defeated Santa Anna at San Jacinto. They watched in horror, from the safe vantage point of the ice colony, as Americans slaughtered each other in the Civil War.

Lune'ah and Luci'ah's parents along with all the other children of Naha'ran and Tia'rah except for one, decided to return to the Mene'ahn system, when the fleet left in 1939. Lune'ah and Luci'ah' chose to remain, as did Uncle Josi'ah, who was married and had seven children. Uncle Josi'ah became a council member and the General in charge of the colony's reserve army.

The girls expected their uncle to arrive at his mother's side momentarily. Naha'ran stood quietly in the shadow of a huge tapestry which hung from the ceiling and divided the large room into two separate quarters. The two women sat alongside their grandmother's bed in silence for several minutes.

The deep wrinkles in her ancient face did not disguise the beauty that she had enjoyed in her youth, nor did it disguise the beauty that remained within her still. She had been an icon of virtue and strength for her entire life.

In a sense Tia'rah had been the "First Lady" of New Mene'ah. Her husband had been nominated and elected to the council by a huge majority of Mene'ahns. He organized the twelve council members here before the turn of the 20th century. Before that, there had been conflict and often chaos within the colony.*

Naha'ran was elected to monitor the most important department in the New Mene'ahn government. Naha'ran was the spiritual leader of

---

* In the Earth year 1907, Naha'ran de Lunon organized the election of one council member representative from each of the twelve districts on the nine planets of Mene'ah. Council members could be recalled at any time, with a vote of "no confidence" by a majority of the citizens of the colony. Each council member had ultimate and final control of one vital department of the New Mene'ahn government. The system has worked almost flawlessly for the past eighty years on Earth and the equivalent of eight thousand years on the Mene'ahn system.

the council and of the entire colony. He had maintained that honor, with dignity for nearly eighty five years. Throughout all those years he conducted all council sessions with great dignity and respect making sure Mene'ah Himself was in charge.

Interrupting the silence Tia'rah finally spoke. "My spirit yearns to be with Mene'ah, my darlings. I have had a wonderful life. I cannot stay with you sweet children forever. I want to go now (she closed her eyes, but continued to speak.) "This old body can do no more for you." Tia'rah gently squeezed the hands of her adoring granddaughters.

The doorway swished open and in came Uncle Josiah. They greeted each other by clasping their hands and touching cheeks in genuine affection. The handsome older gentleman seemed massive beside his thin and graceful nieces. He turned his attention to his mother who was smiling at the sight of her son. He kissed her ever so gently on the cheek. One by one, Josi'ahs wife and all seven of his children filed in and greeted her with similar kisses and forced smiles.

As all of her closest family members surrounded her bed she took a deep breath and said. "Thank you for coming today." She paused and then proceeded speaking slowly and deliberately. "I love you all so much and I am so proud of you. I am going away now, but I will return. You will meet me again in the eyes of someone you love in the future, I promise." At that she closed her eyes and folded her hands across her chest peacefully. Naha'ran came around the tapestry wall and she opened her eyes, looked up at him and smiled. He planted a kiss firmly on his wife's lips. Then everyone held hands in a semicircle around her bed as they recited a prayer to Mene'ah in the Mene'ahn language.

While the family was at Tia'rah's bedside Michael and James were fulfilling the list presented to them by their ladies. They were to find and hopefully to decide on, their contribution to the colony. Apparently this was one of the requirements set by Mene'ah thousands of years ago. Everyone must do their fair share of the work. No slackers! The two young men had a variety of talents and experiences, and it was clear there was much to do to keep a colony of this size afloat. This day they were meeting with Nahish, a Polynesian/ Japanese looking individual who was the council member in charge of the energy supply for the colony. James wanted to learn how the Mene'ahn's convert ordinary water into Hydrogen and oxygen. He thought the department of "Energy" would be a good place to help make a contribution to Mene'ah and he brought his friend Michael along for support.

James made a good impression on Nahish and encouraged him to become an apprentice.

But Michael wanted to make another type of contribution. He wasn't quite sure what that would be, at the time, but he knew he did not want to labor in an enclosed space, away from everyone. He wanted to work with the Mene'ahn people. He wanted to get to know them. They were all his family now.

When Lune'ah and Luci'ah returned from their grandmother's bedside Michael and James knew, without asking, that Tia'rah was gone. Luci'ah softly spoke the news into James's ear and they all shared a moment of silence in a shoulder to shoulder group hug. "Tia'rah is not really sick. She is just tired of living," explained Lune'ah.

"So you are just allowing her to die?" He asked almost scolding.

"We do not have a choice. The decision is hers to make." Lune'ah knitted her brow. She could not help but notice his displeasure and she wanted to explain more, so that he would understand, but this was not the time.

A few awkward moments of silence passed. Michael tried to digest the concept of *allowing someone to die*. It was a bit too much for him to handle so he changed the subject. "Looks like James may have a job working with the Energy Department."

"That would be wonderful, James." said both girls in unison.

"Yeah, James can handle that kind of stuff," said Michael. "You know, he planned to become a doctor. He got accepted to Medical School in Galveston, but his grandfather would not give him the money he had promised, so he couldn't afford to go." Michael had grown to admire James for his brilliant mind and seemingly infinite knowledge of practically everything.

Luci'ah proudly suggested. "You will do quite well helping Nahish to keep this place running smoothly. I just know you will." Luci'ah's adoration of her husband blinded her to his real aspirations.

The feast before the big wedding was the most astounding thing Michael and James had ever attended. At least forty tables were prepared in the dining hall on the second level. Hundreds of guests brought food, elaborate decorations and gifts to the dining hall on the second level. The entire space was filled to capacity with artistic gifts and handmade creations made from colorful sea life. Tiny, bright twinkling lights were set deep inside the solid, semi-transparent into the opal walls of the cathedral. Curtains of transparent and semi-transparent fabric hung from the ceiling, draped from a vanishing point at the top of the altar. Varieties of organic life in the form of flowers and artistic, creations randomly filled the walls and surfaces with bright colors and delicious aromas.

Hours before the ceremony the lights were dimmed and a spotlight was aimed at a slowly spinning ball of tiny mirrored tiles suspended from the ceiling, just like the ones in old dance halls on earth. Thousands of spots of light danced around the room as wedding guests began to take their seats in the large fabulously decorated hall.

The costumes were amazing. Some verged on ridiculous, but they were all worn proudly by those gracious and elegant people. The women obviously had spent hours piling their abundant hair and hair pieces, artistically upon their tall-enough-already heads. Jewelry made from sea creatures, or plucked from some exotic aquatic cave, adorned every arm and every neckline.

Michael sought out the help of Lune'ah's uncle for his wedding ensemble. A few simple alterations changed one of Uncle Josi'ah's tailored military uniforms into the perfect attire. A total of fifteen minutes of preparations took place that afternoon in Uncle Josiah's apartment. Michael looked so handsome, like he had just stepped out of a military issue of GQ magazine, when he stepped boldly out into the hallway and marched in lock-step with his Uncle toward the Auditorium.

Lune'ah's preparations required significantly more time--about two months. All those preparations certainly paid off, because on her wedding day, she was the most stunning creature ever created by the hands of God.

Michael stood erect by the altar in the center of the auditorium, in his borrowed costume. His pale a-symmetrical tunic was collared by short white fur and trimmed with shiny pearl crusted embroidery around the ends of the sleeves and down the sides of the pant legs. The handsome groom's eyes never left the top of the stairway where he anticipated the arrival of his beautiful bride.

His bride took everyone's breath away When she finally arrived Michael's bride took everyone's breath away. Her costume contained every shade of purple known to mankind. One side of her thick auburn hair was left to hang waving nearly to her waist. The other side was piled on her head and secured with a stunning arrangement of amethyst stones and peacock feathers. The thin gossamer fabric clung closely to her perfect frame and was gathered over one shoulder. The flowing skirt was cinched at her narrow waist with a broad and ornate belt, like a work of art hanging from her mid-section. Six or eight long strands of pink and purple pearls draped over her bare arm and across her hip like a beaded shawl. The clingy pastel fabrics flowed to her ankles in layer after layer of lavender and plum with ruffled and irregular edges. She had designed and constructed the ensemble herself.

The entire audience rose as Naha'ran entered the auditorium. He stepped up onto the central stage and stood beside Michael and spoke loudly to the audience.. *"Hane'ah favoy. Sheha Mene'ah rajah favoy. Nieo lo quoree saja sajamo favoy, lewah Michael Ellsworth, wa lewah Luneah Lunon."* Michael was beginning to understand the Mene'ahn language and he knew that Naha'ran was welcoming everyone to the wedding. A few moments later the old council member asked the audience to sit. He could see Lune'ah waiting at the main entrance, at the very top of the steps which inclined upward away from the stage. He asked if there were any objections to this union. After he waited a respectable amount of time, he motioned for Lune'ah to begin her descent toward the stage.

All eyes followed as she stepped slowly down the steps of the aisle.

She carried no flowers. There were no bridesmaids, no ring bearer. She had no veil covering her glowing face. All eyes watched, as she floated slowly down as if in a dream. Michael stood erect, waiting for her at the altar, unable to take his eyes off of the angelic figure as she descended. She finally arrived. She faced him, took both his hands into hers and looked squarely into his eyes, which were exactly at his level. Michael, trapped by the emerald green eyes of his bride, felt a peace and confidence he had never known before. At that moment everything except Lune'ah's perfect face was a blur.

Naha'ran first asked everyone to begin the ceremony with a prayer. All responded by standing and raising their hands into the air and saying in unison.

> *"Orah Mene'ah*
> *e sha Mene'ah*
> *Mon sah ha wa lah Sheha Mene'ah*
> *Ah'men"*

Then everyone resumed their seats and turned their attention to Luci'ah who had appeared as if from nowhere. She was covered from her slender neck to the floor in a white fur trimmed cloak. She began to sing the song she had written and prepared exclusively for her sister's wedding. Luci'ah had a beautiful voice and the crowd listened in utter silence and respect.

> *Orah mon nieo lewah*
> *Orah mon lewah Lune'ah*
> *Sajo quoree*
> *Sajo lasha lewah*
> *Orah Lune'ah*
> *Wa orah Mene'ah*
> *Orah Lune'ah*
> *Orah mon lewah*

When her song was finished Luci'ah smiled sweetly, delicately wiped away her own tears and gracefully stepped down from the stage.

Naha'ran stood center stage, and the bride and groom faced him with their backs to the audience. He spoke for a few minutes in the Mene'ahn language, casually addressing the bride, the groom and the audience. Then he faced Michael and asked him in English, "Michael Ellsworth will you take Lune'ah de Lunon to be your wife?"

He responded prematurely and answered, "I will."

Naha'ran continued with the questions. "Will you live with her according to the laws of Mene'ah? Will you love her, care for her, protect and respect her, and share your life with her until your final day?"

"I will," Michael whispered.

Then he turned to Lune'ah and repeated the same questions. The two held hands and looked deeply into each other's eyes. He gave the two lovers some gentle words of advice. At the end of the service they were allowed to kiss. Naha'ran raised his hands into the air, which signaled everyone to do the same and together they again recited the Meneahn prayer. Then the newly married couple marched, hand in hand, out of the auditorium following the same path Lune'ah had taken in. Then they were followed by virtually everyone.

The reception dinner following the wedding was held on the beach by the salt lake of New Mene'ah. Artificial darkness enveloped the domed lake and artificial stars illuminated the artificial sky, but it was real enough for the two lovers as they faced their life together. Friends and family supplied tropical music with an island luau theme. Lune'ah was able to hike her skirt up and suspend it with a sash at her waist, so that she could dance. Bamboo tables with mountains of exotic foods lined the sparkling shore. A strong salty breeze from across the lake threatened to extinguish the flames of the tiki lamps as Michael and Lune'ah danced and walked along the beach. Their solitude was regularly interrupted by well-wishers and prayers.

Hours passed and Michael was more than ready to retire. He hinted this request to his bride and the two of them bid their guests good night and slipped away. They ran to their apartment and breathlessly laughed as they leaned against the wall to activate the button. The doorway sloshed open and they stepped in. It was a giant step into an entirely different kind of life.

Married life was a new world for both of them, and sex was

entirely new to Lune'ah, though she understood the fundamentals. She had anticipated this night for a very long time. She had studied videos made above the horizon, some of which were even rated XXX. Her passion for her husband had been bridled up until this very moment and she would not hold back. She began seducing him the moment they were safely inside Lune'ah's apartment. Their mouths connected and melded together with magnetism that knocked them to their knees. Without saying a word they moved into the adjacent room where the bed had been adorned with flakes of fragrant flower petals and the room was lined with candle lights.

The newlyweds stood before the floor to ceiling mirror and began to remove their garments. First Lune'ah unhooked and removed the abstract and colorful belt from her costume. Her gown was fastened in the back with a long thin purple cord connecting the two sides of her delicate gown with a series of chain links. When Michael pulled on the tie at the top, the loops quickly slipped through each other to the last one at the base of Lune'ah's spine. He then gently slid the dress off her shoulders to expose her perfect breasts. She carefully removed the large buckled belt from around her husband's waist. When the heavily beaded gown dropped to her ankles she slid her arms under Michael's tunic and pressed her body against his. Then she sat on the corner of the bed and pulled him close, placing her head on Michael's firm chest. She could hear his heart pounding wildly and she smiled to know that her own excitement was matched by her husbands.

Michael did not want his bride to know that he was just as nervous as she. He had known many women but he had never been with a virgin. And he had never really loved the women he had been with. His affairs had been empty. He worried that he might do something that would repulse or scare her so he moved very slowly and cautiously.

The two nervous lovers consummated their union that night by the soft glowing light from the ice wall in Lune'ah's bedroom. The love and tenderness they shared that night brought them closer than either of them had dreamed possible. As they faced an uncertain future together they fell asleep on their wedding night, confident their love would survive.

Chapter 11
LIFE IN THE SECRET CITY

The two young Americans had many adjustments to make over the next few months. They missed things about the world above the horizon, but they both stayed busy. They chose occupations that were tedious and time consuming, but also very rewarding. To the men, time passed by ever-so-slowly. For the Mene'ahns time raced by. They even aged more rapidly on our planet.

James worked at the central energy station on the lowest level. He learned all he could about the technology of the seven - leveled colony above and he became indispensable as a mechanic and general maintenance manager. He was given access to a variety of equipment to repair and replace every part of the vast energy system. This experience enabled him to understand the complex power technology of the hidden city and he kept a personal notebook to record important details.

The central power station was a huge, loud, whirling machine which sucked the heat and energy from the Earth's mantle. A gigantic generator and nearly a hundred miles of special tubing used the heat from the earth's mantle to separate the water into hydrogen and oxygen. This provided the energy to run virtually everything in the colony. Tremendous heat, along with water was forced through magnetic turbines which separated the hydrogen, and oxygen. This process provided all the oxygen necessary for the colony and enabled the entire city to be totally hidden from the world above. Natural cracks in the icy surface allowed for some air filtration. Other than that, it was impossible to see any evidence of a city hidden beneath the surface of the ice.

All of the tools and instruments used by everyday Mene'ahn citizens, were powered by this hydrogen-based form of electricity. James quickly learned how to operate everything. Often he would take a piece of equipment to his apartment, just to disassemble and reassemble it. James was also interested in the mental and psychic powers of the Mene'ahns. Luci'ah was happy to share with James everything she knew. James's beautiful wife became his mentor, as well as his guardian and savior.

Luci'ah explained this psychic phenomenon to James one morning in this way... "Humans, Mene'ahns, and even many sub-species all have patterns to their auras, like an invisible electrical field surrounding us. They are magnetic-like patterns, and no two patterns are exactly the same. This is why some people fall desperately *in-love* at first sight, and why some people dislike each other immediately upon meeting--because their magnetic patterns repel each other--like trying to put opposing ends of two magnets together."

"So did you feel this attraction for me when you first fished me out of the freezing ocean?" James asked his bride.

Luci'ah smiled. "Yes James, it was a very strong attraction, from the beginning."

James was pleased with his wife's answer. "So is that how you can read my mind?" he quizzed.

"Partly," she answered honestly. "I can't really read your mind, but I can sense your emotions. I don't understand how, or why, we have this ability. I think your people call it intuition. For us it is stronger than that. Her expression changed to serious. An uncomfortable long pause ensued.

"So, if you knew that I was going to try to escape, why didn't you try to stop me?" he asked.

Luci'ah thought carefully about her response. "I knew you *wanted* to escape. I did not know that you would *actually TRY* to escape. I hoped you would change your mind. I hoped you could find happiness here with me."

"So, can you tell me," he looked straight into her eyes, "what am I thinking right now?" James was feeling aroused. It didn't take much for James when he was in such close proximity to his stunning bride. He smiled and pulled her hips close to his.

Luci'ah looked deeply into his eyes and smiled, at first. But as she continued to explore the depths of his psyche, her eyes widened, her brows knitted and suddenly she had to turn away. James was still smiling until he turned her face toward his and saw that her eyes had filled with tears and then he wilted.

"What's wrong, babe."

At first Luci'ah was silent. James was beginning to lose his patience. "What did you see in there babe?" He probed, but perhaps he did not really want to know.

Luci'ah turned her face back to his and said simply, "I know James, I know."

"You know what, WHAT?" he insisted.

"I know what you don't want me to know, James. I know that you still want to leave New Mene'ah." Luci'ah's eyes swept the floor, and she gently pushed away from James's embrace.

"No, sweetheart, babe, well, maybe I do miss that world, but I would never leave you. I would never hurt you like that. I am a Mene'ahn now. I may not always be real happy about it, but I am here to stay!" James really believed the words he spoke, but, deep down, he knew he could not hide his feelings from his mind-reading bride.

Luci'ah gladly took her husband's hand and embraced him. "I'll accept that for now, if I can hear the words from your lips," she whispered.

"What words do you want to hear, Babe," James asked.

"Look deeply into my eyes and we'll see if you can read *my* thoughts" she teased.

"I love you," he said knowingly.

"You see, you can do it too." She smiled as she placed her head on his hairy chest and held him close. "I love you, James, more than you will ever know."

While James was picking Luci'ah's brain, Lune'ah was picking Michael's brain about the world above the horizon. She was more than just a little snobbish in her attitude about the civilizations above the horizon. Sometimes her distaste for earthlings became almost racist and often Michael felt offended.

Ever-looming in their future was the awful knowledge that Osaura's fleet was due to arrive in twenty-six years, and onboard was the ability to faze out mankind, in a painless, non-violent way of course, but actually quite mean. The Mene'ahn scientists, the brains of Mene'ah, had created a virus capeable of disabling only the reproductive organs of its human victims. They apparently also had created a vaccine and were able to immunized themselves against this virus. Lune'ah explained to Michael that none of the citizens of New Mene'ah were as yet immunized. The serum to protect them all would arrive with Osaura's fleet in 2016.

Michael did not come from a large family. The family members he still had, were some he wasn't too proud of. His mother had been killed in an automobile accident and his father disappeared shortly thereafter. Michael and his cousin were raised by his Polish grandmother and his beloved Aunt Sweetie. He had wonderful memories of his childhood summers, playing on the beach with his cousin. Lune'ah wanted to know everything about Michael's aunt and he enjoyed telling her stories about the dear lady.

Sweetie had lived in a cabin on the beach at the mouth of the Colorado River, in Texas. Back then Matagorda was a sleepy little fishing village with very little social life apart from Stanley's bait shop. Michael's Aunt Sweetie loved to fish and tell jokes. She never met a stranger. She had been in a rock-n-roll band in her youth, and she could play any kind of tune on her keyboard without missing a note. But Sweetie smoked cigarettes and she died way too young.

"Why do earth humans smoke?" Lune'ah asked.

"I don't know. They just do," he said bluntly as he carefully placed a cup of hot spiced tea on the glassy table beside her.

"Michael," she continued, "Why do your people have wars? What do they fight and kill each other for?"

"That's easy," he smiled proudly. "In America we have always fought for freedom."

"Freedom?" she looked puzzled. "I'm sorry, I just don't understand."

"Well, some countries fight over oil, and some fight over land, and they all fight for power, of course. But in America we just fight for freedom. Sometimes we fight for freedom for other countries, but we are most definitely the good guys."

Lune'ah raised the steaming cup to her lips. She was beginning to feel uncomfortable with discussions about America because she found it difficult to separate the U.S.A. from the rest of the world. According to Michael, America was separate, unique and superior. His pride in having served his country was evident and his wife was wise not to share her true feelings about America with her all-American boy-scout husband. She had studied Earth civilizations half of her life. She was sure that Michael was wrong about his beloved America. She knew about some of the cruelties and horrible corruption within the government. In many ways, she felt superior to the backward, primitive, violent people above the horizon, but she adored her husband. She was sure he was exceptional.

"Why would people fight over their religion, Michael?" she asked.

"There were a lot of wars fought over religion. I guess most people feel that God is on their side so they get brave, they feel invincible, you know." Michael pondered.

"No, I don't know." She looked away and thought for a minute. Michael could not help but notice her perfect profile, as she gazed at a glassy art piece on the wall. "It just seems so silly to me that all those millions of people have so many different names for God and so many different ideas about God. Do they think there are many Gods with many different names or do they know that there is only one God, and they just call Him different names? I just don't understand... Tell me more about your Aunt."

"My Aunt Sweetie was Catholic." Michael said. "She loved Mary and Jesus. She had little statues and Rosary beads all around her place. She kept a huge Bible on her coffee table. She played the organ sometimes, in her church, and she sang too. She had a strong low voice. You would have loved my Aunt."

"You think so? Why?"

Michael reached across the table and took Lune'ah's hand in his firm grasp. He looked deeply into her eyes, which forced her to look deeply into his, and he said "because I loved her." And instantly she understood what Michael was saying. Millions, billions of good people living above the horizon did not deserve to have the futures of their families erased for no reason.

Without words they knew. They would have to do whatever they could to change the course of the Mene'ahn intentions. This could prove to be a daunting task and might even take a lifetime.

Lune'ah was seven months pregnant. They were both thrilled about becoming parents. Lune'ah was planning to have a small room added to their apartment before the baby came.

Michael was learning to be a fisherman, and he loved it. He had gone out several times on short and long excursions with Uncle Josiah. On several occasions, from the co-pilot's seat he had observed his uncle skillfully maneuvering the sleek fishing vessel out of the water tunnel and into the darkness of the icy ocean where they gathered commodities from the vast oceans. It was a submarine about the size of a small school bus. Its smooth rounded sides and shape reminded Michael of similar looking vehicles in the sci-fi movies of the sixties. The cock-pit of the little submarine was a comfortable space, just made for the two six-foot-tall fishermen but there was no additional wiggle room.

One day Michael arrived right on time and was surprised and glad when Uncle Josi'ah offered him the pilot's seat. He happily slid in next to Uncle Josi'ah who on that day, was in the co-pilot's seat. For a few moments Michael sat with both his hands on the sides of the half-round steering panel looking forward. He could hear the purring and feel the vibrations of the engines, so he knew that Josi'ah had already activated the engine. He pulled back on a lever and the unit lurched backward and clicked itself into place. Suddenly the submarine was enclosed in a small aquarium which rapidly filled with water. Sea water poured in around them from all sides; and within just a few seconds the ship was totally submerged. Then the wall in front of them became transparent. When it disappeared completely, a green light signaled ready and a long dark tunnel invited them out to the open sea. Josi'ah gave Michael the go-ahead and after swiping his fingers over some lights on the panel, they shot out of the tunnel like a cannonball.

After several hours of speeding through familiar deep sea pathways, they approached a huge cavern deep within the Great Barrier Reef, east of Australia. The enormous opening was like a long low ebony crack in the ocean floor. Just before they entered its mouth, the whole cave became illuminated and the two pilots could easily see deeply into a wonderland of productivity. Michael slowed the vessel down to a crawl. The first section they puttered through was like a farm but instead of plants, this farm was growing hundreds of individual sheets of organic, carbon, silicon fibers. Rows and rows of colorful, satiny and textured fabrics grew from the ceiling of the cavern and waved freely in the ocean currents. "We will retrieve some hash'ia sheets on our way out." said Josiah.

"They are beautiful." Michael was amazed at the variety of colors and patterns on the rows of fabric sheets as they swayed in the clear water.

Josi'ah pointed for Michael to steer the vessel to the right. A deep cut in the side of the cave contained schools of fish and was completely enclosed by a clear wall with green moss growing around the edges. As Michael approached the wall Josi'ah showed him the round area where their submarine could enter the huge pool. This was where much of the sea life which fed the colony was raised.

Josi'ah reminded Michael of the procedure for ejecting the large net from the stern of the submarine. They could see by the image on the video screen in front of them that the net had scooped up part of a large school of bass. Josi'ah carefully manipulated a joy stick on a panel between the seats and Michael opened the cargo shaft to pull in the catch. Hundreds of beautiful, fighting, striped sea bass filled a basin in the center of the sub.

After the net was safely replaced, the submarine moved on to the next load. Josi'ah put his hands into a pair of thick gloves that were in a slot on the main panel of the cock-pit. Michael gingerly lowered the submarine until its belly was sliding upon the sandy ocean floor. Immediately large crab-like arms, controlled by Jos'iah, reached out from the front of the submarine and began scooping up huge crabs and other crustaceans as they scattered across the sandy cavern floor. He guided the creatures into an open slot just below the cock-pit until the cargo bay was full. After that Michael steered the vessel back out, through the opening and around to the main entrance. There they gathered twenty or more sheets of fine hashi'ah fabrics again using the submarine's crab-like arms. The mechanical arms of the submarine gingerly grasped the end of each hashi'ah sheet near where it grew from the roof of the cavern. Then they reversed the submarine, tearing each sheet down from one end to the other. Some were twice the length of the submarine. The sea water was automatically squeezed out of each sheet as they were sucked into the special cargo hold.

After they returned to the colony and docked the submarine into place, they were met by a dozen or more friendly Mene'ahn merchants who were happy to claim the merchandise. They placed the damp fabrics, crabs, lobster and fish, still fighting, into containers that were supported by anti-gravity devices so they floated away effortlessly. Michael enjoyed meeting the chefs and artisans who would transform these products into useful and edible commodities to be shared with the rest of the colony.

Michael wanted his own submarine and he had made that desire clear to his instructor on more than one occasion. After proving himself on several expeditions Josiah placed a round disk in Michael's hand and announced that the New Mene'ahn council had authorized him to assign Michael one of the newest fishing submarines. The disk, about the size of a poker chip, was the control- key for his new submarine. Josi'ah showed Michael his new, super-fast, economy-sized submarine, which had been updated with the best, most modern Mene'ahn technology. Michael was on top of the world. He could not wait to get home to tell his beautiful, pregnant bride.

He saw his wife leaning over the pedestal table perched on her elbows, her head buried between her arms and her auburn hair disheveled and matted on the surface. "What's wrong?" He rushed over to her and helped her to an overstuffed chair. He brushed the wet hair out of her face. "Baby, are you OK?"

"No, Michael," she sounded almost like she was mad at him, but she wasn't. She was just hurting and worried. "I think I might be losing our baby. I have begun to bleed, and I have an unusual pain. Take me to the infirmary, please."

Michael picked up his bride in one swift scoop and carried her down the hall, up the central spiral staircase and around to the infirmary. He placed her carefully on a narrow padded table and several nurses and interns gathered around her and began administering tests. Michael was escorted out but he stood nearby with his ear glued to the exam room doorway where his wife lay in pain and bleeding.

A few moments later a tall nurse, who looked a lot like Klinger from the old TV series *M.A.S.H.* told Michael that Lune'ah was fine. She was sleeping and the baby inside her was doing well. She advised Michael to go home and get some rest. The nurse felt certain that Lune'ah would be able to carry the child to term if she remained still and horizontal.

The ugly nurse was right. Luneah remained in bed for the remainder of her pregnancy and a fine healthy boy was born about seven weeks later. They named him Gabricl, after Saint Gabril. The entire colony soon heard about the new blessing and prayers of thanks to Mene'ah were offered in every household.

Lune'ah was able to return to their apartment only a few days after the childbirth. They entered and found their home filled with gifts, all sorts of useful and beautiful items for the new citizen of Mene'ah and for the blessed parents. Luci'ah was there too, busily involved in custodial duties in her sister's apartment. She rushed to the door to greet her sister's family. Luci'ah gently pulled back the swaddling blanket to see the sleeping face of her nephew. He didn't look like much at the time. He was still red and flakey and quite scrawny. Luci'ah thought he was the prettiest baby she had ever seen and Michael wholeheartedly agreed.

That night Michael had a strange dream. He saw an angel walking alone along a hazy beach, in a long white sleeping gown and she was holding a baby wrapped loosely in a silky sheet. She waded through the shallow waves close to the shore. Her huge angel wings were almost invisible as she emerged from a dense fog. At first he did not recognize the angel, but as she floated closer he could see that it was Lune'ah. She walked up to him and smiled. Michael looked over her shoulders and wondered why her feathery wings had suddenly disappeared. He reached out his arms, and swung them from side to side in his sleep, trying to feel the wings that were no longer visible. He woke startled, when Lune'h grabbed his arm. "I thought you were going to hit us! You were having a nightmare."

"No, it wasn't a bad dream. It was a beautiful dream." Michael was glad to see his wonderful wife and fine healthy son, Gabriel, sharing his large bed. He smiled and snuggled close to both of them. Then, as they lay there holding each other, Lune'ah and Michael said a prayer to God, whose name they called Mene'ah.

Chapter 12
BETRAYAL

Nearly two years had passed since little Gabriel was born and Osaura's fleet was two years closer to its arrival at the secret colony of New Mene'ah. Citizens of the colony were busy doing their individual jobs, hidden deep within the mile thick glacier at the South Pole. Their main objective, of course, was to wait, and to survive, until Osaura comes with his fleet of new citizens. He was on his way with a dozen ships and a hundred dozen new families. They all would come to populate a new world.

The two American men had twice addressed the council to discuss the dangerous viruses and vaccines that Osaura was bringing. The council, on both occasions had dismissed their concerns with a wave of Naha'ran's hand. "Gentlemen, your concerns are unfounded, no decision has been made about this, and will not be, until Osaura's fleet arrives here. We too are concerned, but you must be patient. Go, and do not bother us with this issue again."

But Michael did not leave it alone. Michael called meetings to address his concerns. He talked to the Mene'ahn citizens about the future of the earth as it concerned the Mene'ahn people. His wife and some friends organized and held a special election and succeeded in electing Michael Ellsworth, the thirteenth council member representing the Earth. The campaign went on for nearly a full earth year.

After Michael was elected the council convened whenever anyone requested it, and Michael was required to attend each and every meeting. He became a very busy man. He continued operating his submarine and was becoming an expert fisherman. He was also a new father and Lune'ah was soon expecting the arrival of twin girls.

Michael and Lune'ah were great together. She was a wonderful mother and joy filled their home. Gabriel, at age twenty months, was running, climbing and mastering simple games. He could speak English and Mene'ahn and was even learning to read in both languages. Their world revolved around little Gabriel. He was active and inquisitive about everything. More than anything, he loved riding in the fishing submarine with his "PaPo"'. The youngster learned about all kinds of fish and sea life on these short educational excursions. Michael promised his boy that, someday he would take him along when he went to the caverns of the Great Barrier Reef.

James and Luci'ah seemed less than happy. Even though he liked his job, James felt claustrophobic and often retreated to the beaches in his spare time. Luci'ah was the most loving, supportive, beautiful wife a man could want on the outside. Inside she often felt worthless and insecure.

Luci'ah was good at making other people happy but she failed to make herself happy. She even felt uncomfortable at the hospital where she spent most of her time. She was sure, others were judging her, and were critical of her marriage to James. This was understandable, under the circumstances. And her jealousy of her sister was tearing her apart. She hated herself for being so shallow. She loved her sister more than anything, but she begrudged her happiness. She envied her sister because Lune'ah had everything she had always wanted. She envied the genuine love that she and Michael shared. Luci'ah knew she would never have one-hundred per-cent of James's love. She knew that James still loved Noreen and Noreen had given him a child. Luci'ah wanted a baby more than anything else in the world, and she made James a very happy man trying so hard to make a baby.

Luci'ah's sister was due to deliver her twins any day. Lune'ahs pregnancy went much more smoothly this time. Luc'iah found herself at her sister's apartment often, especially when she was lonely. She loved helping her sister with Gabriel, and those days Lune'ah needed lots of help.

Occasionally, Luci'ah and James would talk about the world above the horizon. James told her many stories about the wonders of the world he left behind. Actually, Luci'ah, from her childhood, had dreamed of going above the horizon, standing on a mountain top and looking out over green valleys. James promised he would take her up in a hot air balloon one day and they would drift across the mountain tops together. There were times, in the dark privacy of their own ice-carved rooms they would talk about escaping together. Luci'ah knew she would have to be very careful to avoid infection above the horizon, but she had already lived longer than most earth humans. She wanted to be with James more than anything. She made him promise that he would not leave without her. He also promised that he would not seek fame and power above the horizon at the expense of New Mene'ah.

That particular day, in New Meneah, started out as any other day. Luci'ah was keeping an eye on Gabriel while Lune'ah was lying in bed. Luci'ah and Gabriel were playing the Mene'ahn version of hide and seek. That adorable, chubby little boy could be very imaginative and full of mischief. He was often quite difficult to find. Luci'ah was beginning to be concerned about the whereabouts of the toddler when Michael returned home early. She hesitated to tell Michael about the missing boy. She was sure that he was still hiding somewhere in the apartment even though she had exhausted almost every option. *Where was that child?* She thought. Michael dropped his things by the doorway, placed the disk-key to his sea craft on the counter and went into the back room to check on his hugely pregnant wife.

James arrived unexpectedly a few moments later, marched boldly through the open entrance and spoke briefly with Luci'ah. Without a word Luci'ah slipped away. James did not see her tuck the disk into her skirt pocket as she exited the apartment.

"Michael, buddy." he knocked on the wall by the open doorway. "Can I talk to you for a second?"

Michael kissed his beautiful wife on the tip of her nose and then met James in the main room. "What's up?"

"You know that special tool you are learning how to use, the ice-melter, solidifier thing? What do they call it? Anyway, can I borrow it? I'd like to try to expand my kitchen area. Luci'ah loves to cook. You got that thing here?"

"Sure, buddy, I have one I've been playing around with. It is not so easy to operate. I'll show you how to use it, and you can practice with it here, but I don't think I can let you take it with you. It was specifically assigned to me." said Michael.

"OK" said James.

Michael went into a closet, fumbled around and brought out a black net, drawstring bag. He sat down on the floor in the center of the room and dumped the contents of the bag onto the thick fur rug. There were two short transparent hoses and an oval shaped attachment connected to the tool. James sat Indian style next to him. Michael showed James how to use the control lever and how to control the size and strength of the electrical stream. He showed James how the stream could be spread to melt large areas of ice very rapidly. Michael demonstrated the method for connecting the suction tubes to the main gun and how to attach the tube to the drainage system. James paid very close attention.

"Does the thing work without being attached to the suction tube?" James asked.

"Sure, but you're gonna' end up standing in a puddle of water." Michael smiled.

"Come on over here to this wall and give it a try."

James took the tool, which looked like a large water gun, and aimed it at a spot on the wall. James was familiar with a variety of Mene'ahn tools. This one was particularly interesting because it was conveniently portable. He made sure the little green light was on and he pushed the sliding lever. A green beam of light indicated the direction and showed that the gun was ready to fire. James pulled the trigger and a bolt of white light shot a hole in the wall which dripped into a small puddle at the base of the wall. "That's so cool!" said James. He turned the machine off and placed it on the table.

Just then Lune'ah called Michael into the bedroom. "Michael, Love, can you come here for a minute." Michael excused himself to see what his lovely wife wanted, leaving James alone with the powerful tool.

Lune'ah told Michael that he needed to find Gabriel. He had been playing hide and seek with Luci'ah. Michael knew how much Gabriel liked to play this game.

While Michael searched for Gabriel James fumbled with the equipment and tried to put the hoses back into the bag. Suddenly he stood up, grabbed the ice-gun and walked over to the doorway. Then Michael came back into the room.

"James, you can't take that. I told you. It's registered to me."

"I really need this buddy." James was shaking and beads of sweat were forming on his forehead. He held on to the instrument tightly.

"You are not taking that tool out of this apartment," Michael said firmly.

"Yes, I am. I'm sorry. I need it." James answered

The whole scene changed dramatically at that moment. Suddenly Michael knew that his friend James was going to do something stupid. He was trying to steal the equipment and was planning to use it for something, something sinister, Michael guessed. For a few seconds the two men stared each other down until Michael lurched forward and tried to grab the gun away from James. They struggled and crashed against the wall. Four large hands grasped the delicate instrument as they rolled onto the floor. Michael began cursing his friend and screaming at him to release the object, but James was very strong and very determined. They continued to struggle and thrash around on the floor. A stalactite leg of a small table broke and all of the items on it slid to the floor. Lune'ah heard the commotion and came to the doorway of the bedroom. "What is going on?"

The men continued to wrestle on the floor and Lune'ah stepped up and tried to pull James off of Michael. "Stop it. Stop it." No one noticed that the little green light on the instrument had come on. When James resumed control of the gun, he rolled over on his back and jumped to his feet. The green light beam was pointed at Michaels head and then his chest.

"Don't move Michael. I don't want to have to hurt you." said James.

"Why are you doing this? You son of a bitch!" Michael growled. Lune'ah knelt down on the floor by her husband and began to cry.

"What are you going to do with that, James? We can't let you take it, it's dangerous!" Lune'ah begged.

Just then Michael stuck his leg out and swiped it at his friend's ankle. It was enough to make James lose his balance and fall backwards. As he fell a white beam of light shot out of the ice-melting-gun and raced across the ceiling of the ice cave and then across Lune'ahs chest. An arrow straight lightning bolt of electric heat sped across the room, caught Lune'ah at the base of her neck with a deep penetrating burn through her chest where it continued to stream across the wall and floor behind her. James and Michael watched in horrifying slow motion as Lune'ah's body went limp and collapsed in a heap on the floor.

"Oh my God! Lune'ah!" Michael turned his attention to his wife. The heat from the gun had burned her white gown and between the black frayed edges he could see her fried skin. It still bubbled from the intense heat of the gun. Then he turned to James who was still standing there, in shock, holding the ice-melting gun. Michael's eyes narrowed and hatred poured forth as he held his dying wife. He carefully lifted her eyelid and saw that her pupils had already dilated and her beautiful green eyes were black and hollow.

"She's dead. You asshole! You killed her!" Michael screamed at James as he held his pregnant wife in his arms.

"Michael, I'm sorry, I'm so sorry. It was an accident." James looked at the floor and shook his head, but in a matter of seconds he turned away and dashed out into the hallway toward his own apartment. When he arrived Luci'ah was there, frantically packing large fabric bags with clothing and everything else she could think of.

"We have to go right now!" he ordered. His wife did not speak. She passed him with her two bulging bags and started down the hallway. James followed closely behind her after he grabbed some additional bags which were stashed just inside the apartment.. She seemed cool and focused. Of course, she did not know yet, that her husband had just accidently killed her pregnant sister.

Michael, still on the floor, holding his wife, felt the movement in her soft abdomen. His children were trying to get out. They were dying along with Lune'ah. Quickly he lifted his wife up and supported her on his knee. Then he rose up and carried her all the way up to the hospital. He took the spiral stairway around the central elevator two steps at a time. He was met anxiously by a team of nurses and doctors who promptly took over. Lune'ah was placed in a room where half-a-dozen attendants swarmed about and discussed what was to be done. Clearly she needed immediate care if her life and the lives of her twins could be saved.

An orderly came out a few minutes later and told Michael that his twins would have to be delivered immediately. He assured Michael they would survive. "But what about Lune'ah... my wife? Will she...? Is she...?"

The orderly nervously tried to answer when the Doctor stepped in to elaborate on Lune'ah's condition. "Son, I have never seen an injury such as this. Her heart has stopped, and there is no brain activity. Much of the tissue in her chest cavity has been destroyed. She is dead. Yes. But remember, you were dead when we fished you out of the Antarctic, and yet somehow you survived. We will do all we can for Lune'ah, but we must act fast and take the twins first. I will need your permission to have Lune'ah frozen."

"Frozen?" Michael stepped back, tears flowed down and he swept them back into his hair. "Oh my God!"

At that very moment James and Luci'ah were sneaking up the central water elevator to the first level and heading toward the fishing submarines. The two, soon to be fugitives, were loaded down with their bags, awkwardly tossed across their shoulders. There was no one in the stairwell or in the hallways as they hurried through the winding tunnels. "Did you get the disk...the key?" asked James.

"Yes, of course." she answered. "I have never stolen anything in my entire life." Her heart was pounding out of her chest. In a few moments they were standing at the entrance of the submarine port. "Do you know which sub is Michaels?" she asked.

"It's this one over here," said James. "Give me the key." He fumbled and dropped the disk. It rolled across the floor and stopped where the wall curved up. He quickly retrieved the disk. He heard the alarm as he stood up. Overhead lights in green and red began flashing and a loud monotone bell began to sound with short intervals. James told Luci'ah to go around to the other side of the submarine. The vessel instantly popped open on both sides. James and Luci'ah tossed the bags into the cargo hold of the small ship and hopped in as quickly as they could. They buckled up and took a deep breath. Luci'ah seemed confident they were going to escape without any problems.

James slipped the disk wafer into the guidance panel, the engine began to purr and then the vehicle snapped into place. Within a few seconds they were surrounded by water. Suddenly the containment wall dissolved. James accelerated the vehicle and they shot out of the long tunnel and were propelled at a remarkable speed out into the deep ocean.

James and Luci'ah looked at each other as the submarine cruised farther and farther away from the colony. James could see that Luci'ah was smiling but she was crying at the same time. She had never been outside the hidden city, and this was an adventure that she dared not dream of.

James was not smiling. His face was red, contorted and anxious. He was sweating profusely. He was only vaguely familiar with the operations of the submarine but he kept going forward at maximum velocity. He was sure they would be followed. He also knew the Mene'ahns had the ability to track their vessel so he wanted to get far away, fast!

"We did it my love!" She was confused by his sad and frightened expression. "What's wrong? You look like you are ready to cry. Isn't this what you wanted?

You are free now." James said nothing. He stared straight ahead to avoid making eye contact with his mind-reading wife.

Moments later they were startled by a noise coming from behind the seats in one of the storage compartments. It suddenly popped open. Little Gabriel climbed up and grabbed the backs of the pilot and co-pilots seats and said, "Where are we going Uncle James?"

Chapter 13
INDRA AND ANDRE'AH

The glowing whiteness of the tunnels around the infirmary throbbed in silence as Michael waited for information from the doctors who were attending his wife. His mind filled to overflowing with anger, sadness and fear. The rage, ignited by his *best* friend's betrayal and the grief and terror he felt about his wife and children, turned seconds into minutes and minutes into hours. *Would his twin girls survive this awful ordeal? Had he lost his beautiful wife forever? And what about Gabriel? Gabriel? Where was Gabriel?*

Suddenly Michael remembered the last thing Lune'ah said to him was about Gabriel. He was playing hide and seek with Luci'ah. *Where was Luci'ah?* He wondered.

Uncle Josi'ah came around the curved corner by the infirmary and stood tall in front of Michael who was wilted by the stress. Michael straightened up right away and grabbed his Uncle by the shoulders. "Uncle Josiah, I'm so glad you are here, do you know what happened?"

"Yes, but I was hoping the information I received was wrong. Where is Lune'ah?

May I see her?" His voice was cold and serious. His eyes flashed toward the curtained hospital room. They could hear voices, shuffling feet and instruments behind the blue hash'ia sheet drapes.

"They are doing the surgery right now. Afterwards, I have given my permission to let them put her into hibernation." Michael angrily turned to pound his fist into the marbled wall.

"Michael, you must be stronger now than you ever thought you could be." He scolded. At that moment they could hear the healthy crying of a newborn infant. Then Uncle Josi'ah added "I believe you have a baby girl; life goes on, my friend."

"Uncle Josiah," Michael interrupted, "Please, I need your help. I need to find Gabriel. Luci'ah was watching him just before all this happened."

"Where were they when last you saw them" asked Josi'ah.

"They were in our apartment, but Luci'ah left suddenly, when I first got home. I assume she went to her place. Please find her and make sure Gabriel is OK." Michael pleaded.

"Of course, I'll do that right away. I must inform you that your submarine is missing. Apparently James has finally succeeded in escaping from New Mene'ah."

"That bastard!" Michael sneered.

Josi'ah gave Michael a comforting hug and a quick Ahmen Mene'ah, before he dashed off to try to find Luci'ah and Gabriel.

Seconds later Michael heard another baby crying and an intern came through the curtain to talk to the new father. Michael was relieved to find out that the babies suffered no ill effects from their trauma. Their gestation was complete and they were full of life. Michael was thanking the intern when the homely nurse came through the curtain holding a tiny red infant in the crook of each arm. She handed the infants to Michael one at a time and when she smiled Michael thought she suddenly became ten times prettier. He cried silent tears as he looked upon his beautiful daughters. "What am I going to do with you two?"

"Well, the first thing you must do is give these two beautiful little girls names." said the tall, boney nurse. Michael did not respond. "I know you need help, Mr. Ellsworth, I can help you. I recently had a baby boy. I am still lactating and I have plenty of milk. I would be proud and honored if you will allow me to do this service for you." Michael could not help himself, he glanced down at her ample breasts. He looked away as quickly as he could. She added, "Your wife has always been kind to me." She was careful not to put her words into the past tense.

Michael simply nodded. His throat was closed, and the tears continued to flow. He touched the soft faces of his sleeping children with his wet fingers after he wiped away his tears. After several minutes he reluctantly turned the care of the infants over to the nurse who was growing more beautiful in his eyes every minute.

"Do not worry about these little ones. Go, and find your son." The nurse, whose name was Sha'lah, smiled and tried to comfort the worried father. "The doctors are proceeding with the hibernation process on your wife. There is nothing you can do here. I will bring your daughters to your apartment after they are properly examined." Then she repeated, "Don't worry, go now. I will take care of these little beauties."

Michael dashed around the curved wall and took the spiral steps around the water-elevator three at a time going down. On the second level he ran down and stood for a second before the apartment doorway of James and Luci'ah. He was hoping that the doorway would slosh open and Luci'ah would be there, making do-nuts with Gabriel. He gulped and then waved his hand over the sensor and watched in slow-motion as the water sheet slurped quietly into the floor. His eyes entered the room long before his feet. His heart sank to his feet which suddenly were made of lead. What Michael saw both frightened and confused him. It looked as if a small tornado had torn through Luci'ah's otherwise immaculate apartment. Clothes, shoes, pictures, everything was thrown about as if in a rage. Michael called from just inside the doorway. "Luci'ah, you OK? "

He tip-toed through the clutter to the back room of the apartment. He continued to call for her and for Gabriel, louder and louder. Frantically he scoured every corner for any sign of his son.

He began talking to James as if he was there, and he wasn't saying nice things. "You sorry piece of shit! I thought you were my friend! You were my family, for Christs sake! Tell me you didn't get Luci'ah to help you kidnap my son, you damn son of a bitch!" He started kicking stuff around the room. "Where is my son? God damn it." He fell to his knees and sobbed helplessly into his hands, "Gabriel, my boy, Gabriel, Gabriel...."

Uncle Josi'ah showed up in the doorway and waited for Michael to compose himself before he entered. He looked around and Michael could tell by his expression that he did not have good news, but he had to ask anyway. "Did you find Luci'ah? ...Gabriel?"

"No, son, everyone in the colony is looking for them." Michael looked deeply into the eyes of Uncle Josi'ah and saw his fear and sadness. Then he clenched his teeth and straightened his spine. He stood there for a few seconds looking at the floor with one eyebrow lower than the other and a snarl on his lips. "I want to call an emergency meeting of the council, right now. Can you arrange this for me, Uncle?"

"Michael, they could still be found." Josi'ah was not convincing.

"No. James and Luci'ah have escaped from New Mene'ah. They kidnapped my son and killed my wife. You know it's true!"

"It is beginning to be apparent," said Josi'ah and he shook his head in disgust.

Every inch of the seven levels of New Mene'ah was searched thoroughly. Luci'ah, James and Gabriel were not found. A dark and melancholy mood filled the hallways and homes throughout the entire city. No one wanted to believe that one of their own would go against Mene'ah in such a way. Everyone in the colony felt the heavy weight of the anger, disappointment, and betrayal.

Right away the council called for an assembly. All thirteen council members were present within several minutes. Michael was there first, greeting and speaking with each one of the council members as they arrived. Dozens of interested bystanders filed in also. The urgency of this meeting was obvious to all.

The meeting was called to order, and Naha'ran began with the traditional prayer to Mene'ah. All recited the words in unison with hands up-lifted. Naha'ran addressed the council and quickly yielded the floor to Michael. The room began to fill with nearly all the citizens of Mene'ah and the noise and chaos made it impossible for him to be heard. He tried to shout out over the crowd. Finally he suggested to the counsel that they adjourn to the main chapel which was about thirty yards away and on this same level. They agreed and left in single file down the narrow hallway, squeezing past hundreds of concerned Mene'ahn citizens. The huge auditorium was filled to capacity in a matter of minutes and Michael took center stage.

First Michael spoke to the audience. "My friends, my family, by now you have all heard that James McKay has succeeded in the escape he attempted a few years ago. Apparently his wife, Luci'ah and my son Gabriel are with him." The crowd hushed and whispered among themselves. "I have called a meeting of the council to discuss what is to be done, and I am glad you're all here. This involves all of you, all of us."

Then he turned to the other twelve council members. "I respectfully request permission from the council to go after Mr. McKay. I am asking for a few volunteers and I will need another submarine."

The council members leaned across the table and began discussing the request in earnest. Michael could see that some of the council members were shaking their heads in a negative way. His determination did not waver as he pleaded with the council.

"We don't know if Luci'ah went willingly with him, but I know that Gabriel, my son Gabriel, was kidnapped!" Michael said then he paused and gathered his thoughts. "Luci'ah was playing 'hide and seek' with him. She was watching him while Lune'ah was resting. She took my key, the disk that operates my submarine. She took off right away after I got home." He continued after another short pause. "I think she must have encouraged Gabriel to hide in the submarine. I think they must have planned this for a long time." Michael suspected that Luci'ah was jealous of her sister. "She wanted a child of her own." Michael remembered that he and Lune'ah had encouraged her close relationship with Gabriel. "My boy loved his Aunt Luci'." The audience listened respectfully to every word. "Please help me get my son back." Michael choked back his tears as he pleaded with the counsel and the citizens of New Mene'ah.

Uncle Josiah was sitting close to the central stage. When he stood and turned to the noisy audience they were immediately silenced and still for he was a man of great respect and influence. "I have a request to make from the council. May I speak?"

Michael stepped back and said "Of course."

"Brothers and sisters, you all are now aware of the circumstances in which James McKay escaped with his wife, my niece Luci'ah. Our brother here, Michael, has lost his son and his wife. We all share his pain." Josi'ah paused. "I request authorization from the council to assist Michael Ellsworth in retrieving the fugitives and returning Michaels son, Gabriel, to his father. My sons Shavo and Zigmond have agreed to assist us with this mission if the council approves this request. I must remind the council that time is extremely important. The submarine moves farther from the colony every second. We can track the vessel, but I'm sure Mr. McKay knows this." He turned again to the audience. "Is there anyone present who objects to this mission?" Josi'ah looked out over his huge, extended family. The spectators moved and mumbled to each other, and gradually a handful of men stood.

Josiah pointed to his neighbor and asked, "What is your objection friend?"

"I'd rather not say," said the man as he stood to speak.

"So what do you suggest?" said Josi'ah.

"I suggest that you and your sons take a submarine and go out of the colony, go and find those traitors, but leave Michael Ellsworth here," said the nervous spectator.

"WHAT?" Michael shouted. "I object! No, no way, hey Uncle Josi'ah, I appreciate your help and your son's, more than you will ever know. But you guys can't go without me. I object to that suggestion."

Josi'ah put his hand on Michael's shoulder and said, "It is up to the counsel now son."

The twelve council members mumbled in a huddle for a few minutes. Naha'ran stepped forward. Naha'ran argued with several of the members as everyone waited for a ruling. Finally he broke away from the group and stood front and center to address the crowd.

"Fellow Mene'ahns, brothers and sisters. We have an emergency and we have wasted too much time already. The council members have all agreed to allow Michael, Josi'ah and his two oldest sons to have one of our best aquatic vessels, in order to go out of the colony to search for James McKay and his wife. We insist upon the following conditions; number one, Josi'ah de Lunon will be in charge of this mission. Number two, the men will be under our constant supervision. We believe that Michael Ellsworth has the right to be included in this mission. His family has been devastated by this bizarre betrayal. We respectfully request that our brothers and sisters suspend their objections." Naha'ran looked out over the audience and waited for anyone to stand and voice their objections. All remained seated.

"Very well, Michael, do you agree to the conditions we have ordered?"

"Yes, of course, he answered. "Let's do it. Let's go!"

"Go, and make preparations for the expedition." said Naha'ran. Then he began to lead the crowd in the familiar prayer to Mene'ah.

"We will meet you at the dock in one-half hour," Josi'ah told Michael as they hurried out of the auditorium after the prayer.

"Thank you, thank you, Uncle Josi'ah," said Michael as he tried to squeeze through the crowd. "I'll meet you at the submarines in one-half hour."

Michael dashed around the central elevator and flew down the steps. When he arrived at his apartment he was panting like a wild tiger. Inside, his eyes scoured the two rooms and bathroom for anything and everything he might need. He had no idea how long he would be above the horizon and he was not sure what he would need. He found sheets and bags to throw things into. *What about food?* Michael wondered. He looked in the pantry and in the ice-box. It literally was an ice-box. It was a hole in the ice where cold food was kept. Finding nothing in the-ice box he gathered his bags, tossed them over his shoulder and proceeded to the hospital to say goodbye to his daughters.

Sha'lah knew that Michael would be arriving soon so she prepared the babies and carried them out into the hallway. It wasn't minutes; it was seconds and Michael arrived. He threw his colorful bags against the wall of the tunnel and gazed upon the miraculous perfection of his baby girls. He took them into his arms and started weeping again. The girls were awake and looking up at their father. He looked deeply into their eyes, and he promised them wonderful lives. He swore he would do everything he could to get back to them and to protect them. He talked for several minutes, even though he knew they did not understand the words.

Michael kissed his daughters on their tiny fore-heads and

squeezed their tiny fingers and said "Goodbye, sweethearts. Daddy loves you."

As he handed the infants back to the nurse she said, "Wait just a minute. You still need to tell me their names!"

"Oh right, their names!" For a second Michaels mind went blank. *What were the names that Lune'ah and I had agreed to?* He struggled to remember. "Oh yeah, Indrah and Andre'ah. Indrah and Andre'ah." He repeated the names.

"Well it's good to meet you, Indrah and Andre'ah. My name is Sha'lah. I'll be taking care of you for a while. Your father must go on an important mission, but he'll be back soon for his little girls." She smiled and turned to Michael. "So, which is which?"

"Wha'?" said Michael.

"The girls...which one is Indrah and which one is Andre'ah?" she asked.

"Oh, I dunno'. You pick. And thank you. Thank you so much," and he was off.

Michael arrived at the submarine first, but Uncle Josi'ah and his sons were not far behind. He introduced his sons formally, "This is my son Zigmond, we call him Ziggy."

He indicated the tall red-headed boy. "And this is my son Shavo." The boys stood erect and shook Michael's hand like gentlemen. To Michael, the boys looked like they were in their mid-teens, though they were as tall as he.

They began to load their vessel with large bulging bags when a group of men came up with several floating barrels full of food, bedding, and emergency equipment. "We knew you would be needing additional things, so where shall we leave these?" They loaded the barrels onto the submarine and secured them properly. They then departed with a prayer to Mene'ah that they successfully fulfill God's purpose.

The ship that the council commissioned for the four men was not one of the small fishing submarines. It was a huge three story vessel that the Mene'ahns used for major expeditions. Michael explored the submarine as Josi'ah and his sons prepared the equipment for their mission. It was the most beautiful ship Michael had ever seen. The technology of this enormous vessel, constructed in metal and plastic-looking organic shapes, was out-of-this-world.

Michael heard Josi'ah shout from the front of the ship. "We depart in three minutes. Everyone must be seated and secured!"

He found a seat, immediately fastened his seat belt and shouted back, "Ready!"

Water filled up around the submarine and within a few seconds they shot out into the ocean to begin their mission. The inertia of the speeding ship pinned them to their seats but when it reached a steady speed they were able to rise and move freely around the ship. Focused on their mission the four men moved to the front of the ship where they could see, on a 3/D holographic monitor, a tiny moving light indicating Michael's fishing vessel as it sped toward the Eastern coast of Australia.

Chapter 14

SYDNEY, AUSTRALIA

James and Luci'ah were understandably shocked to hear the voice of their nephew Gabriel, coming from the cargo area behind their seats. They looked at each other and then straight ahead. The realization of what they had done seeped in slowly at first, then like an avalanche. Lucia's eyes filled with tears, but she kept a straight face.

The fugitives sped across the floor of the ocean, cruising by bizarre sea creatures that blurred past them in the blackness. The future for them was darker still. Now Gabriel was included. Planned or not, they had to formulate their future around this little boy who happened to be in the wrong place at the wrong time.

"You're going too fast Uncle James I wanna' see the jellyfish!" said the smiling face between the seats. Gabriel was not quite two years old and he already had a huge vocabulary in both English and Mene'ahn.

"I'm taking you somewhere really special Gabe'. I promise you're gonna' see some really cool stuff in just a little while. I can't slow down now." They both assured Gabriel that everything was OK and suggested he take a nap. The excited toddler wanted to look out to see the creatures and wonderful underwater formations but they were streaming by too rapidly.

It wasn't very long before the youngster was snoozing on a soft downy jacket on the floor. This gave James and Luci'ah an opportunity to discuss the decisions they needed to make about their little hostage. He didn't ask Luci'ah about the hide and seek game that she had been playing with the toddler at the time of their escape from the colony. James didn't think he wanted to know. He didn't tell her about the accident back at the colony where he accidentally and tragically killed her sister. He worried how he could keep that from his mind reading wife.

"So, what are we going to tell the boy?"

"Well, we can't take him back," said Luci'ah.

"That's for sure!" James stared straight ahead and kept both hands on the padded steering wheel as he wiped the sweat from his forehead on his sleeve.

"I'm uncomfortable with deception." said Luci'ah. "I have never lied about anything…never in my whole life…never had to."

"So you want to tell him the truth?" He just glanced at her for a second. The question did not warrant a response.

"Don't worry, I have had lots of experience." said James. Memories of his sordid past raced through his mind. He had been a skilled liar for as long as he could remember. He started using drugs when he was in his early teens. When you are a drug addict you tend to need to lie a lot; and you get good at it. James had signed on with the Australian whaling patrol fleet to get away from drug dealers and to kick his cocaine habit. He actually did start medical school in Galveston, Texas. But he left medical school when he was ordered to get treatment for his drug addiction.

"How about this?" James whispered. "Gabriel, I'm sorry to have to tell you this, but your parents had to stay in New Mene'ah, and they couldn't keep you with them, so they asked us to take care of you." James was actually quite serious about this suggestion. His wife said nothing for a while. "How much do you think he'll remember?" James asked, but Luci'ah just shook her head. Her glassy eyes stared blankly out into the darkness.

"We have to make it so he won't ever want to go back." said Luci'ah. "He must forget all about New Mene'ah." She choked on the words because she knew that she also had to forget about the only home she had ever known. And that would not be easy.

James thought for a few moments. "What about this? Gabriel…we got out just in time. The whole colony of New Mene'ah was destroyed. It just blew up, and everyone, was killed in a horrible explosion."

"I hate it, but it sounds reasonable." She could not bring herself to look at him. She was scared and ashamed, but also excited. This was the adventure she had paid a heavy price for, and it was too late to turn back now. It wasn't exactly the adventure she had dreamed about but there could be no turning back.

Luci'ah had studied life above the horizon and she envied everyone there. She hungered for just one peek at a real cloud, and those people up there *she thought*, don't even look up! She had envied her sister more than anyone primarily because her sister had children. Having children was a gift that apparently Mene'ah did not plan to give her. She had grown more and more jealous of her sister as time went by. And Lune'ah was expecting twins. Did she unconsciously intend to kidnap her nephew or was it just a bizarre coincidence? The answer may never be known. She had to live with the circumstances that existed at that moment. Like Scarlet O'Hara, she made up her mind to think about it tomorrow. Contemplating her sin against Mene'ah was more than she could handle at that time.

"So, how will we contact Noreen when we get to Sydney?" Luci'ah really didn't want to know. She didn't wait for an answer before she asked another question. "How much longer, do you think?"

"Probably another hour or so." Her first question made James feel uneasy. James was apprehensive about seeing Noreen again and he was not sure how Luci'ah and Noreen would react to finally meeting. A dark and gloomy cloud loomed inside the small compartment. James hesitated to say anything else for a long while. As the innocent child slumbered behind them, they plotted their future, which now included a son. The powerful engine hurled their vessel hundreds of miles per hour through the icy ocean and skimmed over unseen obstacles like a Frisbee.

"I need to do something Babe, can you control the submarine for a few minutes?" said James.

"Sure, I think so." Luci'ah placed her hands on the control panel and stiffened her spine as she looked forward. "What is it?"

James removed a sheet of paper from his jacket and began to scribble some additional words on a letter he had apparently begun earlier. "I know they will eventually find this sub. I want to leave a personal note for Michael."

Luci'ah understood. James was glad his wife did not request to read the letter.

James quickly resumed control of the vessel after he had written the letter. When they began to see the outer rim of the great coral reef east of Australia he started to slow the vessel down. The change in the roar of the engine woke the sleeping traveler.

Gabriel moved up between the seats and rubbed the sleep from his eyes. His large blue inquisitive eyes searched the black windows for signs of new life forms.

"What's that Uncle James?" He pointed to a large yellow finned fish as it swam by.

James ignored the boy's question and slowed the sub down to a crawl. He turned to the child and began the *Big Lie*. "Gabriel, be still and listen for a minute. Your Uncle James has to talk to you. It's very, very important. After we left the colony, there was a big explosion. Everything went BOOM ! Gabriel ! We are so lucky we escaped!"

"We were blessed that Mene'ah allowed us to get away before the explosion." Luci'ah chimed in. She was surprised to know she was capable of such deception.

Gabriel's face scrunched up and his lip puckered. "My Mommi an' Papo?"

Even James teared up to see that precious little face so sad, so trusting. James had lost respect for himself long ago, but this was the lowest thing he had ever done.

Gabriel returned to his make-shift bed on the floor of the submarine and there he stayed, quietly, for a very long time. "It'll be OK Gabriel, we're going to take real good care of you." said Luci'ah. She patted the little one gently on his back.

James was getting good at deciphering the digital maps installed in the dash of the submarine. Luci'ah had been in similar submarines many times, and she was able to help James understand the control instruments. On an opaque screen of air, hovering just above eye level, he could see the way the underwater terrain was mapped out ahead of them. A bright green arrow showed the location of his vehicle as it traveled through formations along the floor of the ocean. He learned how to move the wheels and buttons on the screen to see long distances. As he randomly explored the applications and icons, he stumbled onto a transparent map. He was able to overlay it on the oceanic map and make out the land formations including roads and the city of Sydney. With a few more twists of a tiny wheel he could see the image of the coast of Australia and the port of Sydney.

It was tricky maneuvering through all the coral reefs and vegetation, near the harbor. There were some close-calls and even a few actual scrapes so James advanced very cautiously. He hoped, if they were being followed, it would be with a larger ship, one unable to navigate the shallow water level. Gabriel moved to sit in his aunt's lap where he buried his head in her warm chest. He kept his eyes closed but looked up occasionally as they cruised past huge schools of fish and large and colorful life forms. Except for the smooth, even rumble of the engine, the cock-pit of the aquatic vehicle was silent for a long time. A heavy darkness filled the space around them as the trio began their family life together based on a terrible lie.

Noreen was making her husband's favorite lime pie that day. The day her first husband, the father of her daughter, rang her doorbell, she was squeezing limes she had grown in her own back yard--a Norman Rockwell wife-- ruffled apron and all. *Ding dong.* She heard the bell, dried her hands on the kitchen towel and casually walked up to the beveled glass paneled door. At first, when she opened the door, she did not recognize him. Then her face turned white as the blood drained down to her feet. She took a deep breath. "Oh my GOD!" James....! Her knees buckled beneath her, but she caught herself on the doorframe.

James stood back and waited for Noreen to accept the evidence of her eyes. "Hi Babe!" He smiled his award-winning smile and shrugged his shoulders.

They looked at each other for a few moments, without touching. "May I come in?"

"Of course!" Noreen straightened herself and stood to one side. "How in the world...? James, you're alive! Where have you been all these years? Did you have amnesia, or what? Why didn't you call me!?"

Before he could answer, the most adorable little girl, came running into the room. "Mommie...." She paused and looked at the stranger in her living room and apparently forgot the important issue she was about to discuss with her mother.

"You must be Grace? I am so happy to finally meet you." He hoped she did not notice the tears in his eyes as he spoke for the first time to his daughter. In her round face and huge blue eyes he could see Noreen and himself. He looked at his ex and asked "May I tell her who I am?"

Noreen did not answer. Instead she sent the child out of the room. "Sweetie, this man and I have some things we need to talk about, serious, grown up things. You go in your room and play for a few minutes."

James and Noreen sat for a few moments before they embraced in a hug that lasted long enough for each of them to feel uncomfortable. James tenderly touched her cheek before he spoke.

"I'm so sorry, babe. I'm sure you know about the attack on the HMAS Hawk. Michael Ellsworth and I were the only survivors. We were saved by a couple of angels." James had gone over his speech a hundred times.

"Angels?" she said curiously.

"Yes, I thought they were angels at first." James knew the story that he was about to tell his estranged wife was unbelievable. Sometimes James himself, had trouble believing it. "This is going to sound preposterous. You won't believe it at first, but trust me babe,. It's true. And I'm just going to lay it out there for you."

A brief look of skepticism flashed across Noreen's lovely face. He took a moment to notice how beautiful she was. "You cut your hair."

"Yes, I had it cut last week. So tell me how is it you are not fish food!?" she said sarcastically.

"What I am about to tell you, you must promise never to tell anyone. It is a vitally important secret, a secret that has been kept for a very long time, hundreds, perhaps thousands of years. You can tell your husband, of course, but you must both promise never to divulge this information, to anyone else. Many, many lives are at stake."

Noreen patiently waited for James to organize his thoughts.

"I know you have re-married. Your husband David, is he a good man, a good father?" James asked.

"Yes, he is. You know all about me. What about you?" she asked.

"I have re-married also." He could see that she was not pleased with this answer.

"And you couldn't have sent me a memo?" she responded sarcastically.

"No, I couldn't, I'm sorry. I came here as quickly as I could because, of all the people in the whole world, I know that I can trust you. You are like a rock. I knew if I told you the truth you would help us."

"Us? You're here with your wife? Where is she?"

"My wife and son are waiting for me in our submarine, down the coastline from the harbor," he answered. "I need to hear your promise."

"Your wife and son! Now this is really getting interesting. OK. I'll play the game. Cross my heart and hope to die, I will never share the secret that my ex-husband is about to share with me."

So James began to tell Noreen the story of his rescue from the icy Antarctic Ocean by the beautiful alien sisters. And how they brought him and his friend into the ice cavern city of New Mene'ah, where they patched them up and ultimately married them.

It was all a bit overwhelming for Noreen. Skeptical, at first, the more she listened to the details and descriptions of his experience in New Mene'ah, the more she tended to believe him. "So what do you need me for? How can I help you?"

James hesitated to respond, "I need you to help me ditch our submarine, and help us find a safe place for our family."

"Why should I? I hate to sound callous, but what's in it for me? All these years you have abandoned us. Why should I help you and your new wife?" Finally his wife exhibited some of the anger and distrust she was feeling.

"I will make it worth your while. Noreen, the things I have learned from the Mene'ahns and the amazing instruments that I have taken from the colony are going to make me a very wealthy man. My daughter will have everything she ever wants and so will her mother. I promise."

"What about your wife? She won't mind your showering your ex-wife with riches?" she said, trying not to show her jealousy.

"My wife...are you ready for this...is seventy two years old." He smiled. "I'm serious. Also, she really is an angel. She saved my life, twice. I owe her....everything. She is a Mene'ahn. She is kinda' like Mr. Spock in Star Trek. Everything, to her, must be logical. She understands me and she really loves me. I will not betray her if I can help it. She knows all about you and Grace, and she is with me one hundred per cent. And money means nothing to her," he added

It wasn't long before David, Noreen's husband, came home and found his wife in the living room sitting on his couch with her ex, who was supposed to be dead! Noreen jumped up and greeted him with a warm hug and a kiss. She introduced her guest and began explaining the purpose of his visit.

At first David, the broad-shouldered Australian, was a little rude. Noreen excused herself and took him into another room to talk to him privately. Her husband was a decent, hard-working man who adored his wife. Naturally he felt threatened by this intruder, who had come back from the dead to haunt them.

James could hear the muffled discussion behind the closed door. The seconds and minutes that were ticking by reminded him that he was a fugitive, and he did not have the luxury of a lengthy visit with his ex and her husband.

David and Noreen emerged from the back room hand in hand. Then they continued the conversation in the living room after a brief and happy visit with little Gracie, who was giddy that Daddy was home. "Mommie and Daddy have a very important visitor today. His name is Mr. James McKay."

"I am so happy to meet you. You are such a pretty little girl." James took the tiny hand that she extended in front of her, and he shook it like a gentleman.

Her mom told her to go back to her room for a while. She promised her they would be having dinner soon. The four year old skipped off without a care in the world.

"This whole story that Noreen has told me is just too much. But if she believes it, I guess I'll try to believe it too. She tells me you and your wife need our help. You need us to rent a boat or something? So what is the deal?" asked David, still keeping his distance.

"Yes, thank you, we need a boat and some help finding a safe place to stay. We are kind-of fugitives. If we are found by the Mene'ahns they will take us back to the colony and I will probably be terminated." James wanted to clarify. "They are not evil people. On the contrary, they are wonderful, Godly people, but if their secret got out, it could be devastating for them."

"There is another thing you need to know," James added. "Luci'ah is a Mene'ahn, and these people are vulnerable to viruses and bacteria an' stuff. We have to make sure that she is not exposed to anything up here above the horizon. Please, when you meet her, do not touch her. Don't shake her hand or kiss her on the cheek. Don't let Grace touch her. We have to find a house or an apartment that is outside the city, preferably someplace recently constructed and as germ free as possible. Money is no object," James continued. "Even though I have no cash money now, I have a solid gold coin that weighs at least three ounces. Take it. It's yours. Everything I have is yours if you will help us." James pleaded as he handed the coin to Noreen.

After staring at the huge gold coin for what seemed like a very long time, Noreen and David looked at each other and two broad smiles emerged.

"David, sweetheart, this coin is real gold and I'll bet it's hundreds of years old." Noreen practically drooled with excitement as she flipped the coin over and over in her palm.

"Yes," said James proudly as he raised his eyebrows. "I think it's a Spanish doubloon or something. I have lots and lots of them."

David's eyes widened as he gently picked up the coin from his wife's hand. He looked at James and simply said, "Well, I'm in."

Chapter 15
THE MISSION

As the huge submarine cruised away from New Mene'ah, Michael, Uncle Josi'ah and his two adventurous young sons began to shuffle around the cockpit and review the monitors and the ship's complex control system. The vessel accelerated to a spectacular speed very quickly for such a large ship but it remained far behind the rapidly fleeing fishing sub. Josi'ah guessed that James was unfamiliar with the guidance devices. But he knew that James had uniquely keen intelligence as evidenced by his work in the energy corridor in the New Mene'ahn colony. Josi'ah was sure that James had a pre-determined plan for his escape. After a few moments he could see that James's destination was the Southeastern coast of Australia. Once James had familiarized himself with the on-board computer guidance system, he had headed straight for the port of Sydney. Josiah informed his three-man crew that they were only a few hours behind the stolen vessel.

Their captain, Uncle Josi'ah, was a seasoned veteran. He had commanded many different kinds of Mene'ahn underwater ships during his long life. Uncle Josi'ah was nearly two hundred years old. He looked like a tall fifty-year-old marathon runner, with his sleek build and short gray hair. His short, bushy eyebrows curled up and bounced up and down as he spoke. Josiah turned in his swiveled captain's chair and glanced toward the tail-end of the long ship. The central aisle of the ship curved gently down like the spine of a gigantic fish and the glassy side panels of the ship glowed with a pale periwinkle blue. To Michael all the surfaces looked like plastic, but in reality, they were made of water, held together with strands of magnetic bonds and sealed with crystallized hydrogen molecules.

With Captain Josi'ah and his two sons standing, Michael felt dwarfed. They all looked quite handsome in their new Mene'ahn uniforms. The tailored fish-skin outfits exaggerated their broad shoulders and healthy physiques. The left shoulder of the Captain's uniform was filled with colorful medals and commendations. Around his neck was his Elrey'ah tube on a silver chain, a mysterious and powerful device, worn by all of the council members. The uniforms, in shades of gray with black and yellow trim carried no decorations except for the large emblem of the Mene'ahn system on the right shoulder. The symbol was a large silver blue "M' with a sunburst in the center and nine small dots of various sizes representing the nine planets of Mene'ah.

"I have accessed the automatic tracking system, but first, I must take this opportunity to brief my crew on the objectives and procedures of this urgent mission. Let me be clear. First of all, our only objective is to capture and bring the three Mene'ahn citizens back to the colony. Force or violence will only be used if necessary to achieve our objective. We will disable their vessel and take the fugitives into our custody as quickly and painlessly as possible."

He paused as he reached inside the front panel of his military uniform. He brought out a small cream colored, draw-string bag containing a silver *Elrey'ah wah Mene'ah* exactly like the ones the council members always wore around their necks.

"Michael, there has never been a thirteenth council member. You have not asked about your Elrey'ah wah Mene'ah. Just a few days ago yours was finally completed, and the council has asked me to issue it to you for this vital and important mission."

Michael knew a little about the tiny jeweled thimble the Council members all wore. Lune'ah had described some of the abilities of the "Triggers of God," as translated in Mene'ahn. Since he had been elected to represent the Earth as a Council member, he wondered if he would ever actually receive one.

"Michael, before I give you this important gift, I must demonstrate its power. "Ziggy, you take the helm and Shavo, monitor the gages." Josiah encouraged Michael to sit, as he prepared to show him the intricacies of his own *Elrey'ah wah Mene'ah*. Captain Josi'ah carefully removed his own device from its protective cover, which hung, like a tube of ladies lipstick on his neck chain. He handled the decorative silver thimble very carefully as he placed it on the end of his finger.

"This device is quite miraculous, Michael." The Captain cleared his throat. "It organizes your own bio-electro-magnetic pulse patterns and keys them into this amazing little tool." Adorned with the impressive finger ornament on his hand, he pointed to the ceiling and said. "The servants of Mene'ah who imagined and created this device were greatly honored for their achievement. It has been credited with bringing peace to the nine planets of our Mene'ahn system sixteen thousand years ago, that is, earth years," he clarified. "This amazing little tool can activate, deactivate and operate almost any electrical or digital device. It can determine areas of weaknesses or malfunction in mechanical instruments. It can reverse electrical streams. It can change the temperature in a room. It can even cook your food!" He smiled. "Most importantly," the captain continued, "it can wage war and destroy whole cities. Therefore it is very crucial that it not fall into the wrong hands."

Michael was overwhelmed. He held his breath and did not speak.

"This one is keyed to react to my own electro-magnetic pulse pattern. You will not be able to use mine. You will need to activate your own. Use it only when absolutely necessary." Then he carefully removed Michael's *Elrey'ah wah Mene'ah* from its soft draw-string bag.

Josi'ah began to explain all the functions on the shiny silver instrument as he sat calmly by Michael's side. It appeared to be quite simple, but as his uncle continued with the lesson, Michael became uneasy and confused. He was afraid he would get the control buttons mixed up and unintentionally fry something or someone!

The Captain placed the delicate instrument on the end of Michael's forefinger. He showed his student the four tiny colored lights on the side which could easily be reached and activated by the thumb. The yellow light controlled gravity and allowed for levitation. Touching the blue light would activate the ability to absorb information from almost any source. That information could be stored within the gadget and accessed by just thinking about it. The third light, the red one, produced heat and energy, could also be used as a powerful weapon. Its power could be adjusted by stroking a ridge that ran from the pointed end to the base of the tube. The fourth light was green. It was basically the ON and OFF button. Holding this button for a short while, programed the instrument to the wearer's own electro-magnetic pulse patterns.

Michael hoped he had retained everything he learned in that short lesson. He held his thumb on the tiny green dot for what seemed like a very long time, until the other lights began to glow dimly, then flicker. When all of the colored lights were fully illuminated, Josi'ah told Michael that his Elrey' ah wah Mene'ah was fully activated.

Captain Josi'ah suddenly stood and Michael did the same. They faced each other and Josi'ah ceremoniously placed the shiny new Elrey wah Mene'ah cord around Michaels neck and said, "Michael Ellsworth, as I place this gift from Mene'ah around your neck, I charge you to honor Him. By doing this you will bring honor to your family and all of Mene'ah as well. Will you accept and protect this instrument of power, this gift from Mene'ah and use it only to do His will?"

"I will," answered Michael, quite seriously. The neck cord hung awkwardly around his neck. As he adjusted the chain linked cord comfortably beneath his uniform collar he added, "Thank you sir. I am honored that you and the council have entrusted me with this Elrey'ah wah Mene'ah."

"Captain, Sir." said Ziggy suddenly, "There seems to be some activity at the target vessel. It has been stationary for a while and now it looks like another vessel is approaching."

Josi'ah eyed the concave monitor panel. "Yes, I see. They must have obtained some help. Do not take your eyes off of that monitor!"

"Yes, Sir," answered Ziggy.

The captain and all three crew members huddled together in the cock-pit. "How much longer before we catch up to them?" asked Michael.

Josi'ah looked over his shoulder and gave Michael a sly smile. "Watch this." He removed his Elrey'ah device from its case around his neck, placed it firmly on his finger. Then he put the pointed tip at the main control panel. Immediately a blurry image appeared in front of them, just over the dark windows of the sea craft. Josiah adjusted the image by moving his thumb across the base of the thimble-tool on his finger. The projection from the Josi'ah's powerful thimble devise enabled the crew to see inside the small submarine. An image of James, sweating and hurrying around in a small space, unfolded right in front of the four men. They could see and hear James and Luci'ah throwing things into several cloth bags. Josi'ah had connected his Elrey'ah to the guidance panel of the stolen sub which enabled them to see into the cockpit.

Captain Josi'ah announced, "We are exactly twelve and one-half minutes away from our target, men. Prepare yourselves. They have apparently obtained some accomplices. They have another boat. They are going to leave the submarine. They know that we can track it."

Michael impatiently added, "We gotta make sure they don't get away from that submarine."

Through the next agonizing minutes, Michael and the young crew members continued to watch as James and Luci'ah abandoned the submarine. Their voices faded as they boarded a ski-boat that Noreen's husband David had rented at a Marina in Sydney. Michael's emotions erupted when he remembered the brief image of Gabriel, calmly, sadly following James's instructions and holding Luci'ah's hand in the cockpit of the submarine. His wounded heart ached to hold his son and protect him from his kidnappers.

As the vessel from New Mene'ah approached from beneath the surface of the ocean, the crew could see, by the tiny green dot on the monitor, that the escape craft was departing.

Josi'ah saw by the veins protruding from Michael's neck and forehead, that he was entirely too emotional to make rational decisions at that time. The Captain took him aside and said. "Son, take a deep breath and close your eyes." With his arm around Michael's shoulder he said, "Now, take another." He squarely faced the sailor and looked directly into his eyes. "Michael, this is more important than just you and your immediate family. The future of New Mene'ah, indeed the future of all of mankind on Earth is in our hands. Mene'ah will guide us. You can be a hero today, or you can be a fool. Think before you act. Pray. Open yourself to the will of Mene'ah and accept it. It may NOT be the will you hope for, or the outcome you would choose for yourself or your family. Now steady yourself, Sir. And remember that I am in command. The Council of Mene'ah has given me exclusive command over this mission. Do not do anything unless I order it. Is that understood sir?" He continued to look straight into Michael's eyes as he waited for a response.

Michael stood at attention and respectfully acknowledged his uncles orders. "Yes Sir!"

"Ziggy, follow that boat!" Captain Josiah ordered.

Luci'ah's emotions were overflowing as she prepared to disembark from the comfortable safety and security of the familiar fishing vessel. She was excited and terrified at the same time. When the hatch at the top of the submarine popped open the cold salt air swirled in through the opening. Luci'ah was holding little Gabriel on her hip. Both of them looked up to the sunlight peeping through, and felt the moist cold breeze of the ocean. Neither had ever seen anything above the horizon and they were about to enter a strange new world. Luci'ah knew a great deal about life on earth. She had been watching images and movies, studying Earth civilization since she was a child, but she was not really prepared for this.

She gave Gabriel a gentle hug, smiled at him and said, "Doesn't it smell wonderful!?" The moist salty breeze swirled through the opening. She grabbed the tot by the waist and turned him around and handed him up to James's waiting arms. "Here you go, sweetie. You go first. Don't worry, little one, everything's going to be just fine." Luci'ah hoped she was telling the boy the truth.

James handed Luci'ah a pair of thin disposable gloves and instructed her to put them on before she climbed out of the submarine. She was so nervous she dropped one and had to go back down to retrieve it. As she scrambled to put on her gloves and get back on the ladder, James called down to her. "Oh Luci'ah, you're not going to believe this! The sunset, it's amazing! I think it's the most beautiful sunset I have ever seen." Indeed it was a gorgeous sunset, with every color of the spectrum boldly hovering over the impressive skyline of Sydney. When Luci'ah braved her head and shoulders out of the hatch she turned to face the sky and froze to take it in. James admired the colorful reflections on her flawless face, as she marveled over the sunset--her very first real sunset. She was speechless as he helped her to her feet, across the curved upper surface of the sub and then on into the small open-air boat. She could not know that beneath their boat, Captain Josi'ah and his crew silently and rapidly approached.

After all of the bags and passengers were safely on the boat, James awkwardly introduced his wife to Noreen and David. As the small craft rose and fell among the ocean swells, Luci'ah held tightly with her gloved hands, on to the outer rail of the small craft. Had she been standing erect, she would have been a head taller than Noreen and several inches taller than her husband, David. The young Australian couple was star struck by the gorgeous Mene'an lady. Luci'ah was wearing a colorful costume which she had made herself, of soft thin hashi'ah sheets. The organic gown was unlike anything they had ever seen. Rows of monarch butterfly wing patterns of yellow and orange with black velvety veins were gathered on one shoulder and draped loosely across the other shoulder. Her black skirt was made of several sheer layers with crinkly irregular edges. She was absolutely stunning as she stared out over the water, with the colors of the sunset reflecting on her perfect complexion.

Little Gabriel grasped the rail, hopping up and down, trying to see the city. "Look, look, what dat?" He did not wait for an answer. He pointed to a sea-gull and said, "What dat?"

James answered, "It's a sea-gull." He scooped up the excited toddler and pointed out over the water toward the glistening city. As the sky darkened, the harbor began to glow with colored lights that sparkled on the surface of the deep navy blue water. "And that is the city of Sydney, Australia. Gabriel, that is where we are going to live."

David shifted the lever into gear and gunned the loud outboard motor. The boat lurched forward, toward the coastal lights just as the large Mene'ahn submarine approached from deep under the horizon. The salt water sprayed across their faces and they held on tightly as the small boat bounced across the huge swells of the churning dark ocean. Luci'ah's eyes widened and she held her breath. She had never known such speed or excitement in her long life

Michael and his crew arrived only seconds later. Captain Josi'ah and his impatient Mene'ahn crew followed the little ski-boat until the undersea terrain became shallow and dangerous. Huge masses of black broad leafed vegetation buried the vessel in a forest of darkness and made navigation impossible. The large submarine slowed to a crawl and was forced to stop when a mountainous reef barricaded their entry into the harbor. Yet, above the horizon, the sea craft sped away like a rocket. Ziggy and the others watched helplessly as the little green dot on the navigational monitor disappeared off the edge of the screen. "We've lost them," he reported.

THE PLAN

All too quickly the little ski boat darted toward the shoreline and disappeared between the swells. The huge Mene'ahn sea craft stayed behind, motionless among the black forest of seaweed near the coast of Sydney. Captain Josi'ah and his worthy crew anxiously watched the opaque monitor as their target sped away. Reminiscent of an old style western, the four eyed each other frantically without saying a word.

Michael spoke first, "What now, Captain? Do you have another boat, like an inflatable boat, or something we can use to go after 'em?"

"We do have such a vessel," Josi'ah responded. "Unfortunately we may not be able to catch up with them before they dock in Sydney. The emergency craft was not built for speed. Michael, do you think we might find some evidence on the submarine, of their intended destination?"

"It's possible, I suppose," Michael hissed through his clenched teeth. His eyes remained glued to the monitor and focused on the tiny spot of light that represented the little ski boat. It appeared by the monitor, to be docking on the north shore near Sydney. Michael knew this port. It was called Watson's Bay, and it was near where the HMAS Hawk had docked regularly. It looked different from this point-of-view, but Michael was sure he knew the inlet. Michael's hands were shaking and beads of sweat were forming on his forehead. He panted and paced back and forth in the small blue space like a cheetah in a cage. Familiarity with this area, coupled with his bitter anger and hatred for the friend who had betrayed him and kidnapped his son, made Michael want to swim to shore. But the darkness above was closing in on them and within just a few minutes they could see that James, Luci'ah, Gabriel and their friends had docked their boat successfully in the harbor and soon would disappear into the crowds of the bustling night-life of Sydney.

"Ziggy, quickly restart the engines in reverse," ordered the Captain. Then he added, "We will go back to their sub and inspect it."

"Captain, sir, we should go ashore, sir, before they get away completely." Michael insisted.

The Captain straightened his spine and squared his broad shoulders and repeated his order. "We are going back to the other vessel." His eyes met Michael with such sternness that Michael backed down immediately.

The small Mene'ahn fishing submarine that James had abandoned, was still resting in the same location, about two miles east of Lady Jane's Beach, a popular nude beach on the coast North of Sydney. The captain raised their Mene'ahn vessel to the surface of the water. The hatch popped open, and they promptly emerged from the curved surface of the submarine. They leapt on to the smaller craft after tethering it to the larger one. The Captain and his sons took a few seconds to look up in awe at the infinite sky to see the last of the beautiful sunset and tiny hints of stars beginning to appear. The young Mene'ahn sailors had never seen the open sky. The team of four had no trouble entering the Mene'ahn submarine through the port hole on its crown. They carefully lowered themselves into the dark chamber of the small fishing craft. Immediately the walls of the vessel illuminated and began to hum with energy as if it had just come to life. The four began to plow through every corner of the vehicle. There were only three main chambers apart from the engine. Captain Josi'ah and Michael thoroughly searched the main control cabin where James and Luci'ah had been seated only an hour before.

Protruding from a section of the control panel was a hand written tri-folded paper. Michael and Josi'ah saw it simultaneously. Michael reached for it and Uncle Josiah nodded in approval. The letter was from James to Michael. At first he wondered when James had taken the time to write a full page hand-written letter. Michael read the letter out loud. Josi'ah and his two sons listened in silence.......

Dear Michael

I had to try to make you understand. What I've done is despicable, inexcusable, but from my point of view unavoidable. I couldn't live in those claustrophobic caverns any more. I was going crazy. I had to get out of there.

Anyway, for what it's worth, I'm sorry. I care for you like a brother, and I know I've made a mess of things. I just want you to know how sorry I am.

You have to know, taking Gabriel was an accident--a stupid accident. Gabriel was hiding in the submarine. He was playing "Hide and Seek." We didn't know he was there. If I can find a way to keep my freedom and return him to you safely, I will. I promise.

I pray that Lune'ah is going to be alright and the twins too. I'm so sorry. You know I didn't mean to hurt her.

I owe Luci'ah my life--everything. No one has ever loved me so much. She sacrificed everything for me. I promised her I would never divulge anything about New Mene'ah. I'm making you and all of New Mene'ah that same promise. Your secret is safe. I know I've gone against the will of Mene'ah, and I will pay a heavy price. For what it's worth, I'm sorry.
Ahmen Mene'ah
James McKay

Michael snarled, crumpled the paper in one hand and shoved it unceremoniously into his uniform jacket. He tried not to think about the letter and continued to search the cabin for any kind of evidence that might lead them to the fugitives. Time raced by as they continued their search.

Ziggy stuck his head out from the cargo bay between the two captain's chairs, and said. "I found this piece of paper. I think it says something about a cruiser--twin engine. Isn't that a boat?"

Michael grabbed the tiny crumpled paper and examined it

carefully. "Yes, it's a receipt. I know this place--Murphy's boat rental. Captain, may I have your permission to take the inflatable boat to shore? I think I can find out who rented this boat and hopefully that will lead us to James."

Josi'ah held out his hand and calmly took the slip of paper from Michael and said. "We must think this through carefully."

The captain called for his crew to join him in the main capsule of the small submarine. "Men, Michael wants to use the emergency vehicle to go ashore to try to find Mr. McKay. He thinks this piece of paper will help lead him to their location. I have some reservations, but I trust him, and he is familiar with this area. If the two of you wish to go with him, I will allow it. I will remain here. We must remain in contact with New Mene'ah."

The eager young men beamed with excitement at the prospect of experiencing the world above the horizon. While the brothers were scurrying around the submarine gathering necessary equipment for their expedition, Captain Josi'ah took a few minutes to remind Michael of some of the functions of his Elrey'ah device. He showed him how he could kill or disable an opponent if necessary. The Captain ordered Michael to practice using the delicate instrument before he allowed him to go ashore. Michael aimed the pointed thimble at a cargo barrel, activated the tool and watched the container melt into a puddle on the floor. "It could be devastating if this instrument falls into the wrong hands. You must be very careful," Josi'ah reminded Michael.

The crew quickly returned to the large submarine which was still hugging the smaller vessel. They boarded and went directly to the tail where the storage area was filled with a variety of equipment. Ziggy grabbed the inflatable boat, a round black object, about the size of a car tire, which was suspended on the curved side-wall of the submarine. He also grabbed the propulsion units, two small silver tubes. Josi'ah explained that Ziggy was familiar with the emergency vessel and would assemble the unit once they were on the water.

Both the boys were nervous, but thrilled to go with Michael. They quickly gathered the emergency equipment as well as some food and extra clothing, shoved the items into a cloth bag, and proceeded to the central shaft. Like emerging from the blow hole of a whale, one at a time, the three men once again climbed out, on to the curved upper shell of the enormous craft. Right away Ziggy twisted something on the rubbery, vacuum compacted boat, and it instantly inflated. He then attached the two tubes, one on each side of the craft. Uncle Josi'ah rose up, out of the submarine, examined the vessel, and added a few last minute warnings before the three men set out on their own.

Ziggy started the jet-like engines. The raft shifted awkwardly as they began to move forward. They all promptly squatted down and held tightly to the straps. The young Mene'ahn sailors looked up at the infinite sky with astonishment. The nearly full moon illuminated the sky, and the reflection glittered on the black water as they headed toward the colorful lights of the port of Sydney. The silver engines of the little black craft rumbled and propelled it rapidly toward the shore as its passengers held on tight.

Michael, in charge now, guided the vessel toward the sandy beach of Lady Jane.

The raft slid silently onto the sugary sand as the waves gently lapped up under the flat bottomed boat. The three men jumped out and secured the dark floating craft by tying it to the post of an abandoned pier. He told Ziggy and Shavo to remain by the raft. He intended to go a short way into town, obtain some Australian cash, and purchase some T-shirts for them and return quickly. He checked the communication bracelet on his wrist to insure that he would be in constant contact with his comrades.

As he was about to depart, Shavo stopped him. "Sir, shouldn't we call upon Mene'ah and offer a prayer before we continue with this mission?" The young man's face was red with excitement.

Michael thought for a second. "Yes, of course," he answered.

Then the three of them stood and faced each other, lifted their hands and recited the familiar prayer to Mene'ah.

"Orah' Mene'ah
Esha Mene'ah
Monsah ha wa lah Sheha Mene'ah
Ah'men."

Michael then dashed off along the coast toward the lights of the harbor, leaving the two disappointed sailors waiting on the shore by their black raft. His slick dark gray Mene'ahn boots sank deeply into the dry sand as he crossed the narrow strip of dunes. In a matter of minutes he arrived at a pub which was rowdy with smelly fishermen and middle aged, overweight women. Fishing nets filled with real and plastic sea creatures were mounted on all the walls between colorful neon advertising. Michael thought it odd to see a large round clock on the wall. It read ten-fifteen. It had been a long time since he had paid any attention to time. For inhabitants of the hidden city, time had grown nearly irrelevant.

Michael walked up to the bar and sat on a dirty wooden stool. The bar-tender was a slim, large-breasted woman in her forties. In her prime she had probably been a beauty, but now as they say in Texas, she looked as if she had been *rode hard and put up wet*. Her stringy brown hair clung to her neck and pointed to her cleavage and when she leaned forward to speak to the handsome new customer she seemed pleased when he stared at her breasts.

"You're new. What can I get for ya', handsome?" she said with a flirtatious grin.

"Could you help me? I don't have any money, but I do have some gold coins. Do you know where I could sell these gold coins in order to get some cash." Michael reached into his pocket and pulled out three large gold coins. He guessed they probably weighed as much as five ounces all together.

"Those are beautiful." she exclaimed. "They look really old"

"Yes," Michael responded without offering further information.

"Well, let me see... George." she called to her friend across the smoke filled room. "Come and look at this." At that a leather-clad biker put his amber, long necked beer down on the table with a thud, stood up, adjusted his manhood and walked over to Michael.

"Interestin' lookin' outfit there, mate." he said with a decidedly Australian accent. The man dared to criticize Michael's attire as he stood there with a spiked collar and braided sideburns.

"He's got a couple of gold coins to sell George. They look like Spanish doubloons or something." The woman motioned for the man to look at the coins in Michael's hand. "You like this kind-o stuff. I know you do. He wants to sell 'em."

Michael knew that the coins were probably worth thousands of dollars each but he was not in a position to barter that night. George's eyes widened as he examined the coins but Michael did not let them leave his hand. "Those are beautiful. How much you want for 'em?" He tried to hide his enthusiasm.

Michael was surprised when the hairy biker pulled out from the pocket of his black leather pants, a roll of bills that would choke a horse. It didn't take long for the two to reach an agreement and Michael left the tavern with six hundred Australian dollars. The biker got a very good deal that day. Those coins were from a Spanish galleon which sank in the South Atlantic in the 1500's. Uncle Josi'ah was wise to grab a stash of spendable commodities, gold coins, pearls and uncut diamonds, before their rushed exit out of New Mene'ah. They were worth far more than the smelly biker had paid, but Michael was happy to have the spendable, cash money.

As he left the bar he thanked the helpful bar-maid and asked her if Murphy's boat rental was still operating down the street.

"Yeah, I think so. It probably ain't open now though. Too late." she winked and encouraged him to stay and have a drink. "Come-on, don't go runnin' off so quick!" but he was out the door before he heard her.

The wet street glowed with the reflections of the business lights. Michael was happy to find a small convenience store nearby, stocked with a wide variety of necessities from booze to bathroom tissue. There was a rack of tie-dyed T-shirts in a corner. He grabbed three, all size large, along with a chocolate coated ice cream bar from the freezer box. After paying for the merchandise he scarfed down his favorite ice-cream treat with gusto. He had not had one of those in nearly four years. Then he hurried on to Murphy's with the boat receipt still in his pocket.

Parallel rows of floating docks creaked and moaned as the current gently ebbed below. The boat docks were securely bolted to the stationary pier just outside Murphy's. As Michael approached, he could see that the business had expanded in the last few years and now included a bait and fishing tackle shop. Apparently Murphy's now sold fresh and frozen sea-food as well. A large new brightly lit neon sign hung above the double-glass door entrance to the business. The word Murphy's was spelled out within the shape of a large cartoon fish. There were at least a hundred boat stalls in Murphy's Marina. Almost all of them were occupied with a variety of sea-worthy vessels, from sail boats to merchant vessels. It was quite late and the business was closed, but that did not stop Michael from looking around.

At first Michael walked down the pier and gazed out over the water toward the lights at the opposite end of Watson's bay. He had not seen real stars and the real sky for years, and he breathed in the salt air, deeply. He was not anxious to return, right away, to his comrades by their raft on the beach. As he walked along the wooden slats between the boat stalls he reached into his pocket and examined the crumpled receipt again. He began to look for the specific boat that he was sure his ex-friend James had used to escape into Sydney, a Sea-ray, twin engine Cruiser #19. He did not see it at first. The hair on the back of his neck bristled as he paced up and down looking for the boat. *Was someone watching him?* Suspiciously he looked all around the marina. The air was unusually still and silent except for the noise from the bar down the street. His eyes searched every black shadow, but he saw nothing.

Then there it was, the Sea-ray Cruiser, in the last row of boat docks, at the end of the pier. It was a shiny, new, white boat with red and silver stripes and white plastic interior. Michael hurried over and jumped in to examine it closely. When he paused and grasped the chrome rail, his heart filled with pain as he imagined his son holding that same rail only a short time ago. Angry, helpless tears filled his eyes. He grumbled and cursed his friend as he searched the squeaky clean boat for some evidence of his son and the kidnappers. Finally he collapsed on the cold white plastic bench in the back of the boat trembling with anger and desperation.

After several minutes he gathered himself together and stepped with renewed determination, out of the cruiser and walked toward the weathered building. His head and shoulders hung low and his eyes watched his boots as they stepped, one foot in front of the other, until he reached the main building of Murphy's Marina.

Not knowing what to do next, or where to go, and in no hurry to return to his comrades on the beach, Michael walked around to the back of the wooden building where a covered shed was available for fishermen to gather and clean their catch. He sat down on the long bench by the filthy picnic table and looked past the marina out across the bay, and noticed a thick fog gently rolling in from the south. His mind drifted far away. He thought about his wife and the twins back in New Mene'ah and the near perfect world that the Mene'ahns had created and hidden from the world for centuries. He thought about his new faith and found himself actually praying, to Mene'ah, as he sat alone in the black shadows of the marina, watching the fog move slowly onto the shore.

"I knew you'd come," said a low voice from the darkness on the side of the building.

Startled, Michael turned and stood up quickly. He recognized the voice even though he could not see a face. The voice continued to speak as the man stepped out from the eerie shadows and into the glowing yellow light. "I knew you'd come, Michael, but I wish you hadn't." It was James. Michael's heart began to pound as his nemesis came clearly into view, surrounded by a yellow haze.

Instinctively, Michael reached for the powerful little thimble which hung from the cord around his neck. He quickly snapped the silver tool from its case and slipped it on his forefinger. His eyes never left the silhouette of the man who had killed his wife and kidnapped his son.

The hazy shadow continued to speak and slowly approached Michael through the fog.

Michael pointed at his enemy, with the Elrey'ah thimble on his finger, and touched his thumb to the colored button on its side.

There was a swift loud *thud* and then the world went black.

David had come up suddenly, from the darkness behind Michael, and struck him on the head with a wooden post. Michael lay helpless on the ground.

The two men stood over their victim and looked at each other.

James shook his head and squatted down beside his friend. "I'm sorry, Michael," he said honestly. "I didn't want to do this, but you have left me no choice. I have to make sure you never try to find me again."

James walked over to the back screen door of Murphy's Marina, opened it, and kicked at the main door with his heavy boot. At first it did not open. David offered his assistance. He used the wooden post to crash through the back entrance of the bait shop. They went to the cash register, quickly pulled out all of the cash and left the cash drawer open and some of the money strewn over the wooden floor. David grabbed a bottle of rum from under the cabinet. Then they went back outside and stuffed Michael's pockets with the cash. They unceremoniously poured some of the contents of the liquor over his chest, face and hair and left the ugly scene behind.

The two men then silently disappeared into the darkness. Seconds later, though, James returned to his unconscious friend lying in a puddle of rum on the nasty deck of the fishing pier. He reached down and grabbed Michael's hand and eyed the silver tool on his forefinger. "So you managed to get one of those Elrey'ah's for yourself, Michael! What a piece of work you are!" He carefully twisted it off his friend's finger and placed it on his own finger. He did not bother to take the neck cord or it's silver case. "Pretty cool. Thanks buddy." Then he joined David, and they slithered off into the night.

Chapter 17
THE RESCUE

As they anticipated Michael's return, Ziggy and Shavo drank in the new and unique experience with gusto. Like a couple of teenagers at a YMCA or church camp, the two boys stayed up all night talking by a primitive camp fire, which they had built themselves with driftwood and dry grass from along the shore. They waited patiently for Michael to come back and bring them news that would facilitate their mission. Then they could finally begin their adventure. As time crept by they enjoyed the strong salty ocean breezes, the lights, the smells and the noises. The fog rolled in and dimmed the stars as the two young Mene'ahn sailors waited for their officer in charge to return and give them the orders they needed to complete their assignment. But Michael did not return.

The sun rose peeking above the horizon with spectacular splendor exceeded only by the sunset on the other side of the horizon just the night before. The two brothers had finally dozed off just before sunrise, but the noise of the seagulls and the light of the sun stirred them awake. Shavo regained consciousness first, as he reclined on the soft satiny blanket of a yellow and green hashi'ah sheet. Completely startled by what his eyes were witnessing he jumped up to his knees and shook his brother who was still snoozing.

"Ziggy, you must wake up. This is not to be believed. Where in the world are we?" Shavo squealed with excitement.

Reluctant to awaken Ziggy complained, "What's wrong? I was having a wonderful dream. Has Michael returned?" Ziggy's back was turned toward his brother and did not see at first.

"Turn over, brother, you must see this!" Shavo insisted.

Grumbling, the young man rolled over on the fabric cloth, shifting the soft sand beneath him. He opened his eyes. Then he opened them wide. He watched as the beachcombers began filling the dunes and the shore. Young and old, beautiful and homely, fat and thin, men and women-- all happily parading up and down the sugary beach, in the light of the brightening sunrise, carrying their coolers and colorful beach towels, except they were all completely naked!

With eyes glued to the unbelievable scene in front of them the two young men sat cross-legged and speechless for quite a long while. For the time being they forgot about their mission. Their mouths hung open as they watched the comings and goings of the nude sun bathers who frequented Lady Jane's beach. A few young ladies were worthy of their admiration, but most of the people who arrived on the beach that morning were simply ordinary people who just enjoyed being naked outdoors. Ziggy and Shavo could not imagine such freedom.

Shortly after dawn Ziggy pressed his finger on the opal dome on his wrist bracelet, in an attempt to contact Michael as he had done several times during the night. Again, there was no response and the two continued to worry. They decided, if they did not hear from Michael soon, they would notify their father who was alone, waiting for them in the submarine nearby.

As they sat admiring the view, they began to realize that they were the oddballs on the beach. They still retained their clothing though not your typical Australian attire. So after the sun rose and the temperature increased, the two removed their jackets and knit polo shirts to expose their pale white skin to the morning sun. They continued to wait for Michael to return but they grew more and more uneasy as time flew by. Something unexpected must have happened to Michael, they thought. They wondered why had he not returned or tried to contact them. *Why was he not responding to their attempts at communication*, they wondered? Finally they contacted their father who was still aboard the Mene'ahn submarine just a short distance out in the bay.

Ziggy pressed the cabochon on his silver wrist bracelet and closed his eyes. Instantly the crystal dome on Josi'ah's comfi'ah began to glow and tingle with urgency. He touched it with his forefinger and responded. The voice of his father came out clearly "Yes, Ziggy. I am here."

"Sir, Michael left us late last night. Shavo and I have been waiting here all night for his to return. We have tried repeatedly to contact him but there is no response." Josi'ah could hear the urgency in his son's voice. "Something is wrong Sir. What should we do?"

"I can see exactly where you are." Josi'ah turned to review the monitor as he continued the conversation with his son and in only a few moments he had located Michael also. "Michael is in north Sydney. He is on North Parkway about two miles from you."

"Should we go after him?" Ziggy asked nervously.

"No. Gather your equipment, come back to the submarine. I will prepare our strategy and we will go in to the city together." ordered the Captain.

"Yes, Sir." said Ziggy, somewhat relieved. Then he asked his father about the naked people on the beach. "Sir."

"Yes, son."

"Sir, I don't understand. All the people here are...well... they are all naked"

"Naked?" Josi'ah questioned. "What do you mean son? They really don't have any clothes on, at all?"

"That's right," said Ziggy. "Totally naked--all of them!"

"Well, I have seen much of the world above the horizon, but I have never seen a city where all the people are completely naked?" Josi'ah directed his son to activate his bracelet and enable him to see for himself. Immediately the bizarre image of a long golden beach with hundreds of totally naked people, soaking up the sunshine, unfolded in front of Josi'ah. "Amazing," he said, his thick dark eyebrows bouncing up and down.

Following the Captains orders, the boys threw all their gear into the sleek black raft and shoved off through the rolling waves at the edge of the Lady Jane's beach. Shavo watched the activity on the beach for as long as he could as their raft quietly slipped away. Ziggy guided the little boat toward the open sea where Captain Josi'ah waited in the submarine.

While he waited for his sons, Josi'ah studied the holographic monitor and downloaded the necessary information into his Elrey'ah thimble. He was able to pinpoint the exact location of Michael's wrist communication device. He could not know, however, that Michael's delicate but powerful little thimble had been stolen, and his wrist band was in a drawer in a Police Station in Sydney.

Josi'ah became truly worried as he continued to fondle the glassy domed stone on his confi'a bracelet, again attempting unsuccessfully to contact Michael. Deep creases in his forehead revealed his concern. The opalescent jewel glowed with a soft light and emitted a strong electrostatic pulse within a small dark metal drawer in Captain Jenkin's office, alongside an unusual looking neck cord with an empty silver tube attached to it. But the tiny green dot on Josi'ah's monitor did not budge from 273 Pacific Highway, in a place called *Crow's Nest*, near Lavender Bay in North Sydney, Australia. It was the location of the North Sydney Police Station.

Uncle Josi'ah had other reasons to be concerned about venturing above the horizon. He had to put aside his fear of infection that the open air above the horizon brought with it. And he knew the dangerous situation that would ensue if the secret of the hidden colony of New Mene'ah were to be discovered. But he had to rescue Michael. He had no choice. He still coughed occasionally from the nasty upper respiratory infection he had contracted on his last mission. He shoved a hand-full of rubbery gloves into a large shoulder bag as he quickly formulated his plan to rescue Michael from the police station in Sydney.

When his sons arrived and climbed down into the submarine Captain Josi'ah began grilling them for information, they actually knew very little. They all feared the worst. "Michael ordered us to stay at the raft, Sir. He said he was going to get some money and clothes that were more appropriate. He said he would return in an hour or two," said Ziggy.

The boys looked at each other for the briefest of seconds and smiles crossed their faces as they shared the same thought. They wondered why they needed clothes. They wondered why they couldn't just shed all their clothes. Then they'd fit right in. They even tried to convince their father that they didn't need to wear anything at all.

"In all seriousness Sir, we were there. We *saw* them. It has been a very long time since you went up to the surface. Things have changed Sir. We will look conspicuous if we are wearing coverings," Shavo insisted.

"Trust me," said Josi'ah, with his arm around his son's shoulders. "I don't know where you were, but believe me the vast majority of people above the horizon do wear clothing."

"Yes Sir," the young men answered in unison, shaking their heads. The polo shirts their father had supplied were outdated and the khaki pants were way too short.

"Sons, this may be the most important mission of our lifetimes. We must call upon Mene'ah for strength." The three stood face-to-face, close together with the palms of their hands raised upward and they recited the familiar Mene'ahn prayer."

After the prayer the two quietly sat and began receiving individual instructions, which came on a bed of cautions and recommendations, directly from Captain. He showed the two sailors maps of the city and the bay. He briefed them on their path. He showed them where they would turn into an inlet called Lavender Bay, just after they passed under a huge arched bridge at Highway # 1. At the shallowest end of the bay they planned to disembark, leaving Shavo to guard the raft and other equipment, while Ziggy and Captain Josi'ah would then go on foot on to the Police Station. The tiny green dot on the monitor screen continued to indicate Michael was still at the same location.

"What does it mean, Sir, that we are unable to contact Michael, either by his wrist band or by his Elrey'ah?" asked Shavo as they organized their equipment at the base of the exit shaft in the submarine.

"It may mean that Michael no longer has possession of them. If the Elrey'ah were in its case around his neck, or on his finger we would still be able to access it and we could see exactly what was happening." Josi'ah shared his concern with his sons. "He is in the Police Station. That is all we know. We don't know his condition. We must be very careful. We must assume that he is in a dangerous and difficult situation. Most likely he has been incarcerated. Or he may even be dead." Josi'ah frowned as he struggled with the bags.

"What about Michael's Elrey'ah? What if it has been taken?" asked Ziggy.

"It must be re-programmed in order to be used by someone other than Michael, and someone would have to know how to do that. It will be a useless toy to whoever has possession of it." Josi'ah tried to reassure his sons, but the deep furrows in his brow clearly showed the depth of his concern about Michael and his Elrey'ah thimble. "If someone tries to activate it we will be able to see it on the monitor." Then he added, after a pause, "If we can retrieve it, of course, we will. We must wait for the cover of darkness."

Waiting was difficult for young men eager for adventure, but they did as their father ordered. They used those hours to prepare and eat a large meal of crusted pearl melons and dried salted fish. As they waited they contacted some of the council members in New Mene'ah to update them on the progress of their mission.

Soon the three anxious Mene'ahns were hurrying toward the brightly lit Australian coastline in their sturdy black raft. Hunkered down on the damp floor of the vessel, dressed in their 1980's preppie costumes--pleated tan pants, green knit polo shirts and London Fog jackets--the three finally embarked on their rescue mission at sunset.

The cold salt-filled gusts of wind sprayed the breaking waves straight up into the air as they bounced along the crests of the rolling ocean. By the time they reached the bay, their hair and jackets were wet with cold salt water. Thick blackness surrounded them as the damp ocean breeze blew a blanket of dark clouds across the starry, moonlit sky. The team decreased their speed as they passed through the bay under the bridge at Hwy #1.

The main highway that connected the suburbs of North Sydney with a huge arching bridge that spanned over a half-mile across the Watsons Bay. As indicated by the tracking monitor they steered the vessel to the right just after the bridge and continued to the shallow end of Lavender bay. The heavily weighted craft clumsily slid onto a steep incline on the grassy shore of a small public park. The boys scoured the area for any sign of humanity, no doubt looking for some of those naked beachcombers. There were no spectators lurking in the darkness. Ziggy and his father carefully removed some equipment and started walking up the hill toward the freeway, leaving Shavo behind to guard the raft as planned.

Uncle Josi'ah carefully placed his Elrey'ah wah Mene'ah on his forefinger as they left the safety of the shore and moved toward their destination. The North Sydney Police Station was only a few blocks from the edge of Lavender Bay. The two marched silently side by side, through the empty blocks toward the Pacific Highway. Once there, Josi'ah positioned himself across the street from the main entrance of the police station. Ziggy stayed close by, within the dark shadow of the crumbling brick building across the street, as his father approached the blue brick building. The double glass doors and large windows with no curtains enabled Captain Josi'ah to see clearly into the main lobby of the weathered and outdated building. He used his Elrey'ah to look deeper into the offices and scan the layout of the entire structure. He pointed the device and a transparent screen emitted a 3/D layout of the two story structure.

His father's low voice came from Ziggy's wrist stone. "Son, I'm going in. I need you to find a position at the rear of the building and wait for further instructions there. I am going to disrupt their communication system and their access to electrical power. This diversion may enable you to open a back entrance and find Michael. If not, just wait there until I call you again."

Looking like an American tourist, Uncle Josi'ah calmly opened the heavy glass doors and stepped into the stark gray lobby of the shabby neighborhood police station. The officer at the front desk, a large black man with shiny round cheeks and a bald head, looked up from his computer monitor.

"May I help you, Sir?" the man asked with an unusually high pitched voice.

"I am looking for Michael Ellsworth. I understand you have him here. May I see him?" As Josi'ah spoke he touched the silver thimble on his finger to the back of the officer's computer, instantly downloading all information about the mechanics of the entire police station. Then he immediately deactivated the computer.

"Wha' tha'?"... Distracted momentarily by his computer screen which now showed only dancing points of light on a black background, the flustered officer responded.

"Michael Ellsworth? Yes, we have a prisoner here by that name. Are you his lawyer?" The officer asked.

"I am his uncle. May I see him?" Josi'ah responded.

"Visiting hours are from 10:00am to 2:00pm. Come back to...."

Before he could finish his sentence, his head hit the desk with a thud. Then Josi'ah calmly pointed, and touched the rotary phone at the corner of the desk with the end of his Elrey'ah tool. The lights, indicating activity on the lines, all immediately went out.

Seconds later another uniformed guard came frantically through a heavy steel door, and upon seeing the officer passed out on the desk, reached clumsily for his side arm. The skinny young man didn't have time to remove the gun from its holster.

Josi'ah quickly pointed his bejeweled finger and the young man collapsed in a heap on the floor. Then he reached down, unhooked a mass of keys from the officer's belt loop and moved him out of the way with his boot so that he could pass through to the hallway behind him.

Josi'ah moved quickly but cautiously to the back of the building. According to the information he had extracted from the front officer's desk computer, Michael Ellsworth was in "C" Block in cell #1. He peeked into several empty rooms through small rectangular glass panes as he continued down the main hallway. The sharp cold edges of the perfectly straight corridors seemed terribly odd, eerily quiet and a huge contrast to the smooth, rounded and curved passageways of New Mene'ah.

Just inside the back entrance Josi'ah disabled another young guard. Then he signaled for Ziggy to come up to the back of the building and he let him in through the heavy metal door at the back entrance. "We must work quickly. Michael is in Block "C." I passed Block "A" and "B" so "C" will be this way." Ziggy followed close behind his father.

The large steel door at the entrance of Block "C" was locked. It had one of those small glass panels, but Josi'ah was unable to see anything through it. He fumbled through the keys until he found one clearly labeled with a "C." Seconds later they were inside.

When Michael saw them, he jumped up from his gray striped cot and shouted, "Josi'ah, Ziggy! Thank God you're here! How did you find me?"

"We were able to see the location of your wrist band on our monitor, but I can see you are not wearing it," said Josi'ah as he searched through the jumbled keys for the one that would open Michael's individual cell.

"No," said Michael. "I guess it's around here someplace."

The old drunk in the cell with Michael woke up and rubbed his long narrow face with his wrinkled hands and said. "What tha' heck is goin' on here? You breakin' us outa here?"

Josi'ah pointed his powerful finger tool at the old man who stumbled back to sit on his bunk, slumped over and closed his eyes peacefully. "Not you. Sorry," said Ziggy.

Michael was wearing one of the tie-dyed T-shirts he had purchased in town. His own clothes were soaked with blood and rum and crumpled in a locker in Captain Jenkin's office. Josi'ah did not mention Michael's missing Elrey'ah right away but Michael could see by his expression that he was quite concerned. His wrist band and the cap and neck cord of his missing Elrey'ah were locked inside the desk drawer in that same office.

Josi'ah carefully touched the thimble on his right hand and slid his thumb along the ridge until a clear 3/D view of the Police Station appeared before them. A small green light indicated the location of Captain Jenken's office where Michael's neck-cord, and confi'ah lay locked securely in a desk drawer.

"It's not there," said Michael

Uncle Josi'ah knew Michael was talking about his Elrey'ah." A look of horror spread across his face.

"James took it. He attacked me at the marina." Michael hated admitting his utter failure but here was no time to think about the terrifying consequences.

"Ziggy, you and Michael go out the back entrance. I will meet you there."

Josi'ah located Captain Jenkin's office and was attempting to find the appropriate key to unlock the door, when he suddenly heard sirens and noticed flashing lights arriving at the curved driveway in front of the building. He made a rapid decision. He abandoned his search, dropped the keys and hurried to the back of the building and out to meet his comrades. When Ziggy and Michael escaped out of the back exit Ziggy had placed a floor mat in the doorway, the kind made from strips of old tires, so that the door would not close completely. When Josi'ah dashed out into the alley behind the police station, he joined Michael and Ziggy in the shadows. There they crouched behind a smelly, dripping dumpster until they could safely return to Shavo on the shore of Lavender Bay.

The flashing lights and the ear piercing sounds of the sirens faded in the distance as the three renegade Mene'ahns moved cautiously between the buildings and freeway structures. Josi'ah briefly contacted Shavo who was waiting for them by the black raft. "We are on our way back and we have Michael." Shiny black and white police cars crept through the cramped city streets flashing their huge spot lights down each alley and cross street narrowly missing the three fugitives as they darted in and out of the dark shadows.

While he waited for the team to return from the Sydney police station Shavo closely watched the holographic monitor screen emerging from his wrist band. He was able to follow tiny dots of light as they moved in and out of the streets of northern Sydney. From his location on the inlet bank Shavo could hear the sirens and see the flashing lights coming closer and closer. In a panic, he shoved the sleek black raft as far as he could, under a smooth weathered boardwalk. He squeezed on board and cautiously peered out above the soft wet sides of the raft, as he waited. He had done such an excellent job of hiding that Ziggy, his father and Michael did not see him when they first arrived at the park on Lavender Bay.

When Shavo saw his team, he slid out of the raft and pulled it toward the waterline as quickly as he could. Josi'ah rushed up and greeted his son with a nod as they prepared to board the small vessel.

"It's good to see you Shavo," said Michael breathlessly.

"What happened?" asked Shavo.

"No time for discussions, we must go now!" barked Captain Josi'ah.

Just then two, then three, four and five police cars, sirens screaming and lights flashing, sped onto the grassy slopes as far as they could go, before a low rock wall impeded their advance. Deafening sirens and red and blue lights flashed across the pier and temporarily blinded the four as they tried to shove off. Eight uniformed officers jumped out of their vehicles and began their pursuit on foot, guns drawn and pointed at our heroes.

"Stop now, or we'll be forced to shoot," shouted one of the police officers standing on the muddy shore of the inlet. But Josi'ah and his team were already gliding and spurting across the waves toward the open ocean.

Two of the officers took aim and fired a couple of rounds, narrowly missing the men as they made their escape. As the bullets whizzed by, Josi'ah made a brief adjustment on his Elrey' ah thimble and pointed it at the officers on the bank. Suddenly the officer's knees buckled beneath them. They collapsed on the wet grass only to awaken hours later in the police station wondering what had happened.

Chapter 18
SANCTUARY

The heavy hearted crew of the Mene'ahn submarine retreated home to the safety and security of the hidden city. They had failed in their mission, to capture and bring back James, Gabriel and Luci'ah. They nearly lost Michael as well, but they had been able to rescue him from the Sydney Police Department where he was being held on charges of robbery and public intoxication.

But James was still at large, and now he possessed Michael's Elrey'ah thimble. And if he were able to activate the device and wield its potential power, he could become the most powerful man above the horizon. Regretfully they would just have to wait, wait for James or someone else to try to use the device. Then its location could easily be seen. They prayed to Mene'ah to keep the knowledge and potential of the powerful device away from James. They prayed that Luci'ah would not share the secrets of the powerful tool which could threaten the security of New Mene'ah and of the entire earth above the horizon as well.

A dark shadow of uncertainty clouded the atmosphere as the four men returned to the colony. They were met by the other eleven council members who had been notified of the failure of the mission. The powerful tool that had been entrusted to Michael as a result of his being honored as the thirteenth council member representing the earth was now in the hands of a traitor. Some of the members were angry and voiced their concerns and disappointments by verbally thrashing Michael for quite some time.

Michael slumped and hung his head between his broad shoulders as he endured the admonishments. They had entrusted to find James and return him to New Mene'ah. He had failed. Oh no, he hadn't just failed, he had made things much, much worse. He had jeopardized the safety of the entire world, above and below the horizon with the loss of his powerful Elrey'ah thimble. And he feared he would never again see his son, Gabriel. Rage and hatred eked from every pore when he thought about James and his utter betrayal. With anger and disappointment weighing heavily on his shoulders he excused himself and made his way through the winding halls of the city toward the infirmary to check on the condition of his wife.

With a little help from his friends above the horizon the fugitives managed to secure a small newly built house in Sydney just a few miles from Noreen and her husband's home. James paid cash for it after selling half-a-dozen rare Spanish coins to a dealer in Sydney.

Before long James was off to Seattle, Washington from Australia leaving Lucia'ah and Gabriel behind in Sydney. Noreen turned out to be a valuable friend and teacher for Luci'ah and her newly adopted child. Noreen saw to it that Luci'ah had everything she and Gabriel needed.

Even though Luci'ah had studied earth civilization all her life, the actual experience of life above the horizon was not easy for her. Her fear of contamination, her guilt, loneliness, and separation from her Mene'ahn family and the ideal life she had experienced in New Mene'ah, catapulted her into valleys of depression she had never known before. Luci'ah's friendship with Noreen provided little comfort to her during James's long absences.

Over the next few months James met with the CEO's of several up-and-coming computer and communications companies. He was able to make a very lucrative deal with Microsoft, when he demonstrated the wrist communication devices that he and Luci'ah had worn as they escaped from New Mene'ah. The men in charge of research and development were impressed and wanted to know the origin of the devices, but James simply said "Don't ask." After the brainiacs of the company examined the two bracelets for only three days, Microsoft contracted to lease the two devices from James for fourteen thousand dollars a day.

James was curious about the Elrey'ah thimble that he had taken from Michael. He had never seen it being used for anything except decoration, so he was uncertain of its capabilities. At first he hesitated to show the device to Luci'ah. He didn't want her to know about his encounter with Michael in the Marina.

When James had first arrived at the colony of New Mene'ah, he had noticed the Elrey'ah devices suspended around the necks of the council members. He had assumed the tiny tools had unique properties, but he hadn't known for sure. James was jealous of his friend when Michael was elected to the council and was due to receive one of the impressive ornaments. Now James possessed it. He spent countless hours fiddling with the little silver object, touching the lights and stroking the curved edges. Occasionally a few of the lights would begin to glow slightly, but he was never able to get them to remain activated. Finally he shared his new toy with his wife.

When Luci'ah saw the Elrey'ah in James's hand she tried to hide her shock, but her high-pitched voice and saucer eyes belied her intention. "How? Where did you get this?" she squeaked. "These are special tools awarded only to the council members of Mene'ah.

You took this from the apartment of Michael and my sister?" she concluded.

James had prepared a series of lies to justify his possession of Michael's Elrey'ah thimble, but he decided at that moment, it was best to say nothing. It was best for her to assume that he had taken the device from Michael's apartment, along with the ice-melting tool, before they escaped from New Mene'ah. James was learning clever ways of deceiving his mind-reading wife. He avoided looking directly into her eyes and used his hands to express himself. He did not want her to *ever* learn the truth. But he worried that Luci'ah might someday be able to read the feelings of shame and regret which haunted him.

"What does it do?" He asked Luci'ah, ignoring her questions.

Luci'ah held the delicate instrument in the palm of her hand as if it were a baby bird newly fallen from a tree. As she contemplated her response, she carefully rolled it over with her finger, touching it with reverence like an object of great monetary value.

"It is an Elrey'ah wah Mene'ah, *a trigger of God*. It is a highly prized award, a decoration, reserved only for Mene'ahn council members. You should not have taken this," she whispered. "I did not know that Michael had been issued one."

"Right," said James unapologetically. "Those little lights on the side, do they mean anything? Sometimes they start to glow a little, is there a special way to turn it on, to see how it works? What can you tell me about this thing?"

Suddenly Luci'ah came to a frightening realization. The man she loved, the man she married, could not be trusted. After she picked her heart up from the floor she opened her mouth to speak. She also realized that he had perfected his skill at deception. She was no longer able to read his thoughts. "I can tell you that you should not have this. You do not deserve to have this."

"OK, babe, I get it," said James. Then James threw the delicate instrument unceremoniously into a kitchen drawer, slammed it shut and stormed out the door.

Luci'ah calmly retreated to her room, sat quietly on the side of her brand new king sized bed and began to weep. She had betrayed her family, even her God, for the love of a man who had used her. Little Gabriel heard her crying and gently knocked on the door. It creaked open. He stepped in and held his pudgy little arms out to his new mom and asked "Why are you crying?" Luci'ah embraced the toddler squeezing him so tightly he began to squeal. "I'm alright Gabriel, don't you worry about me," she said, through her tears, gaining little comfort from the precious little boy's heartfelt embrace.

When James returned home he pretended nothing was wrong. Luci'ah was in the kitchen struggling with the unfamiliar equipment, trying to make some scrambled eggs for her son. James sauntered in and gently kissed his wife on the cheek as he embraced her from behind. "I love you babe."

Luci'ah looked at him through her red and puffy eyes and said nothing. She forced a smile and continued to stir her eggs.

"I know I should not have taken that thing and I'm sorry." said James being careful to avoid eye contact. "I just saw it lying there and, well, I wasn't thinking." Then James closed the book on that conversation and never mentioned it again.

The unbelievably powerful little ornament remained in a drawer for the next several years relatively undisturbed. Occasionally James would pick it up and press the tiny crystals in various patterns trying to enlist some sort of response from it. He would stroke the seam on the side and once he even rapped the tip on the counter in frustration but the tool was keyed specifically to Michael's magnetic pulse patterns. Only someone with an identical or practically identical pattern would be able to activate the device. He was sure that the tiny instrument had some secret use or purpose. He held a bit of resentment against his wife for not offering any information about it. He was sure that she knew more than she was willing to share, and of course, he was right.

Life for the little McKay family rapidly and drastically improved over the next few years. James purchased an island in the South Pacific Ocean where he and his wife and child lived like royalty, secluded from the rest of the world. Their friends the Blankenship's, Noreen, David and little Grace moved there too, and shared the luxurious, Polynesian lifestyle resulting from James's amazing, stolen, technologies, and his shrewd investments.

The island of Sanctuary was one of the most beautiful islands in the South Pacific. It was only about nine square miles but was it growing. James had two construction teams working for three years to build a series of piers and jetties for his fishery. He connected these with panels of sheer netting material that he had fused to transparent sheets of film mysteriously made in a secret laboratory on Sanctuary.

The house on the side of the steep emerald mountain on the island of Sanctuary, was literally dug out from side of a sleeping volcano. Large cavernous rooms scooped out of shiny black volcanic rock were veined with rich red earth and crystals. Outrageous, colorful art highlighted every room. Luci'ah loved her home. Her stark white windowless apartment in the colony of New Mene'ah was like a prison compared to her glass castle. She could stand in her main living room and look out over the Pacific Ocean and watch the sun, moon and stars rise and set. From her crystal palace she could watch ships come and go and busy workers at the island's fisheries, hauling in their catch. She came to understand quite well why James felt so imprisoned by the ice caverns of New Mene'ah.

James thoroughly enjoyed the life of an entrepreneur and private investor. He had irons in many fires. One of his favorite ventures was in ocean farming. His little tropical island was home to a thriving seafood business; a farm where he raised nine kinds of fish along with crabs and lobster, exporting tons of pricy edibles every year. Another one of James's favorite things was the world of politics. He developed close friendships with several prominent politicians. He particularly enjoyed the prestige derived from friendships with diplomats and royalty. He considered one of the princes of Saudi Arabia a close, personal friend. Abdul and his three wives were often guests on Sanctuary. He attended the parties and swearing in ceremony when Bill Clinton was elected President. He allied himself with a number of wealthy Democrats and had people like George Soros help him invest his money in extremely lucrative opportunities.

Two or three times a year James would leave his tropical paradise and fly to Philadelphia to meet up with his friends in the Hindenburg group, an incredibly powerful and secretive organization. He grew to understand that the United States was not run by the government, elected by the people and for the people. America was controlled by this group of money gods and He was proud to call himself a member.

When James was around he was a good father. Gabriel and Grace had private tutors and all the benefits that money could buy. Gabriel was so young when he was taken from New Mene'ah he had no concrete memory of his biological mother and father. He never questioned his basic understanding that James and Luci'ah were his Pappo and Mammi' and that Gracie was his half-sister. Their lives were far from what anyone would consider normal. The life they lived on the island of Sanctuary was paradise, indeed.

Gabriel and Grace were the best of friends. They roamed the island without any fear, exploring the fisheries, caves and hidden corners of their own private world. There were other children on the island, of course; sons and daughters of all the employees and guests, but they came and went. Gabe and Gracie hardly ever quarreled with each other like most siblings. They adored each other, whispering together and plotting all kinds of mischief for the unsuspecting guests of the island. Sometimes they would travel with their father on his beautiful new jet, to America and other exotic places, exploring the world, a prince and princess in modern times.

James turned out to be an honorable husband as well, at least for the first ten or twelve years. He lived up to almost all of his promises to Luci'ah. He showed her, from various altitudes, all the incredible sights she wanted to see. Her favorite thing to do was to float up above the clouds in hot air balloons and glide silently across the landscapes of some of the most beautiful places above the horizon. She saw the Grand Canyon in this way, and Niagra Falls and the skyline of New York City, before 9/11. James was very careful to shield her from contamination. He became obsessed with sanitation. Luci'ah remained quite healthy for the years they remained on the island.

Luci'ah regularly swam in her own personal, private lagoon. She would drive her little yellow golf cart or ride her dapple gray Arabian stallion from her palace on the side of the mountain all the way down to the edge of the horseshoe shaped lagoon on the opposite side of the island. Often she would be accompanied by Noreen, Gabriel and Grace.

When the two youngsters were very small, Little Grace, two years older than Gabe, was horribly cruel to her baby brother, teasing him constantly, tormenting him with live critters and daring him to perform dangerous and humiliating tasks. They reached a turning point in their relationship when Gabriel was about seven. One day he placed a pale full of sand crabs in one of her bureau drawers. He had captured all the live crabs, in a trap that he had constructed himself. She opened the drawer she reached in without looking. A big sand crab clamped down on to her tiny finger. Screaming, she flung the crab across the room. The other creatures quickly escaped out of the dresser, and skittered around the room forcing the screaming little girl to leap onto her bed. After that, Grace developed a healthy respect for Gabriel and their relationship began a new and more positive direction.

Occasionally Noreen would join Luci'ah in the crystal clear

tropical waters of her lagoon where they would swim and dance together beneath the gentle waves. Luci'ah would close her eyes and imagine she was swimming with her sister in the cool salt waters of Lake Mene'ah.

David and Noreen kept James grounded and reminded him, from time to time, who he really was and where he came from. Sometimes, especially when James had been drinking, and when he found himself alone with Noreen, he would flirt with her shamelessly. But Noreen never gave him any encouragement. She was wise. The two of them had been married, though it seemed like a very long time ago. They shared a passion from the past that was difficult to forget. But they both adored Luci'ah. Luci'ah was a saint, an angel on earth. Not only was she patient, wise and loving, she was stunningly beautiful, flawless. She was painfully honest and brilliantly insightful, logical and, of course, faithful. Noreen would often say this about her good friend, "The only thing I really hate about Luci'ah, is that she is too damn perfect!" Together they all did a pretty good job of raising the two children in spite of their luxurious lifestyle and near royal status their families had come to enjoy.

Meanwhile, in New Mene'ah, Michael was struggling with the uncertainty of his wife's condition along with the shame of his recent failures. Lune'ah was unaware of her own suffering. She was being kept in a coma, at a temperature just above freezing, floating in an anti-gravity chamber about four feet by nine feet and attached to more than twenty yards of tubes and wires. Tethered and sedated in this way she would remain for the next several years. Healing tissue for her horrendous wounds would have to be grown from her own cells and would take a very long time.

When Michael first returned to his apartment nanny Sha'lah was there calmly caring for the tiny infant girls. He walked in through the familiar waterfall sloshing doorway. The nanny greeted him warmly and invited him to hold his beautiful daughters. The utter sadness and hopelessness on Michael's face discouraged Sha'lah from any conversation. As he held Indrah and Andre'ah, close to his chest, memorizing their delicate, soft faces he thought about their mother.

The image of her perfect body clinging to life in that cold clear cylinder full of gasses and tubes, flooded into his brain and he was no longer able to control his emotions. Michael began to weep as he had never done before. He began to shake so hard in his sorrow that Sha'lah had to remove the newborn babies and place them safely in their crib. Michael hoped that, in time, he would be able to breathe again for the sake of his children.

Day by day, hour by hour breathing became easier for Michael. His dependency on Sha'lah grew as well, and along with it, a strong friendship. Michael learned a great deal about Mene'ahn/humanity through the patience and amazing insight of his friend Sha'lah.

She made him feel proud to be a father, a council member and a Mene'ahn citizen. The more they talked, the more he listened to her wisdom and the more beautiful she became to him.

Uncle Josi'ah and his sons returned to their routines. Zigmond got married and his red-headed Mene'ahn wife gave him an adorable carrot-topped daughter right away, followed by two more equally red-headed daughters. Shavo remained unmarried but he and his friend shared an apartment for many years. So he was not alone.

Late one evening, as Michael and Sha'lah were preparing to put the girls to bed. They were about three years old (earth years). Michael asked his favorite nanny, "When the girls get old enough to ask the important questions what do you think we should tell them about God, and about their mother?"

Sha'lah looked up and smiled, making those prominent front teeth stick out far too much, and she said, "That's easy Michael, we will tell them the truth--the truth that Mene'ah is the only God and their mother is in His strong and capable hands." Michael nodded and smiled. "Yes, of course."

Chapter 19
THE SON OF GABRIL

Michael retreated to his apartment and remained secluded there for several months after he returned to New Mene'ah. The only thing that brought joy into his life during those uncertain times was being with his beautiful daughters. Sha'lah continued to care for the twin infants and her friendship with Michael grew daily. He resumed his fishing services with Uncle Josi'ah but a dark cloud hung over him constantly. He could not stop worrying about his son Gabriel. Not being with him, not being able to protect him, made Michael crazy. And he worried about his lovely wife. Would he ever again look into those beautiful green eyes, hold her and share his life with her? Would she ever know her daughters? And he worried about the future of New Mene'ah and the future of the world above the horizon. Indeed the problems of his family and of the whole world weighed heavy on Michael's broad shoulders.

Michael could see the indistinct shadows through the dense ice wall of his apartment as Sha'lah was preparing the children for bed. He joined her one evening as she carefully placed the sleeping infants into their cribs. "Have I told you how much your help means to me Sha'lah? I don't know what I would do without you." Michael spoke softly as they tucked the satiny hashi'ah blanket around the tiny sleeping angels.

"There is no need to thank me, Michael. I love them. It is a joy and an honor for me to care for these adorable little ones." Her broad smile accentuated her large protruding teeth as she spoke. Then her expression changed to serious as she looked deeply into Michael's eyes. "Is something wrong?" She asked.

"I'm a mess, Sha'lah. Sometimes I just don't know which end is up." He knew that she would not understand that particular term. He needed to talk to someone and she had always been a good listener. They walked over and sat on the long white cushioned divan which curved along the side wall of the cavernous room. Michael dug his elbows into his knees and held his head up with his hands. Sha'lah sat quietly waiting for Michael to speak. After a long silence Michael tried to put into words the feelings of emptiness and desperation he was experiencing. "If I had a problem when I was young I always turned to Jesus. I prayed and asked for help from Him. Now I just feel so lost. I have tried to pray to Mene'ah, but it just isn't the same. It's like Jesus was kind-of human. He could understand my problems. Don't get me wrong. I really do believe in God, in Mene'ah. It's just that He is so vast, so distant. So...I don't know. I just can't tune in to Him like I could when I prayed to Jesus."

"Would you like to meet him?" she asked quite seriously.

"Meet who?

"Meet Jesus." Sha'lah smiled and explained. "There is a series of wonderful journals produced by Gabril himself which document his experience above the horizon. They are very moving. You should continue your relationship with Jesus. You should continue to depend on Jesus as you have always done, if it helps you. Mene'ah is still working through the spirit of Jesus. I think if you see Jesus... if you meet him for yourself, it will help you."

"I can see Jesus?" Michael repeated in disbelief. "I can actually see and meet Jesus, the real, actual historical Jesus? Will you show me how to access those video documentaries?"

"Of course" said Sha'lah, smiling confidently.

Sha'lah proceeded to show Michael how to access the specific documentaries directly from the historical files in the main library. He was surprised to learn how easy it was. By just using his wrist phone he could retrieve thousands of years of video history and project the images with 3/D holograms right there in his apartment. Surprisingly, all he had to do was think about the year, the name of the author and number of the documentary as he touched the domed crystal bracelet on his arm.

The tall Mene'ahn nanny sat with Michael for a long while and shared with him the amazing background story of Gabril and his remarkable experiment with the people of earth. Sha'lah left Michaels apartment after dictating a list of names and dates that he could use as codes to access video documentaries from the library. "If you wish more information or if you wish to research other things you can go down to our library. There you can record and store additional codes which you can use here in your apartment." She smiled sweetly as she exited the apartment and then added, "I hope you find the comfort you seek."

Michael remembered how James had helped him retrieve the Meno'ah documents from the main library when they first came to the secret city. He remembered Lune'ah spoke of her knowledge of Jesus during their courtship. His life had become very complicated since his marriage and his election as Earth's diplomatic representative. He never seemed to find the time or the interest in advanced Mene'ahn technology. Michael was not prepared for what he was about to experience.

That day a world of ancient history opened up to Michael in a way he could not have imagined. Right there on an opaque screen of air, in his spacious opal-walled apartment he came face to face with Gabriel, the angel from his beloved New Testament, as well as his Lord and Savior, Jesus Christ.

He closed his eyes to increase his concentration as Sha'lah had instructed. With the forefinger of his right hand, Michael touched the warm round stone of his wrist band. Then with his left hand, at the same time, he touched the tiny diamond crystal atop the computer-transmitter. A golden sphere floated inside the elegant looking instrument, within a diamond studded band that was anchored to a heavy marble stand. The delicate looking instrument had rarely been utilized in Michael's apartment, at least by Michael. He continued to touch the diamond and repeated in his head the code words that Sha'lah had helped him to memorize...*Gabril, Earth year 136, series #12, Gabril, Earth year 136, series #12.* The metal ball became transparent and began to glow. Within just a few seconds a blinding light erupted and displayed a 3/D image centered in the large room.

A tall elegantly attired Mene'ah gentleman in a pale green ankle length robe fastened at the hip with a wide braided belt and brassy buckle, materialized only a few feet from where Michael stood. Right away he began to speak in the Mene'ahn language as he faced straight ahead looking past Michael. Instinctively Michael reached out across the image causing waves like ripples on a glassy lake. Then Michael touched the stone on his bracelet to enable him to hear Gabril in English.

"This is transmission number 12 in the series I have dedicated to the region of the Eastern Mediterranean called Jude'ah. I have chosen, at this time to concentrate on a Jewish community for reasons I have expressed in previous transmissions. Transmissions one through eleven clearly document my mission here."

Sha'lah had explained to Michael that Gabril had been chosen by the council two thousand years ago to research the growing and evolving civilizations on the Earth's land masses. There was great concern about the tremendous conflict among the peoples of Earth. Gabril's important research on earth happened long before the colony of New Mene'ah was established. His mission lasted well over one hundred Earth years and the data he produced established a broad historical base for the Mene'ahn-Earth relationship. It was Gabril's concern for the oppressed people of Israel that influenced him to concentrate on that particular group of people. His request to interfere directly into the lives of a Jewish family was opposed by the council at first. Gabril was sure he could advance the civilizations of the area, or even the whole earth, by introducing the people to Mene'ah. Gabril was the first council member to have traveled to Earth. As a council member he was elected to represent the ice planet of Lunon. Later it was he who recommended the establishment of the secret colony within the South Polar ice sheet. His ultimate goal was to unite the world within the sheltering canopy of faith. The council eventually agreed to Gabril's proposal.

"As you know, I have been overseeing the growth and training of my son from a hidden distance up until today. On this historic day I plan to begin his training. Jesus is now nearly thirty years old." As Gabril spoke his hologram turned and began walking slowly down a gravel path between two steep treeless cliffs. "My son is considered a rabbi or teacher and he has studied and committed to memory the ancient Hebrew Scriptures of his tribe, throughout his life."

The pathway of the arid terrain disappeared and was replaced by a series of large rocks which made walking quite difficult. At that point Gabril removed the silver cylinder from his neck cord and placed his Elrey'ah on his finger, pointed to the ground and elevated himself gently over the rocks.

"I have enticed Jesus through his dreams to leave the village and venture into the desert. There I hope to instruct him in the ways of Mene'ah." Gabril paused and gently lowered himself on to a large flat surfaced rock. "I will wait here for his arrival."

At that point the image blurred and seemed to disappear by shrinking into a tiny dot.

A few seconds later the spot grew again to an image of Gabril. The deep shadows showed that many hours had passed. "Jesus approaches!" Gabril slid off the rock bench and floated over the rocks and down the surface of the steep cliff to face his son as he appeared around the curve of the barren hillside. Gabril's joyful expression clearly described his excitement and anticipation. He had never come face to face with Jesus though he had been watching him all his life.

Jesus, upon seeing the elegantly clad floating Mene'ahn, became filled with fear, dropped to his knees on the rocky ground and buried his face between his outstretched arms. "My God, my God, I have received your message to come. I am your servant Lord!"

Gabril immediately used the device on his forefinger to lower himself to the ground. "Stand up my son and speak with me. I am not God. I am simply God's messenger. My name is Gabril." He held out his hand to the astonished rabbi and motioned for him to rise.

Jesus rose slowly and stood, still shaking, with shoulders arched, afraid to speak and unwilling to look the Mene'ahn council member in his eyes.

"You have been chosen by God to be His representative here on earth. I have been chosen to instruct you. Follow me and I will share with you the truth of your Father in Heaven." A reassuring smile met

Jesus when he finally looked up to meet the imposing stranger's clear blue eyes.

"I am not worthy." The young Hebrew quickly responded. "Why have I been chosen?"

"Neither am I worthy of this gift, my son. We are not to question God. Ours duty is to obey his will. However, you do have a choice. You can turn from me and go back the way you came and forget you have seen me. Or you can come with me. You can learn from me and together we can fulfill God's purpose for us." As he spoke he turned and began walking slowly deeper into the wilderness. Jesus followed closely by his side. "Can you make this decision today my son?"

"I want nothing more than to do God's will." Gabril was hoping for exactly that response.

"Your assignment is a gift from God and an honor. By accepting this honor, you will also receive a huge responsibility. If you accept this mission we cannot know the final outcome. After your training I will not be allowed to help you in any way. My assignment is to prepare you to go into the world to share the truth about God. First you will go to your own people but you must also share your knowledge with gentiles and Romans." Jesus listened carefully as they walked along the path. "Are you prepared to go into the wilderness with me now to learn the truth about Mene'ah that you will use to enlighten the world? Can you accept the gift as well as the task?"

"Yes Lord." He responded without hesitation.

As Michael looked upon the face of Jesus his eyes filled with happy tears. It was the face he had always imagined. His eyes were dark, almost black. His face was thin and his full beard was parted at the ears and in the center of his chin so that it hung in two short segments. He was taller and paler than most of the Hebrew men of his village, but his features were predominately Middle Eastern. He wore an ordinary one-piece tunic with a hemp belt and a hand-woven red cloth draped across one shoulder. His long dark brown hair was parted down the middle and crusted with dust from the arid desert winds. The experience of seeing the face of Jesus brought Michael to a spiritual place he had never been before. He felt honored to be meeting his Lord and Savior in such a close and personal way.

Michael continued to watch and listen carefully as Gabril and Jesus walked, side by side deeper and deeper into the mountains. He remembered the Sunday school lessons he had learned as a child, of Jesus's experience in the wilderness for forty days. Seeing the scene from this perspective reminded Michael about the story of Satan and how he had tempted Jesus. He wondered how that would play out in Gabril's documentary.

When their conversation became softer and muddled Michael turned up the volume on his confi'ah in order to hear more clearly. "Jesus, what do you know of your birth?" Gabril asked.

"When I was young I asked my father why the elders of the temple did not want to include me in some of the services. He told me that he would explain when I was older. Then when I became a man and began to seriously study the ancient prophecies I asked my father again, why was I treated differently than the other boys? My father told me a story I did not believe until now. My father told me…" Jesus suddenly looked Gabril straight in his eyes and then he turned and stared toward the horizon. The sun was setting and the cloudless sky slowly dimmed to a soft purple. "My father told me that my mother…I didn't believe it and apparently no one else believed it either…that my mother had experienced a miracle and had been blessed with a child of an angel of God. My father said that he did not believe it himself, at first. But then he said he was visited by the angel in a dream. The angel told him it was true, to trust in God and to marry his betrothed as planned. He married my mother and raised me as his own son." Then Jesus locked his eyes on Gabril's and asked "So, it was true?"

Gabril nodded. He did not know if he should tell Jesus all the details of his encounter with Mary but he knew there would be questions to follow so he explained it to Jesus in this way. "I was honored to bestow that miracle on your mother. It was done in a way that she remained pure."

"Are you my Father?" Jesus stepped back.

Gabril did not expect this question to come up so quickly but he answered honestly. "I am."

The two walked on in silence for a long while. Michael memorized the features of the man Jesus and as he stared closely at the hologram there in the main room of his apartment. He remembered the words from the Bible that Jesus had repeated over and over when he described himself as...*The son of man*. Suddenly Michael had a clearer understanding of the nature of God. He began to realize that Gabril's *experiment* had not been a failure after all. In spite of the suffering that Jesus endured he had indeed changed the world and united the world above the horizon in a way that could not have been done without a miraculous intervention.

"Before we begin your instructions do you have any questions for me? Gabril asked Jesus as they stepped carefully along the narrowing gravel pathway.

Jesus thought for a minute and then asked a question that had plagued him all his life. "I want to know about Heaven. What paradise rewards us after we leave this earth?"

Gabril contemplated for a long while before he answered. He knew that Jesus had been raised according to strict Jewish traditions and beliefs. The Hebrews believed that they were the "chosen people" of God and that only *they* would have the reward of everlasting life in paradise.

He composed his answer carefully and began his parable. "A farmer plants a field with fine, healthy seeds. He prepares the soil with compost and turns and fertilizes the earth as he learned from his father. The plants grow and put forth flowers and then fruits that feed and nourish the people of the city. In the winter the brown and lifeless leaves and stems are turned back into the soil. In this way the soil is nourished and life continues." Gabril could see the confusion on his student's face. "Heaven, my son, is all around us. Life endures only when the seeds you have sewn produce life."

Gabril knew there would be more questions about that subject and often the truth would be hard, if not impossible for Jesus to grasp. "Tell me what you have learned from the Holy Scriptures about paradise?" he asked.

"I was taught that the reward for lifelong obedience to God's Holy commandments was eternal life in a heavenly, peaceful and spiritual place." Jesus responded. "Was that wrong?"

"Wrong?" Gabril pondered his response. "I don't know. I have never seen evidence of the kind of paradise you speak of. What I do know is the paradise around me. God has created an amazing world, full of happiness, life, beauty and love. Heaven is all around us. And I have always wondered why mankind on Earth ignores these things and focuses on death." Gabril stretched out his arm toward the horizon as the two rounded a steep mountain slope. "Just look at that amazing sunset. How could anything in death be any more beautiful than that?"

The terrain became more and more desolate as the teacher and his student walked deeper into the mountains. By nightfall Jesus and Gabril were standing on a plateau overlooking a gray and empty valley. The cold dust-filled air curled up the side of the cliff and the two men gathered dry leaves and sticks to start a fire. Gabril aimed his jeweled finger at the mound of dry shrubs and ignited it instantly.

Michael watched and listened as the two men continued their conversation with the light of the campfire dancing on their faces. The hologram began to blur unexpectedly and then disappeared completely into a tiny dot of light floating in Michaels living room. That was the end of episode number twelve of Gabril's Judean documentary.

Michael wanted to know how Gabril's mission failed and how and why Jesus had to die in such a painful and horrible way. But like someone who has already read the book and knows the ending, Michael's apprehension was based on what he knew from the Bible. He knew the question he had about Jesus's tragic and horrible death would be answered by watching that last episode of Gabril's holographic documentary. *Why did Gabril not rescue his son from the Romans?* Michael wanted to know the answer so he skipped episodes #13 through #15 and went straight to the end of the series.

Within just a few minutes Gabril was again standing in the middle of Michael's living room in front of a background of rocks and brown weeds. This time the expression on his face was contorted and tearful. He began to speak but his voice cracked and his phrases were confusing. The translation Michael was hearing seemed jumbled and often did not make any sense to him. When Gabril began to speak he wrung his shaking hands in front of him. "This may be the last episode of this series...this journal of my experiment with the Hebrew...not an experiment, this was so much more than an experiment. What should I say?" At that point Gabril hid his face with his trembling hands and began to sob quite uncontrollably. "Mene'ah! Why must my son endure this trial? Is there no other way?"

Gabril tried to collect his thoughts. He seemed to draw in strength after calling upon Mene'ah. Then he straightened his spine and continued. "This episode, is number sixteen in the series based on the Judean territory of Earth." He stared past Michal then turned to look out over the image of the valley below. "When the council first gave me permission to proceed with my research I had to give my word that I would not interfere after Jesus's training. The Council refused to hear any part of my request unless I agreed to allow the will of Mene'ah to determine the people's reaction to Jesus's teachings. If I had been clearer in my lessons...if I had been a better teacher...if only I had not promised the council...If only I had had more time with Jesus. If only..." Gabril's voice trailed off to silence, deep in thought for a few moments. Then his eyes narrowed. "If only the people had not been so primitive, so ignorant, so corrupt. I hoped to prove that these people could learn to accept Mene'ah. I wanted them to stop their senseless wars based on their ancient religions. I hoped my son could unite the world...instead we have succeeded in tearing it apart. Now they are going to crucify him."

Gabril gazed out over the valley and pointed to a procession of people moving through the city and out of the enormous gates. "How can I watch this and not try to save him?" he said tearfully. Michael was able to focus more closely on the crowd. He gasped and held his breath when he realized he was witnessing Jesus, himself, dragging his cross down the street amidst the angry jeers of the onlookers. Blood streamed down from Jesus's head as a ring from a thorned branch cut deeply into his skin. He stumbled and the heavy wooden beams pinned him to the white gravel roadway. Angry shouting soldiers in dust covered uniforms grumbled and ordered the crowd to disburse. A few spectators obeyed, but most stayed and continued to harass the prisoner with mean and insulting remarks that were not translated for Michael to understand. Jesus lifted his cross and continued his journey toward his execution. He did not moan or complain. He seemed to accept his fate without question. Michael wondered *where were Jesus's disciples. Why did no one help him with his burden?* Michael felt his own tears trickle down his cheeks. He knew all too well the horrible fate that awaited his Lord and Savior when he reached the crest of the hill.

The scene suddenly doubled back to Gabril who stood watching from the cliff at the edge of the wilderness north east of Jerusalem. "I cannot bear to witness anymore." He turned away and floated down the steep pathway. "My heart is broken. My son has done nothing to deserve this. He has shared what he learned of Mene'ah by telling the stories I taught him. He used the skills I taught him to heal the sick and blind. His miracles and healing powers exceeded even my own expectations. Mene'ah worked through him in ways I never dreamed possible and yet, they rejected him. Why?" Gabril looked back with an expression of disgust. "These are indeed miserable, crude, godless people." Then the holographic image suddenly disappeared into a tiny dot.

Michael sat motionless for a while waiting for the image to pop back into view. As he waited he wiped the tears from his face with his sleeve. Then he said the prayer to Mene'ah that he had memorized… "Orah Mene'ah, e sha Mene'ah. Mon sah ha wa la sheha Mene'ah, Ah'men. Saying the prayer comforted Michael and he held his breath until the hologram resumed.

The hologram zipped into view again in Michael's apartment with an ear piercing scream from Gabril as he stood dangerously close to the edge of the rocky cliff looking down on the crucifiction of his beloved son. "NOooo!" he screamed. He held his hands above his head and pointed with his bejeweled finger at the clouds. The beam of white light that ejected from his thimble brought the clouds together into an angry swirling mass of dark gray. Lightning and thunder erupted from the center of the storm clouds. More clouds swirled together until the entire afternoon sky was black and the wind howled through the streets of the city. Then Gabril pointed his silver finger at the ground below and the stream of blinding light that erupted from it caused the ground to tremble. Rumbling and hissing the earth cracked open from the edge of the gully to the base of the hill where Jesus was strung up bleeding and dying on the cross.

Michael watched in amazement as swarms of frightened people scattered in all directions. The grumbling black clouds began to pour down streams of drenching rain. Three Roman soldiers scrambled up to the tall wooden crucifix where the lifeless body of Jesus hung. They quickly cut his limp and broken body down from the cross. Jesus, the Lord and Savior of all mankind, fell into a puddle of mud at the base of the bloody wooden beam. The tallest of the soldiers barked orders at the other two in a language not translated by Michael's confi'ah. Then the other two men grabbed Jesus's hands and feet and carried him to his tomb, his long hair dragging on the rain soaked ground.

At that point Michael had to turn away from the horrible image displayed in his living room. Shaking and distraught he placed his finger atop the diamond crown of his transmitter and the image immediately disappeared into a tiny white dot which floated in the room for a few seconds before it finally vanished. He could not bear to watch any more.

Michael tiptoed into the room where his baby girls slept peacefully. He stood in the doorway for quite a long while as he thought about the path Jesus had taken and the price he paid for his dedication to God. *What an amazing man he must have been,* Michael thought to himself. He knew he wanted to go back later, to see the other episodes and to learn more about the teachings and the life of Jesus. But now, he had to go back and play out the episode he had been watching, to its end.

He returned to the long narrow sofa in his main room, took a deep breath and calmly placed his finger on the diamond device to continue the documentary. The image immediately burst back into view. Lightening crackled from out of nowhere and shattered a small tree near the soldiers on their path to the burial ground. They carried Jesus like two hunters carrying their kill, often dragging his lifeless body across the ground and through the mud. Michael shuttered. He watched the emotionless soldiers as they tossed Jesus's mangled and tortured body onto a flat rock within a hollow space in the hillside. Then the three used a huge pole with a large stone as a lever to hoist a gigantic boulder into the mouth of the tomb. The three soldiers hurried away grumbling and complaining as the rain continued to pour down in heavy sheets.

Gabril still stood on the edge of the cliff, watching as his beloved son was carried off and thrown into a filthy hole in the earth. Michael could see, even at such a great distance, the anger and bitterness written across Gabril's face. The sky was still blanketed with churning, angry black clouds. Bolts of electricity crackled and jumped through the blackness and the rain continued to fall. Soon all the people on the ground had sought refuge and the only sounds left were the sounds of the storm. When Gabril was sure he would not be seen, he floated down and stood weeping by the crude grave. He lifted his hands skyward and shouted, "Orah Mene'ah, e sha Mene'ah. Mon sa ha wa la she ha Mene'ah." Michael's wrist band moaned, "God be praised and his will be done!"

Michael watched in awe as Gabril pointed his powerful thimble at the boulder. It slowly rolled away and toppled over the crest of the hill and became wedged in the gully below. Gabril ducked down as he entered the hollow cave, scooped up his lifeless son and floated up the side of the hill, away from the city. Then he turned and the holographic image seemed to move directly toward Michael. When Gabril stood directly in front of Michael holding Jesus in his arms the scene was so real and seemed so close that Michael had to step back.

Gabril, dripping and flushed, looked through Michael and spoke. Tears flowed down his wrinkled cheeks as he made the final statement to conclude episode number sixteen in his video documentary. "This is my beloved son with whom I am well pleased. He tried to teach the truth about God to these ungrateful people and they have killed him." He looked up and away from the limp and bloody body he carried. A somber expression of determination swept across his face. "But I can bring him back. I can heal his wounds." Then he added with hopeful enthusiasm, "When he has recovered I will not allow him to return to these shallow, empty people. There is a land across a vast ocean where the people live peacefully on the gifts of Mene'ah. I will take him there. Perhaps the Lamb of God will be accepted in that primitive land and the teachings of Mene'ah will thrive there." The heart-wrenching image of a sad and bitter father holding the body of his tortured son, was then instantly sucked away into a bright speck which disappeared with a little *pop*.

Shocked and disheartened by the closing testimony of Gabril and the disturbing images he had witnessed, Michael sat for a long while contemplating the images he had just seen. He knew then that Jesus had indeed died on the cross that day as history and the Bible have repeatedly verified. Michael understood that Jesus had been resurrected, miraculously and brought back to life by the angel Gabriel just like the angel Lune'ah had resurrected him a few years before.

Suddenly Michael felt very proud to be a Mene'ahn. He no longer mourned for Jesus. He knew that Jesus had served God's purpose and the world was a much better place because Jesus had fulfilled his mission. A calming feeling of peace came over him as he thought about what he had just witnessed.

Throughout the next months and years Michael often returned to learn more about Jesus by watching practically all of Gabril's holographic documentaries. Understanding the way God worked through Gabril gave him the strength and courage he needed to overcome his own discouraging failures and fears of inadequacy. It helped him understand the importance of his own vital part in fulfilling God's purpose for him and for the powerful political position he held within the colony.

When his daughters were old enough to start school in New Mene'ah, Michael became a teacher. He instructed his own children as well as a small group of Mene'ahn children in the Government systems around the world. Ironically, Michal had hated that subject when he was in high school. He felt strongly that the young people of the colony needed to be prepared for the ultimate takeover of the Earth in the near future, by the Mene'ahns. He believed, and the council agreed, that understanding the structure and history of earth civilizations would be beneficial in securing a peaceful takeover of the planet. He was able to easily access everything he needed for his lessons from the New Mene'ahn library.

As his daughters grew, respect for Michael also grew within the colony. The Mene'ahn people learned to depend on Michael in many ways because of his knowledge of life above the horizon and his devotion to the teachings of Jesus. His insight into the religious principles and doctrines of the earth formed a basis for Mene'ahn understanding of civilizations above the horizon.

Michael had been elected to representative the Earth as councilman number thirteen. He balanced the awesome responsibilities of his station with the equally daunting responsibilities of a single parent. He monitored the news broadcasts and made regular reports to the council on the conflicts and conditions above the horizon. He met regularly with the council to inform them of important events around the world and conducted educational seminars for the adults in the colony who wanted to learn more about earth civilizations.

When his busy schedule permitted, Michael would venture out of the colony in his hydro-craft to retrieve seafood and hashi'ah sheets. Often he would bring his daughters along. The twins thoroughly enjoyed their excursions out of the colony and into the open seas around Australia. Indrah and Andre'ah received an exceptional education from their father, learning all about the earth above and below the horizon and about everything in between.

Even though the girls appeared identical their characters were miles apart. Indrah was the mischievous princess and Andre'ah was serious and even-tempered. As they grew, their personalities evolved, as did their love for each other. By the age of ten Andre'ah had grown tired of being confused with her twin sister and being called by her sister's name so she took some scissors and whacked off all of her beautiful strawberry blond hair. She cut it off so short she could have been mistaken for a little boy were it not for her perky little nose and ridiculously long eyelashes. Because their personalities were so different, as time went by, the twins were rarely mixed up again, even after Andre'ah's hair grew back.

Michael considered his job as a single parent for his adorable twin daughters the hardest job of all. Of course Sha'lah remained close by and continued to help him in every way possible. The twins from early childhood on, had Daddy wrapped around their little fingers. Together the girls filled their father's days and years with mountains of laughter and tears as they waited patiently for their mother, like sleeping beauty, to awaken from her slumber.

Chapter 20
AN UNCERTAIN FUTURE

The transmission was received in the Earth Year 2001, day #8 of the ninth month. The message was sent seventeen years before, from the "Prevailer" while in route to the Earth from the Mene'ahn system.

Michael donned his official uniform and prepared to meet the others in the main council chamber at the appointed time to hear the important message. The gray and maroon coat of the uniform was made of starched hashi'ah sheets and was cinched at the waist with a dark woven belt and a perfectly round buckle. The buckle sported twelve sparkling colored stones and embossed organic shapes that depicted the major continents and governments of earth. Michael's pride was apparent as he stood before his reflection in the main room of his apartment. His thoughts briefly traveled a thousand miles away as he eyed the new Elrey'ah wah Mene'ah hanging from a silver cord around his neck. It was exactly like the one James had stolen from him in the dark shadows of the damp and fishy marina in Sidney. He was grateful the other council members had trusted him enough to give him a replacement. He promised himself he would be worthy of their trust.

One by one the stately council members filed into the council chamber to hear the important message. No one spoke. The seriousness of the upcoming transmission was apparent. They knew that the convoy of nine huge ships, the "Prevailer" was due to arrive on Earth in the spring of 2016, only five short years away, Mene'ahn years of course, fifteen earth years. This was sure to be an immensely important message preceeding the future mass colonization of earth.

There had been no communication from the fleet in nearly half a decade (in earth years).

The transmission was witnessed by all thirteen members of the New Mene'ahn council that day. All were seated at a huge table, a flat semi-transparent slab on an intricately carved pedestal centered in the private council-chamber. The mushroom shaped stools, on which the council members perched were anchored to the marbled floor. A hologram, suspended directly above the table, appeared at the designated time. Distorted at first, within a few minutes the perfect image of a handsomely decorated officer came into view from all sides of the table.

"Greetings to the citizens and council members of New Mene'ah." The low voice came from the image along with a deafening squeal. He faced his audience squarely in his white asymmetrical uniform, adorned on the shoulders with an array of decorative medals. The slightly transparent image rotated as he spoke. He wore a square short brimmed white hat with a narrow gold band. It had an odd shaped gold button in the center, the symbol commonly used as a symbol of Meneah, a pointed M with a bright star in the center and nine round shapes encircling the center star. His white hair and clean-shaven face emphasized his ocean blue eyes.

After a short pause he continued. "I am General Osaura. This message is for the people of the earth. It is to be shared with the people of earth through communication devices of your choice, at a future appointed time. Begin recording this message now."

During the General's pause one of the council members rose briefly and placed his hand over a panel near the end of the table, activating a recording device which formatted the transmission for common Earth technologies. All of the council members sat in silence, stone faced, as they received this important transmission. The impressive looking speaker formed his words carefully in the Mene'ahn language. Michael had tuned in to the speech using his wrist band, so that he could hear the transmission in English even though he had been speaking and understanding the Mene'ahn language almost effortlessly for several years.

"I, General Osaura de Lunon, have been appointed by a unanimous vote of the Meneahn council to command this, the ninth fleet en route to the planet earth.

This data is to be translated into many languages and is to be broadcast and published, simultaneously around the earth, at the appropriate time.

It is with the guidance of Mene'ah and the approval of the main council, I make this announcement. Ahmen-Mene'ah.

At that point all thirteen members of the elite council audience bowed their heads and repeated in unison, "Ahmen-Mene'ah." Then he continued his speech.

People of earth...

I am honored and humbled by the challenge of this important mission.

Our fleet of twelve ships is scheduled to arrive on your planet in the year 2016 by your calendar. Your people must prepare for our arrival.

First let me emphasize, lest you panic and make unnecessary complications for us--we are human. You should not fear us. We are a peaceful, non-violent people. We come in peace.

Our civilization evolved along a path not unlike the Earth. Our planets contain the same atmosphere and solid mass constitution as your planet, minus the large variety of dangerous micro-organisms which your people have managed to overcome.

We have visited your planet many times despite the immense time travel distance and found it to be a planet of exceptional beauty and variety, almost perfectly suited for colonization by our people. However, our observations over the past several centuries have not been favorable for your people. You're people have abandoned God. You are destroying this planet that Mene'ah has blessed you with. The choices your people are making will result and are resulting, in worldwide pollution.

Cruel and evil leaders have amassed enormous wealth at the expense of their citizens. Your cities are overpopulated and diseases plague your planets. If allowed to continue with these destructive patterns, your magnificent, abundant lands and oceans will no longer be able to sustain life.

It is our intention to dismiss the control of current governments on your planet and replace those governments with Mene'ahn control. We hope to do this without violence. We do not wish to harm the resources of this planet, BUT we will do what we must, to ensure that the stability and health of the Earth is no longer jeopardized.

Our technology far exceeds that of your people. Your weapons will be ineffective against us. After we have taken control of the planet we will incorporate ourselves into the government offices and educate your people in the ways of Mene'ah. Those who will not cooperate will be quarantined.

I must say again. You have nothing to fear from us. We come in peace to SAVE the planet. We will teach you how to live in peace with your neighbors. We will transform your planet into the land of milk and honey that your legends speak of. Your beautiful planet Earth, is now and will forever be, the thirteenth territory of Mene'ah. It is the will of Mene'ah …the will of God.

Ah'men-Mene'ah.

Michael and the audience of other devout council members, stood and raised their hands above their heads and chanted, in unison "Ah'men Mene'ah, Orah Mene'ah e sha Mene'ah, mon sah ha wa lah sheha Mene'ah, Ahmen."

After the meeting Josi'ah and Michael remained to discuss Osaura's transmission.

"What does this all mean, Uncle Josi'ah?" Michael knitted his brow. "Don't you think there will be violence when the Prevailer fleet arrives? I know a lot about Earth history and none of the leaders are going to just lie down and allow the Mene'ahns to walk in and take over."

"I'm sure the mission has been carefully planned, we have not been apprised of the details, but I can assure you, violence will be used only if absolutely necessary. We have the ability to disable every conceivable type of weapon." Josi'ah countered matter-of-factly.

"But what about the people? How will the Mene'ahns win over the hearts and minds of the people of earth?" Michael had become a Mene'ahn in every way but he was also a proud American, and an ex-marine. The concern he had for the upcoming takeover could be heard clearly in his voice. He had seen people dying for their beliefs and for their countries, and he knew that war was inevitable.

"You are the Mene'ahn council member representing the Earth's populations. It will rest upon you to bring about a peaceful transition." Josi'ah responded matter-of-factly, without showing any emotion. As he spoke he rose and calmly moved toward the doorway. Over his shoulder he added. "My prayers are with you today Michael, with you and your family. I understand Lune'ah will be revived today. Will you notify me of her condition?" Michael followed close behind, his head still swimming with the weight of his overwhelming responsibility.

"Of course," he answered.

After the meeting Michael waded through the fog of his apprehension for the future, putting one foot in front of the other as he had done every day for the past twelve years, until he arrived at the infirmary. There he gazed upon his beautiful wife, still frozen in the transparent gaseous chamber. Her peaceful expression gave no indication of her long suffering.

Briefly Michael put aside his burdensome responsibility for the fate of the world and replaced it with concern for his wife, because that day would be unlike any other.

It was finally the day that Lune'ah was to be reborn. Michael had not seen his wife's lovely jade green eyes or held her delicate hand for twelve full years. According to the doctors, she was ready to be revived. Beads of sweat emerged from his forehead as he hurried down the winding hallways.

Lune'ah's heart and lungs had been rebuilt from tissue grown from her own cells. Through the years she had undergone countless procedures and Michael watched and agonized through each and every one of them, but she was never allowed to regain full consciousness. She remained in a frozen state until that very day. Michael had put all his trust in the Mene'ahn doctors, and they had reassured him repeatedly, that in time, his wife would recover from her devastating trauma.

Michael hesitated to enter at first. He stood before the glassy entrance of the infirmary, still wearing the official council member's uniform, only now the jacket fell open in front. He held the belt tightly in his left hand. His long hair, silver at the temples, was tied in a tight band at the back of his neck. Indrah and Andre'ah floated up quietly behind him.

The twins preferred different styles and generally everyone could distinguish one from the other, simply by their attire. Indrah loved satiny, flowing, organic, feminine dresses with colorful accents and cool colors. Her sister preferred more tailored fashions with earth colors, like red, gold and brown. She rarely wore flashy ornaments. The twelve-year-olds chose outfits that generally matched their personalities. Andre'ah was quiet and serious while Indrah was soft, sweet and vulnerable. The sweet one, in a lavender shift, wrapped her arms around her father's chest from behind, and placed her head on his back between his shoulders.

Michael caressed her arms and held them close, "Hey Indy." He turned and held his arms out to embrace both his daughters in silence. At that awkward, pre-teen age both girls, with tall heeled shoes, stood shoulder to shoulder by their father, exactly his height.

The girls promised to be every bit as beautiful as their mother, when they matured beyond their present lanky, pre-puberty stage. In Michael's eyes they were gorgeous, and when he looked at them on that particular day his throat closed as he choked back his tears.

Together they moved into the large, open space where Lune'ah lay waiting for so many years in her icy cocoon. The doctor was crouched near the end of the transparent chamber adjusting the gauges. When he noticed the family entering, he stood and walked toward them. The smile on his face indicated, to the three, that everything was OK.

"Everything seems to be on schedule. She should be waking any minute now."

"Remember," the doctor added, "She is going to be very weak and probably confused as well." The doctor had deep wrinkles and huge, dark, bushy eyebrows that did not match his thin, white hair. "Your mother will not know you two. It will be a shock for her to see you all grown up like you are. Perhaps you should stand outside and allow her to see your father first."

"Doc, would it be OK for them to stay here until she starts to wake up?" said Michael without taking his eyes off his wife.

"Of course." Then the doctor walked up to sleeping beauty's crystal chamber and carefully released more of the frozen gasses. "This should be enough. The temperature should stabilize quickly now. When she regains consciousness my assistant and I will take her out and place her on a gurney. She will need to remain here for quite some time, until we know her condition is stable. Are you ready for this?" He smiled and placed his hand on Michael's shoulder.

"Doctor, I am so ready, *we* are so ready. Thank you so much for everything you've done." Michael choked up a little as he spoke.

The doctor stepped out and said, "I'll be close by if you need me."

Then the three stood like statues watching and waiting for the fairy tale princess to awaken from her peaceful slumber. Minutes turned into hours. Slowly, Lune'ah's hands began to move, and a few seconds later she made fists with her hands. Her chest began to noticeably heave up and down as they could see by the monitors that her heart rate increased. Her eyelids fluttered and finally opened, tiny slits at first, then wider as she focused on the curved surface of the capsule around her.

The girls gently touched their father on his shoulder to signal their departure, but Michael's eyes did not leave Lune'ah's pale profile. A few moments later he could see the emerald eyes of his beloved as she turned her face toward him with a slight smile at the corners of her pink lips. Michael wrapped his arms around the cold cylinder to embrace her. "Doc! She's awake! Can you come back here and get her out of this thing please."

The old doctor hurried back into the infirmary chamber after summoning his assistant. The two of them promptly moved the floating gurney up to the end of the icy prison chamber and gently guided the delicate female figure onto it. Super soft, white, hashi'ah sheets, swaddled her perfect frame as Michael watched her grow aware of her surroundings.

Michael took her hand, still cold, and warmed it in his own. "Don't try to speak Sweetheart. You are doing fine. Do you know who I am?" Her crooked smile and slight nod indicated that she was regaining consciousness and was returning to him.

For a long while he just sat there, talking quietly to her and caressing her hand, as her body warmed and her mind began to focus. She turned her head and opened her jade green eyes to drink in the familiar image of her handsome and loving husband. Suddenly a puzzled expression crossed her face and she reached her hand up to touch the unfamiliar gray hair at his temples. She looked away and closed her eyes, squeezing tears down the sides of her face into her auburn hair. Questions flowed into her head but her mouth was still unable to respond.

"It's OK Sweetheart. Baby, don't worry. You're back now. You've been away for a long time. You're gonna need some time to get your strength back." His eyes filled with tears that he did not want her to see, so he smeared his face on the satiny sheet covering her shoulder.

Lune'ah moved both her hands to her abdomen. Without words she was asking Michael about her twins, and he was quick to respond. "They are fine, my love. Your twin girls are beautiful, and healthy and very anxious to meet their mother. Are you ready to see them?" She answered with an enthusiastic nod.

Michael briefly stepped out and motioned for his daughters who were waiting nearby. When they rounded the corner Lune'ah tried to sit up a little, her eyes widened and filled with tears- tears of joy- tears of surprise and tears of sadness. Clearly she was not prepared for daughters who were already nearly six feet tall. She tried to speak, but her voice was silent. She whispered, "You can't be my babies! No! What happened to me...where have I been all these years?"

Lune'ah began to tremble. She reached for Michael and strained to speak but could only whisper. "Are these girls really our twins? How old are they?"

Michael gently held his wife's hand and answered with a breaking voice, "They are twelve years old."

"What are their names?" Michael leaned in to hear her question.

Indrah stepped up and flashed a beautiful smile at her mother. Both girls had their mother's smile and abundant wavy hair, only several shades lighter than Lune'ah's. On this special occasion Indrah had her hair piled atop her head, secured with an outrageous group of pluckings from the ocean floor. Her blue eyes sparkled as her father gently handed her mother's hand to her. "Mother, I'm Indrah. It's wonderful to see you. You look beautiful."

"I wish I felt beautiful," she whispered softly and smiled as she held out her other hand to Andre'ah who was standing on the opposite side of the floating bed. "And you are...?"

"Mother, I am Andre'ah." She took her mother's hand and leaned forward to hold it gently to her breast. Her copper tinted hair fell across her flushing face.

"Michael, they are so beautiful," she said with her soft voice beginning to return. She turned back to look again at her daughters and asked, "And where is your brother?"

The girls looked at their father. Michael rarely spoke of Gabriel but they knew all about him.

"Michael, where is Gabriel?" she insisted.

He was not prepared to answer her questions about their son. He knew that her condition was still delicate. He didn't want to upset her, but he did not see how he could avoid the questions about Gabriel. He quietly asked the girls to step outside for a few moments so that he could speak privately with his wife. He could see in her face that she would not rest until he answered her question. Michael paused to gather his thoughts and carefully considered his response.

Uncle Josi'ah appeared at the entrance of the infirmary. "Michael... is she allright?" he asked as he quickly stepped up to her bedside. "Well, you look beautiful!" then he abruptly turned again to Michael. "I need to speak with you NOW."

"What is it?" said Michael worriedly.

"Excuse us Lune'ah. I'm so glad to see you looking so alive and lovely, my dear. I'm terribly sorry to interrupt, but I need to speak with Michael on an urgent matter." Josi'ah was literally pulling on Michael's arm as he crouched by his wife's bedside.

When they arrived in the corridor outside the infirmary, Josi'ah got right to the point and announced "Michael there has been an attempt to activate your Elrey'ah!"

Michael's expression suddenly changed and the wrinkles on his forehead deepened. He looked directly into Uncle Josi'ah's eyes and he understood the importance of this information. "Where is it?"

"Our monitor indicated that it is on an island in the South Pacific Ocean. We cannot know, at this point, if James still has possession of it." Josi'ah answered. He could see the hatred that still burned within Michael's spirit. "The council will be meeting in the council chamber right away, to determine how we should proceed. I'm sorry, I know this is bad timing. I know you want to be with your wife."

"I understand. This is important. I'll meet you there as soon as I can," Michael said as he looked over at his wife.

Josi'ah dashed off quickly. Then Michael returned to his wife's bedside to try to answer her difficult question. The twins had been visiting with their mother while Michael was speaking with Josi'ah. Their faces revealed their confusion. "We didn't know what to say Papo," they said in unison. "She wants to know about Gabriel."

"I know. I'll talk to her. You girls leave us for a while."

"Michael, where is Gabriel? Where is our boy?" She feared that Michael would tell her that her son was dead and she tried to prepare herself for what she was about to hear.

Michael gulped hard and tried to find the words. He knew better than to try to lie to Lune'ah. "Sweetheart, do you remember how you were injured?"

Lune'ah tried to think back through years of darkness to that day. "I'm not sure what happened. It was James, wasn't it? He was trying to escape again, and the two of you were struggling with the ice excavating tool. It was an accident. Did he succeed in escaping?"

"Yes." Michael looked away.

"Did he take Luci'ah with him?" she asked.

"Yes, she helped him escape."

"She loved him so much," she said. "I am not surprised."

Michael's throat closed and he found himself unable to speak.

"Michael, where is Gabriel?" Lune'ah reached up and turned his face toward hers.

"They took him." Michael spoke so softly she was not sure she had heard correctly. He repeated. "They kidnapped our son that day, Lune'ah."

"Oh Michael, they took our beautiful little Gabriel?" She knew that Michael would not lie to her about something so important, but she did not want to accept his words.

Michael laid his head gently on her chest, and they held each other for a long while, crying silent tears. "I'm sorry, I'm so sorry," Michael whispered, over and over.

Chapter 21
GABRIEL

Gabriel and Rahsheed ran down the steep paved road from the glass palace deep in the side of the mountain on the island of Sanctuary. They raced toward the white sandy beach after their morning tutorials. The sun was shining brightly that day but a dark and ominous cloud blanketed the southern sky as they dashed along the shoreline.

Rahsheed had visited the McKay family on this amazing tropical island many times over the past few years, often spending entire summers with his best friend, exploring, sailing, surfing, fishing and laughing. His father was a powerful lawyer and politician in Saudi Arabia. Abdul Amier Hareem Mustafa had important friends in high places and in low places as well. Rahsheed and his family were faithful Muslims. Gabriel would often stand by, a bit confused, when his friend would stop suddenly, flop down on the ground on his knees in the fetal position and mumble a string of words in Arabic. But the two boys never discussed their beliefs about God, they were too busy enjoying their youth and freedom to contemplate such matters.

That particular afternoon was like so many others, except that Gabriel had something special to show his friend. He had found an unusual item, earlier that morning, nestled among a pile of tools and outdated electrical equipment in a closet in a card board box. He had been looking for a power cord to an old computer he had recently disassembled, when he ran across the strange looking metal thimble. Gabriel, anxious to show his friend the delicate treasure in secret, stepped behind a group of palms and hibiscus bushes and motioned for his friend to come closer. Gabriel smiled and reached deep into the pocket of his baggy tropical print, knee-length swim trunks and brought out an old-fashioned white handkerchief . He carefully unfolded the cloth to reveal his prize. "Look at this, Rahsheed. Look what I found."

"What is it?" said the young man as he eyed the little silver tool. Rahsheed looked up and flashed his large, pearly white teeth in a broad smile. Even though he was a year older he was several inches shorter than his friend, Gabriel. They was an odd contrast between the two teenagers. Rahsheed was dark and scrawny, while Gabriel was tall, and tan, with an athletic physique, and pale gray blue eyes.

"I have no idea, but isn't it cool?" said the sweaty teenager, panting like a tiger, after having run half the length of the island down the beach. "I have fooled around with it a little, and it's doing some weird things. These little crystals start to light up when I put it on my finger like a thimble. Pretty cool, huh?"

"Where did it come from?" his curious friend's face was bright with enthusiasm. Gabriel held the object close to him like Gollum holding his *Precious*.

"I don't know, but it's been in that box for a long time. It was covered with dust." He eyed the colored crystals on the side as he placed it on his finger. "I want to see if it will light up again." At first nothing happened, but Gabriel began to stroke what appeared to be a green light on the side of the shiny instrument. Patiently he waited for the tiny colored lights to begin to glow as they had done before. Within a few minutes all four lights were completely illuminated.

"Stand back, I'm not sure what it's gonna do. Something tells me this thing is more than just a junky, battery-operated toy, made in China." Gabriel placed his thumb on the red light and aimed the thimble at a short palm tree. Suddenly a ray of blinding light, like a bolt of lightning, shot out of the pointed end of the little silver tool and the palm tree split in two. POW! It exploded so quickly and with such force that it did not fall over, it snapped in two, and the top half landed eight or ten feet away.

"Holy crap!" Gabriel whooped. "Did you see that?...Oh my God!"

For the next few minutes he continued to experiment with his newfound toy. He destroyed half a dozen palm trees in the process, and made some sea water boil!

Gabriel and his friend couldn't believe what the strange little tool could do. When he held his two fingers together tightly and pointed directly down, he actually levitated off the ground! When he released the pressure he stumbled back to earth.

Rahsheed begged his friend for an opportunity to test the tool for himself, but Gabriel wisely refused.

At prayer time, his friend fell to his knees and began his ritual prayer to Allah. Gabriel casually pointed the tiny tool at Rahsheed and suddenly over heard his prayers in English!

At first the boys did not notice when Luci'ah approached from the South, riding freely on her beautiful dapple gray Arabian stallion. Like a scene from a black and white Hollywood movie, her flowing white gown blurred with the ocean waves as she galloped across the shoreline. The scene was colorized with a background of crystal blue ocean, flat blue sky and Luci'ah's loose, flowing copper hair. When he saw his mom approaching, Gabriel calmly slid his hand into the pocket of his colorful shorts, hiding the conspicuous instrument.

"Beautiful afternoon boys. What are you doing?" said Luci'ah from her prancing stallion. She had heard the booming noises and saw the trails of black smoke from the palm trees. She was concerned but she did not pressure the boys any further. She was glad to see that the teenage pranksters were safe.

"Nothing Mom, just hangin'," said Gabriel.

As the morning sun shone through Luci'ah's hair, it outlined her silhouette with an aura of white light. Gabriel and Rahsheed were accustomed to Luci'ah and her stunning ten-plus beauty. Any other man or boy, upon seeing this goddess, would have held his breath and been speechless. These two pre-occupied teenagers just ignored her, caught up in their own world of youthful exploration. "Down the beach, by the black boulder, I saw a dozen or more sea turtles, just hatched, scrambling toward the water." She said excitedly. "You boys should hurry down there to see them."

"Sure thing, Mom. Sea turtles! Wow. How exciting. Thanks." They looked at each other and smiled.

"So, tomorrow you both will be going with your fathers to New York. Have you completed packing your things?" she inquired.

"Don't worry, Mom," the fourteen year old responded disrespectfully. "I'm a big boy now. I can pack my own suitcase."

"That's fine, son," said Luci'ah. She hated the fact that Gabriel had grown up so fast. Her only child, no longer a child, seemed to have no need for her now and the emptiness seemed inescapable. She twisted in the black, silver-studded saddle and gazed out over the horizon steadying her prancing stallion with a gentle pat on the side of his neck. Using only her fingers she turned back and waved good-bye to the teenagers, who seemed occupied with more important matters. "I'm off. We'll all have dinner together, so be home before nightfall." Then she guided Legacy back to the water's edge. The boys barely looked up to acknowledge her departure.

Luci'ah had developed a love for horseback riding similar to her love of swimming. Having lived her whole life within the confines of the hidden city of New Mene'ah, Luci'ah cherished the feeling of freedom and communion with Mene'ah that she experienced as she galloped her stallion up and down the beach. Often she felt her horse, Legacy, was her best friend and she was sure that he understood every word she spoke to him.

The following morning began well before sunrise. James, Gabriel, Rahsheed and his father, along with the pilot and his assistant, boarded the small jet plane just before dawn. After fueling and loading all the passengers and supplies, the sleek white jet, with a silver horizontal stripe along each side, taxied down the paved runway. The dual engine jet airplane rolled away, darted past the rows of palm trees and lifted off just as the sun began to peek over the horizon in the East.

The nineteen hours in the air proved to be boring and tedious for the two teenagers, but they bided their time with video games and internet explorations. At mid-day the pilot stopped briefly at a small airport on the island of Oahu, to re-fuel. Afterward, they were off again, headed toward the glistening city of New York, where the twin-towers still defined the skyline.

Gabriel had hidden his tiny silver toy in a pocket inside his suitcase. During the entire trip he never stopped thinking about his amazing treasure. Getting through customs when they arrived at La Guardia airport in New York might prove to be a problem and Gabriel was worried. He and Rahsheed whispered quietly together as they approached the airport. "If they find it, Gabriel, what will you do?" Rahsheed pressed his friend.

"I don't know, it's so weird looking and so small, I just hope they don't confiscate it. We'll find out soon," said Gabriel. Then he added, "I guess I shouldn't have brought it."

As the hours dragged on, aboard the shiny new jet, the boys entertained themselves the best they could. The small private jet was artfully upholstered with tan leather seats. Chrome and glass trim, lined the wide center aisle, in the ultra- modern airplane. Unable to sleep, the fidgety teenagers bounced from one end of the airplane to the other, passing the time between games and movies by talking and laughing, and scrounging for snacks.

During the long flight, James and his Saudi Arabian friend occupied themselves at a round, thick, glass table spread with graphs, charts and computer generated forms. The two business men rarely looked up from their papers, as the boys endlessly moved up and down the aisle. Abdul Mustafa, Rahsheed's father, was wearing his most royal Middle Eastern garb, minus the elaborate headdress. Purple and yellow delicately embroidered bands encircled his broad sleeves and lined the edges of his robe to his collar. While on the island Abdul would dress quite casually, in linen floral camp shirts, or knit polo shirts and short pants, but he wanted to present himself in his formal, princely attire, upon his arrival in New York. After the plane landed at La Guardia, he donned his huge white scarf, twisted on the black and gold head band and the four of them walked down the steep steps and into the glass walled airport. Abdul's attire sharply contrasted with the ordinary street clothes worn by James and the boys.

Gabriel had visited New York on two separate occasions, with his father, in the past. Their arrival had always been uneventful. This time was no different. As usual, James was treated like a VIP. Everyone called him "Sir," and his foreign friends were given the utmost respect as they breezed through customs. Upon their arrival all the luggage had been X-rayed and thoroughly inspected. Gabriel's treasure had not been spotted and Rahsheed noticed the relief on Gabriel's face afterwards. A shiny black limo waited for them just outside the baggage pick-up area. Within minutes, they were headed down the sparkling crowded streets of the city, toward the elegant Manhattan Arms Hotel.

This was Rahsheed's first experience in the Big Apple, and his eyes grew wider and wider as the limo meandered through the noisy streets of New York. Gabriel pressed the button and the sun roof opened. He and his friend then stood on the seat and exposed their upper bodies to the sounds and images of the city streets. James and his business associate tried hard to ignore the youthful excitement of the boys who grinned and waved at the pedestrians as they approached their first-class hotel.

The hotel, one of the finest in New York, was situated south of central park near the corner of Park Avenue and 23rd. The three bedrooms of the penthouse surrounded an elaborate living area of mauve and tangerine, with modern accents of glass and shiny copper. A shaggy cream and brown oval carpet was centered in the middle of the room under a heavy marble coffee table, between two white leather sofas. Thick, striped tapestry curtains opened to reveal the amazing New York skyline with the Empire State Building at its center. The two teenagers, anxious to get out and explore the city, scrambled to unpack their suitcases into the drawers of their shared room. James gave the boys some last minute instructions, and in time that could be measured in micro-seconds, they were hurrying out and down the wide hallway to the elevator.

When the two spilled out of the double glass doorway of the hotel onto Park Avenue and headed straight toward the Empire State Building which was only a few blocks away. The two young men, unimpressed with the elaborate mosaic tile floor and three story metallic illustration on the wall of the lobby, pressed the button to activate the elevator. Within a few moments they were admiring the amazing view from the observation level. They had no way of knowing that, in only two days, the New York skyline would be drastically altered by the elimination of the majestic twin towers of the World Trade Center.

The rest of their day was spent in a whirlwind of typical tourist activities. Gabriel talked his father into allowing him and his friend to purchase two-day passes to ride the red, double-decker buses around the city. This enabled them to check out the entire city in the least amount of time. They hopped off and on the busses all afternoon, always climbing the narrow metal staircase to get seats on the upper level where they could have a three-hundred-and sixty degree view of the city as it passed by. The weather was cooperative as well. As the boys explored the city, the first signs of fall offered cool breezes and the sun sparkled through the skyscrapers.

Throughout the day Gabriel had traveled around the city with his special thimble at the bottom of his deep pocket, not daring to use it, but deriving comfort knowing it was safe.

The men had a three o'clock business appointment on the second floor of the New York Federal Reserve building at 33 Liberty Street, just a few blocks from the famous Twin Towers. They asked the teenagers to join them there afterwards.

Shortly after four thirty Gabriel and Rahsheed hopped off the double decker bus on Liberty street, where they were allowed to enter the grand building, after giving their names to the armed guard just inside the doorway. They took the steps up the curved marble staircase two and three at a time, to one of the main conference rooms. James was there, sitting at a huge black marble table, with half-a- dozen distinguished looking gentlemen. All the men wore dark suits and ties, except for Abdul Amier Hareem Mustafa who wore his traditional royal maroon robe and white headdress. There were no women present. The boys stood patiently in the open double doorway. James motioned for them to enter and introduced the boys quite formally, to the other gentlemen, but did not introduce the men to the teenagers. "We are almost finished with our business here, boys. You two just have a seat," said James. The boys cooperated and took seats at the far end of the oval table where they waited for the men to conclude their business.

All the men seemed pleased with the agreements that were made that afternoon. Papers were passed around the table and promptly signed by all parties. Three or four large screened table-top computers revealed graphs and columns of numbers. As the men were finishing their meeting Gabriel sat quietly with Rahsheed for what seemed like a long time. He began to get bored. He reached his hand deep into the pocket of his cargo pants and slipped his powerful little toy inconspicuously onto his finger. Within a few minutes he felt it growing warm. He had seen it perform very curiously on his own home computer and he, in his youthful naivety, wanted to see if he could access some top secret, highly, confidential information from one of the computers on the table. Just when he was about to give up on his idea all the men suddenly stood up and began milling around the room shaking hands and congratulating each other on their potentially beneficial economic venture. Gabriel stood also and calmly walked over to the men. He touched the back of one of the lap-top computers with the silver device on his forefinger. Instantly the monitor screen went black.

"What did you do Gabriel?" James saw Gabriel standing by the computer and he panicked as the men began to crowd around the malfunctioning computer.

Gabriel rapidly shoved his hand into his pocket and responded innocently, "Nothing, I just touched it." He stepped back from the table and stood against the wall, and as the group huddled around the computer Gabriel zapped even another computer with his magic thimble. At first no one noticed, but soon they discovered that it too had shut down unexpectedly.

Within a few moments both computers were booted up and running smoothly again, but what they didn't know then, was that Gabriel had unknowingly downloaded all their bank information and could soon have the ability to access that information, as well as all the money in their accounts.

After the meeting at the Federal Reserve building Rahsheed and Gabriel enjoyed a pepperoni pizza at a hole-in-the-wall joint on 23rd while James entertained his gang of elite businessmen at Carmines, a high-end Italian restaurant in the heart of Manhattan.

Exhausted and stuffed, they all returned to their suite at the luxurious Manhattan Arms Hotel. James opened the heavy drapes to reveal the spectacular city skyline. They all fell asleep that night as the Empire State Building stood guard over them through the massive glass window of their hotel.

Before he fell asleep that night Gabriel secretly took his silver thimble out of his suitcase for one last look before he closed his eyes. It could take Gabriel a long time to figure out how to use his elegant and powerful little toy. But if and when he did, he could easily become one of the wealthiest, most powerful men in the entire world. And that might be a lot to handle, for a fourteen year old boy.

Chapter 22
A PLAN OF ACTION

The Mene'ahn council met in the main council chamber to discuss a plan for the retrieval of Michael's stolen Elrey'ah device. It had remained dormant for over twelve years. A large semi-transparent screen projected from above the central table displayed a three-dimensional world map in the council chamber. The huge slowly spinning globe showed intricate details of every nation, every city, every village, every river, and of course, every island as well. The Mene'ahn council members were able to zoom in so closely that houses and cars could easily be identified.

Naha'ran stepped up after all the council members were present around the massive oval table. "For those of you who do not already know the purpose of this meeting, I will explain as clearly as possible. It is imperative that we act on this information quickly. An attempt has been made to activate the Elrey'ah thimble that was stolen from our fellow Council member Michael, twelve years ago." He pointed to the map and moved it where the South Pacific Ocean was centered before the council members. Then he opened his fingers, which enlarged the area. He repeated this motion again and again until an aerial view of the tiny island of Sanctuary reached the entire length of the oval table. It hung motionless before the concerned council members. "About eight hours ago, our monitor indicated an attempted activation of the device on this island."

"Eight hours ago!" Michael stood up and interrupted. "Why are we just now hearing about this?"

"The signal was very weak, at first, and then it disappeared completely." The old gentleman responded calmly. "We have been watching carefully since the first indication was noticed. The Elrey'ah has not been fully activated. There has been no additional signal since. Please sit down Sir." Naha'ran continued, "We are here at this time to formulate a plan that is unanimous."

"What is there to discuss? Let's go get 'em." Michael urged impatiently.

"Michael, we don't know who has the device at this point. Of course we will attempt to retrieve it. When the signal reappears, and we are sure that it will, we need to have a plan in place," the old gentleman reasoned sternly.

Then Uncle Josi'ah rose to speak. "I wish to volunteer myself and my two sons for this mission. We should use our air transportation vehicle. I therefore respectfully request the assistance of General William. He has the most experience piloting the vehicle."

The large council member at the end of the table immediately stood and announced. "I will be proud and honored to participate in this important mission." Council Member and General, William de Siano represented Territory # 2 on the planet of Siano in the Mene'ahn system. The impressive looking gentleman with broad shoulders, very short, thick, curly gray hair and a double chin, had for the past forty-two years, been in charge of several above-the-horizon expeditions. He had more experience flying the Mene'ahn air ship than any other citizen.

Suddenly the distinguished group was hushed as all eyes quickly focused on the bright green sparkling light emerging from the island map suspended in front of them. The light, which grew brighter every second, indicated the Elrey'ah thimble was being activated at that very moment. The light seemed to be originating from a section of the beach on the Eastern shore of the island. Naha'ran promptly enlarged the area as much as possible. On the white sandy beach of the tiny island they could see two small figures. The light emanated from the larger figure and often encompassed the person entirely. The other figure, a smaller and darker individual, remained close-by and moved all around excitedly. The facial features could not be seen clearly, but they appeared to be a pair of young men or boys playing on the beach; *Playing* with perhaps the most dangerous toy in the world. The council members watched for several minutes, speechless, as the green light dimmed and glowed, occasionally exploding with bright yellow and green light.

"Look, over here. Someone...looks like a lady with red hair, is riding down the beach on a horse, toward the other two," said one of the council members.

"Yes, she is riding right up to them," said Michael. "Luci'ah. Could it be Luci'ah?" Anger that Michael had tried to bury for years suddenly welled up inside him as he watched the blurred image ride up to the other two figures.

"Perhaps," Josi'ah answered. "Is the council ready to make a decision on this mission?"

Naha'ran responded, "I propose a rescue mission be immediately organized to retrieve the stolen Elrey'ah, and if found, bring Gabriel, Luci'ah and James back here as well. William, Josi'ah, and of course, I assume...Michael, have volunteered for this mission." He looked over at Michael for confirmation and Michael nodded. "Josi'ah will ask his sons, and I am sure they will also agree to participate in this very important assignment. If there is any member here present, who objects to any part of this mission, will that member please stand?"

No one stood to vote against the mission, and after a brief pause Naha'ran continued. "Now, may we stand and offer a prayer to Mene'ah." All the council members rose up and raised their hands to recite the prayer in unison. "Ah'men Mene'ah, Orah' Mene'ah, e sha Mene'ah, mon sa ha wah lah sheha Mene'a, ah'men." Then everyone left the chamber excitedly talking among themselves. Michael, William and Josi'ah exited together already planning their strategy. They agreed to meet at the air ship as soon as they could all say goodbye to their loved ones and gather their equipment.

Michael knew a little about the air transport vehicle. He knew it had not been used for a very long time, perhaps as long as twenty years. He knew that it had become dangerous to take it out and to expose it again and again as they had done in the past. As technology and air travel above the horizon increased, the threat of being discovered increased also. He understood that the aircraft counteracted gravity and was able to achieve incredible speeds. Uncle Josi'ah had shown it to him several years ago. It had been stored in a huge hangar on the primary level for a very long time. Michael was looking forward to seeing it again, and riding in it. *How many earthlings had ridden in such a vehicle?* None, ever, Michael guessed.

Michael held his breath before entering his apartment. His mind raced with too many random thoughts and questions. *How would he tell his girls goodbye? Would he recognize his son if he saw him? What would he say to Lune'ah? What would he do if he ran into James? Would he be able to control his anger? Had he learned enough of the lessons and teachings of Mene'ah to control his inner–self, or would he relinquish his hold on the beast within, and lose his cool completely? Would he honor Mene'ah with his service?* He found himself reciting the standard prayer over and over, in the Mene'ahn language, as he packed his things into the heavy hashi'ah draw-string bag.

It wasn't as hard as he thought it was going to be, to say goodbye to the girls. The twins were very supportive. They understood the urgency of the mission. Lune'ah was more difficult. She did not speak, but her expression spoke volumes. She understood everything all too well. She and Michael held each other closely for those few long minutes. Her mobility was increasing rapidly. She had been transferred to a standard hospital hover chair. Michael knelt down on one knee holding her hands and speaking softly with his wife. She cleared her throat to speak and whispered "Bring our son home, my love. Please bring him home."

"I will Sweetheart. I promise," and he kissed her gently on the lips.

She began to speak again and Michael leaned closer to hear her soft voice. "Tell her...tell her...if you see her... (he knew she meant Luci'ah) tell her ...I'm sending Fran's letter to her, Fran's letter to Stepha'niah." Michael looked confused. He repeated the phrase, still holding her hands.

Michael hoped he would not see Luci'ah but he made another promise. "If I see her, I will tell her." Not surprisingly He hated his wife's sister.

The teenage twin girls stood on each side of their mother and said in unison, "You need to go now Papo. We'll take good care of our mother." Then Michael stood and squared his shoulders, walked away and wiped the tears from his cheek. To walk away from Luni'ah at that time was the hardest thing he had ever done. He took the stairs up to the first level and tried to focus on the immediate needs of this mission.

The three older gentlemen stood in their cream and maroon colored Mene'ahn uniforms before the massive terminal entrance on level one, where the main air exploration vehicle had been quartered, undisturbed for decades. Josi'ah activated the button with a sweep of his hand, and the automatic water doorway slurped open. Michael called it a "flying saucer" because it was shaped like a pie or a round sea shell. Josi'ah had explained the mechanics of this very special flying machine to Michael, in this way. "Son, Mene'ah has given us a miraculous gift. He guided our ancestors and helped them to transform ordinary water into Hydrogen, which provides power for almost everything, and oxygen...which is quite handy for breathing. The hydrogen in this vessel propels magnetized lutanium balls around and around the perimeter of the ship. You see that channel?" Josi'ah pointed to the tubular ring around the ship. Michael thought it looked like the ring around a child's blow up, wading pool. "It operates very much like an old fashioned spinning top. The spinning of the metal weights generates the reverse magnetism, like trying to force two negative magnets to connect. That is how it works. It's really quite simple. Gravity is just a form of magnetism." Michael pretended he understood.

William went right up to the unearthly looking vehicle and activated the opening and the lights with a remote key. Josi'ah followed him into the ship, climbing a pair of floating steps on the side. He motioned for Michael to come along. It was the most beautiful, most colorful space he had ever been in. Light glowed through the stained-glass swirls that concentrated above and wrapped around a central column. Mother of pearl equipment with red and orange exotic leathers and fabrics made Michael feel like he was inside a genie's bottle.

William went to work right away at one of the four central

terminals, attempting to prime the engine. Josi'ah stood at his shoulder checking out all the equipment. Michael looked over and immediately did not like the expressions on their faces. He promptly joined them at William's other shoulder and tried to make sense out of all the bells and whistles on the high-tech instrument panels. "Is something wrong?" he was quick to ask.

"I'm not sure, at this point, Michael. This ship has been idle for a very long time. Hopefully she just needs a little boost to get her warmed up. Let's use our Elrey'ahs and see if we can't stimulate her." William continued to move his fingers up and down, testing the panels and manipulating the levers and lights as he spoke. Though his voice sounded calm, the deep furrow in his brow gave a different message to Michael and Josi'ah.

"I need both of you to activate your Elrey'ahs right now. When they are fully activated we will touch this disk right here in order to charge the engine." He pointed to the small raised section of the control panel. "Josi'ah, you understand what we need to do, right?"

Josi'ah nodded as he removed his silver thimble device from its case around his neck and placed it on his finger. William did the same. Michael understood and he followed their example. Soon they could see by the bright glowing lights on the sides of their thimbles that the three "Triggers of God" were ready for action.

William focused all his energy and touched his Elrey'ah to the quarter sized, raised disk on the panel in front of him. Josi'ah and Michael did the same. The disk began to erupt with streams of light shooting across the tiny space, like a room full of shooting stars. William sensed that Michael was about to pull his hand away. He grabbed his arm firmly, and without saying a word, signaled to Michael that this process needed to continue. When the fireworks stopped, they pulled their hands away. "That should do it" said William looking confident.

Josi'ah instructed Michael to stash his bag under one of the benches that ringed the perimeter of the air ship, to take a seat, and to strap himself in. Michael was quick to comply.

A few moments later the familiar red head of cousin Ziggy popped into the doorway. "Don't dare go without US!" he shouted as he entered. "Shavo is on his way; he'll be here in just a few minutes." Neither his appearance nor his jovial, positive attitude had changed in the slightest over the past twelve years. He could not contain his excitement about being included in this important and *flying* mission. "I'm so honored to be included in this mission. Thank you. he said.

Shavo came in right away, more quietly than his brother. They huddled together intently discussing their mission, but after a while they began to grow concerned when they saw William still struggling with the control panel. He asked Michael and Josi'ah to once again try to prime the central power generator. Josia'h sent out a request for help from Naha'ran to add umph to their efforts. Soon he arrived and added his powerful touch with his Elrey'ah. The group held their Elrey'ah thimbless to the disk for quite some time. The light show, while lovely, at first, became quite tedious after a while. Finally Michael asked William "How long is this gonna take?"

He did not like the answer he got from William. "As long as it takes," he said as he shook his head in disgust. The four men crowded around the energy panel and continued their efforts to stoke the powerful engine. A very long hour or more passed before the men could hear a change in the sound coming from the outer ring of the ship. It became smoother and the pitch became sweeter. "Another few minutes should do it I think,"

Michael's patience was wearing thin, and he finally had to speak. "We need to go. We need to hurry this up. Should we try to get another council member to bring another one of these Elrey'ah things?" He didn't mean to sound disrespectful. "Is there another ship we can use?"

Naha'rahn spoke abruptly. "These *things*--these *triggers of God*, are working and the engine will be ready soon. Son it has been twelve years. A few hours will make no difference."

Naha'rahn did not know, of course, that in a few of hours James and Gabriel would be leaving that tropical island, boarding a small jet and flying to New York City. "And to answer your other question... Yes, we have many additional ships in storage all around the South

Polar region, but it would require an hour or more to acquire one of them. This one will be operational soon. Be Patient."

When the engine began to purr and tremble, William and the others knew that it had been fully charged. The men graciously thanked Naha'ran as he climbed down out of the ship. "Ah'men Mene'ah," shouted all.

Soon the flying pie was air tight, and all passengers were buckled in and ready for flight. William and Josi'ah checked to make sure all passengers and all equipment were secure. The pilots tightened their harnesses and placed their palms firmly on the colorful panels before them. The huge domed panel above the ship suddenly liquefied and flowed onto the upper surface of the polar ice sheet revealing the clear blue sky above.

The others could see Michael's frustration as he held his breath for the departure. The engine hummed loudly but he could feel no movement. He was sure the aircraft was malfunctioning--that it was unable to access the energy from the four Elrey'ah devices, and that their mission would have to transfer to another ship, hours away, or move to a submarine for an underwater mission. Finally, after several agonizing minutes, he had to speak, "What's wrong? Why are we not flying yet?"

Knowing smiles spread across their faces. Michael realized, by their expressions, that they were already in flight. "We'll be flying over New Zealand in about an hour." They almost laughed. "You can get out of your seat harness now, Michael. It'll take several hours to reach the island."

"What?" Michael quickly unsnapped and jumped up to see the monitor in front of William. From the crystal clear view in the monitor he could see that they were miles above the horizon and rapidly gliding through the atmosphere toward Australia. "Wow, look at that! It's beautiful. This is great! I can't feel any motion at all!"

William explained the phenomenon as if he were speaking to a kindergartener, as if it were the simplest of concepts. "The gravity of the earth has been stabilized. You will feel it more when we stop which will be in about three hours, standard earth time."

Michael felt his heart stop beating, and he held his breath for a few seconds. *"This is it,"* he said to himself. Then he shouted to the others, even though shouting wasn't really necessary as the air ship was very quiet in its operation. "I want to land on the island, on the beach, exactly where we saw the Elrey'ah being activated!"

"I believe that will be quite possible, Sir." William approved of the suggestion. "The beach will be an easy, flat surface, on which to land."

When the air disk arrived at the island that morning it hovered over the beach at the designated spot for several minutes. They began their descent which felt, to Michael, very much like an elevator, going down, that is, except for the swaying. A short distance away, and on the other side of the island they did not see the small airplane take off just before the early morning sunrise. As their craft floated only a few feet above the ground the passengers backed down and out of the vehicle one by one, onto the sugary beach. William remained onboard.

Only the tiniest sliver of a moon remained in the pre-dawn sky as the men began to explore the area. At first no one noticed anything strange about this beach as they wandered inland, but it didn't take long for them to see the palm trees, six or seven of them, blown to pieces. Michael felt the black stub end of a large palm tree and noticed it was still warm. The four men followed the tracks leading back to the fishery. From there they could see a road leading up the side of the dark green mountain. The men crept silently up the paved roadway where they finally reached the glass palace where Luci'ah slept alone.

They walked around the wide slate walkway and stood on the broad ledge where the curved glass wall faced the ocean unobstructed by any curtain or blinds. Using the light beams emitted from their Elrey'ah thimbles, they scoured the entire room. The men recognized the typically Mene'ahn decor with bright colors, flowing lines and textured surfaces. William touched the massive door lock with the tiny tool on his finger and quietly slid the door open. They calmly stepped in and began exploring the spacious room without hesitation.

In one of the interior doorways a stunning female silhouette appeared, wearing a slinky white gown. Michael recognized her instantly even though he could not make out her facial features. The shapely woman scratched her head and stretched in her bedroom doorway. When she saw the men she stopped in mid-stretch and said, "Michael, I always knew this time would come," her voice echoed with resignation and relief. "James is not here. He is on his way to New York City."

Michael was not prepared for her casual greeting. "Gabriel, where is Gabriel?" He said through clenched teeth.

Luci'ah looked down and finally spoke. "Gabriel is with him."

"When are they comin' back?" barked Michael.

"They will return on the eleventh, in two days." She answered. "You all are welcome to wait here for them. Honestly, I'm glad you have come. It's been far too long. Would you like some coffee or tea?" said Luci'ah, as she floated across the stone floor. She had to hoist her skirt up, in order to walk without tripping over the long ruffled edge of her exotic nightgown. "Hello Uncle Josi'ah, Ziggy and Shavo." She offered a slight smile as she passed them on her way to the kitchen area. She wanted to greet her beloved uncle and cousins with a warm embrace but she felt uncertain of their response. The gentlemen stood erect on each side of the doorway, quite seriously guarding her exit. They did not respond to her greeting but they did acknowledge her invitation.

"We may take you up on the hospitality, Luci'ah," said Michael, but he added, "I'll have to confer with the others." He walked over to the men and asked, "What do you think? We gonna go to New York City? Or we gonna wait here?"

"I think we should wait here and see if the Elrey'ah is used again," said William.

Luci'ah overheard and interrupted the men. "The Elrey'ah, you mean the one that James took from Michael's apartment. James never used it. He couldn't activate it, and I wouldn't tell him anything. It's been in my closet. It's here and it's perfectly safe. No one has had access to it."

"You are wrong. It was used on your beach just yesterday," said Michael. Lucia's face went pale when she suddenly realized that Gabriel must have gone into her closet, found the device, and figured out how to use it on his own. "It is how we were able to pinpoint your exact location here," Michael added.

"Oh, Michael..." she stumbled with her words. "Michael... Gabriel. He has it. I'm sure. I should have buried it somewhere. It's my fault. I always hoped that someday I'd be able to give it back to you."

"Yeah, well that's a nice thought. And I do appreciate it," Michael responded with a great deal of sarcasm. "But James didn't take it from my apartment, he took it from me when he jumped me in Sydney."

Luci'ah faced him with her mouth open, clearly surprised by this latest revelation.

Michael could see that this was news to her so he continued, "We followed the submarine when you and James escaped. You remember, when you and your husband kidnapped my son. We followed you as far as we could. I met up with James at the marina on Watsons Bay. He knocked me out and had me thrown in jail! Your husband turned out to be a *really* good friend!" he added sarcastically.

"I didn't know, Michael. I'm so sorry," said Luci'ah, obviously surprised by more unhappy news. "I don't know how he could have kept that from me."

"You're SORRY!" Michael was allowing his feelings to control his inner spirit. Suddenly he began to erupt with all the anger and pain he had buried for so long. "So you are sorry for not taking very good care of the Elrey'ah thimble that your husband cracked me over the head and stole!" He didn't stop there. "So, how about Gabriel? Are you sorry for kidnapping my SON?! And what about Lune'ah? Are you sorry that your husband nearly killed her!"

"What?" She wasn't sure how much more she could take. "James nearly killed her?"

"Michael, please tell me what happened. Is Lune'ah alright?"

Uncle Josi'ah stepped in and tried to calm Michael's rage. Michael stepped aside and Uncle Josi'ah calmly explained to Luci'ah the grisly details of the awful accident that occurred the night they escaped from New Mene'ah. He left her weeping on her bed.

Michael's heart remained hard toward his sister-in-law. As he left the room he suddenly turned and remembered the promise he had made to his wife and said. "Your sister wanted me to give you a message. I have no idea what it means."

Luci'ah lifted her head off the satin pillow and looked sadly into his eyes. Her chin quivered as she waited for what she feared might be more bad news.

"She wanted me to tell you she was sending Fran's letter to you." He added, "The mail service from New Mene'ah is not so good, so I don't know exactly how she is going to send you that letter."

Luci'ah looked like a brokenhearted little girl, her face flushed, her eyes puffy and her lower lip quivering. She wiped her teary face on her pillow and said "a letter, from Fran?"

Michael shrugged his shoulders.

"To Stepha' niha?" she asked.

"Yea, that's it, Fran's letter to Stepha'niha." He confirmed.

Luci'ah remembered the poem that The High Priestess Fran de Zebron had written to her friend Stefa'niah in the Mene'ahn year 342. She had memorized the poem when she was in school. She went over the words of the poem silently and a sad smile crossed her face. Then Luci'ah sat up on the side of her bed and straightened her spine. That sad little girl face suddenly changed to a look of determination and she paused to organize her thoughts. She searched for the courage she knew was going to need. She called upon her God and said a silent prayer to Mene'ah to give her strength. A blanket of calmness and strength came over her. "Michael, you must know how much I love your son. We didn't mean to take him. I do hope you believe me. I'm so very sorry. I understand if you can't forgive me." She gracefully rose up from her bed and stood facing Michael squarely, almost nose to nose with Michael and said. "I will help you get your son back, Michael. I want to do the right thing."

Chronicles of our Sister Fran de Zebron
Chapter 1242, Book II of the Meno'ah
Mene'ahn year 342

Dear Stepha'nia
           Too much time between our meetings
                 makes my heart weep.
           You are my beloved sister, my friend.
Did not we, just yesterday, laugh, love, and cry together?
           Did not we, just yesterday, share and
                 trust and try each other?
           Did not we, just yesterday, promise
                 friendship, always and forever?
Take your anger and your fear and put them in a box.
           Bury them in your garden and watch the
           weeds grow forth, and I will do the same.

    You are always in my prayers.
    Love Fran

Chapter 23
NEW HOPE

A few hours after their meeting with Luci'ah, Michael and his crew were back in their little round space ship and headed toward the Big Apple. Luci'ah loaned all of them appropriate, American type street clothes from James' closet and gave them the information they needed to find James and Gabriel in New York City. Her help proved to be indispensable. Shavo was ordered to stay behind with Luci'ah even though she assured them, and they believed her, that she wasn't going anywhere. It would be dark by the time they arrived in New York's central park. The crew had a few hours in flight to rest and prepare for their mission.

As they passed over the landscape they were astounded by the glittering rows of lights that stretched from horizon to horizon connecting the cities. The big city lights were even more spectacular. The sparkling strings of lights caressed the rolling hills and then shot straight up to illuminate the sky with mountains of lights. When they finally arrived in New York, dawn was about to break and the lights of the city had dimmed to a pale gray. William activated a cloaking device which made their craft virtually invisible and they managed to land the vehicle on a flat grassy area by the lake in Central Park. The few visitors of the park, the winos, the street people and a few hard-core early morning joggers, did not notice the nearly invisible, silver disk, defying all city ordinances landing right in the middle of Central Park. The crew knew that, sooner or later, someone would come by and notice the ship so William deposited the team quickly and retreated to a safe distance. Michael, Josi'ah and Ziggy proceeded on foot. William remained on the ship to provide the get-away vehicle for the expedition.

The team exited the park on foot at 71st street. Michael suggested they hail a cab to the hotel. Why not? They looked like ordinary Americans. Even though it was only about 5:30 am, there were plenty of cab drivers zigzagging through the city and the three men looked quite appropriate in their business attire. Michael jumped out, into the street and flagged a yellow cab right away. Josi'ah and Ziggy had never been in an automobile before. The cab driver did not seem to notice how awkwardly the men entered the cab. Within a few minutes they arrived at the Manhattan Arms Hotel. The Indian cab driver was thrilled to be paid with a solid gold coin.

Once there, it became a waiting game. The three hours from six-o'clock to nine o'clock passed quietly, without incident. Rich, sophisticated Americans and foreigners passed through the spectacular lobby of the hotel, eyeing the four tall tourists who looked a little odd in their short slacks. But they passed the time patiently and confidently. They had acquired verification from the attendant at the front desk. This was definitely James's hotel. The men chose not to go up to his room lest they risk passing him on the elevators. They chose instead, to wait in the lobby of the grandiose hotel knowing that sooner or later James would emerge from one of the elevators.

At precisely 9:15 am on the morning of September 10th 2001 James McKay and his adopted son, Gabriel stepped out of the first floor elevator of the Manhattan Arms hotel into the lobby. Immediately Michael, Josi'ah, and Ziggy stood up and faced the elevator.

James stopped abruptly and grabbed his son by the shoulder and held him back. The three tall Mene'ahns approached and blocked their exit. James locked eyes with his adversary and his defense collapsed. He had known one day his old friend would finally catch up to him. It had been only matter of time. But it was still a shock and he required a moment to pull himself together, before he was able to speak. "Michael, I always knew you would find me. How have you been?" and he dared to add, "Old friend."

This enraged Michael and he immediately relinquished control of his inner spirit and let loose with a few choice, unprintable verbs and adjectives intended for his most heinous enemy.

"Hold on," Josi'ah interrupted. "Gentlemen, shall we adjourn to this private room to continue our conversation?" He pointed to a consultation room nearby.

All the men, including the puzzled teenager, filed quietly into the adjacent room. It was a stylish but totally empty room filled with about twenty, eight-foot tables in parallel formation. Michael watched his son as the group moved into the conference room. His joy at finally finding Gabriel, after all these years, had to be curtailed for now.

"What's going on Papo?" said Gabriel to James, trying not to appear concerned.

With a snarl on his lip Michael turned his gaze away from his long lost son and responded. "Yes, James, why don't you tell Gabriel what is going on!" The teenager stood by James, ready to defend his father.

The room was silent at first, all eyes darting back and forth, until finally James spoke, "Gabriel," he stated quite honestly, "This man, is Michael Ellsworth. He is…or was…a very good friend of mine before you were born. He is your father." Gabriel's eyes opened wide. "He is your biological father."

Gabriel stepped away from James and looked squarely at Michael. "This is for real, isn't it?" he asked. "You really aren't kidding, are you?" He looked back at James, his mouth hung open.

"No, son. It's true. I'm sorry you have to find out this way. I've wanted to tell you for a long time now. But, it's been so many years. I thought…well…I guess I thought we were home free!" Then he turned to Michael and asked, "So Michael, how did you finally find us?"

"The Elrey'ah, you took from me, the night you and your goon attacked me at the marina in Sidney, has recently been activated," said Michael.

"No, that is not possible," said James, honestly. "I never was able to figure the damn thing out, and Luci'ah wouldn't give me any clues. We've kept it in our closet all these years. Nobody else has had access to it…really."

Michael looked at Gabriel. Gabriel stared at the floor in front of him. "Gabriel has it, don't you Gabriel?" said Michael, knowingly.

"What? I don't know what you are talking about?" lied that innocent face.

Michael, breathing hard, stepped up boldly in front of the handsome young teenager and said, "Gabriel, you have a small tool, like a thimble, but quite delicate, carved in a swirl, with crystals on the side that light up." Gabriel looked at him directly in the eyes and then he looked at his feet. He was only inches shorter than his father but their profiles were identical. "How could you possibly know about that!"

"It is a powerful tool. You played around with it yesterday at the beach, didn't you Son? You blew up some palm trees. I think you know…I think you have already seen…at least a taste of its power. I want you to give it to me right now." Michael softened his voice and added, "Son…please."

The boy reluctantly reached deep into the pocket of his Dockers, and pulled out an old fashioned gentlemen's hankie with a delicate silver thimble within its folds. He handed the wad of cloth to Michael and looked away. With eyes full of angry confused tears he looked at James. "So…what's going on Papo?" he said sarcastically. "Why the bouncers?"

James did not bother to answer.

For a moment Michael just stood there looking at the tiny tool that had caused so much angst and concern in New Menc'ah. When he finally put it in his pocket he looked up at James and asked "Will you be going back with us voluntarily, or will we be forced to subdue you?"

"Well, gee, let's see. Do I want to go with you, to an icy prison, where I will be treated like a slime-ball for the rest of my life? Which probably won't be that long for me anyway?" James sighed. "*And* you want me to go willingly? *That* may be a bit too much to ask for, my friend."

"I am not your friend! *WE* are not your friends!" said Michael angrily.

"Well then no! I will *not* go willingly! So…Ya' gonna shoot me?" growled James.

"You know that Mene'ahns do not kill." saidMichael.

"No, they just put people out on the frozen ice in sub-zero temperatures to let Mene'ah take them. Yeah. I know," snapped James. Understandably he feared the fate that awaited him in New Mene'ah. He became quite nervous. Beads of sweat began to drip from his forehead, and his eyes darted around the room. Suddenly he poured forth a litany of desperation. "Michael, I won't go with you. You'll just have to kill me! I am so sorry about Lune'ah. You know I didn't mean to kill her. I understand that you hate me. God, I'd hate me too, and I deserve it."

He looked pleadingly at his wife's uncle and begged. "Luci'ah came with me of her own free will. She wanted to come with me. She loves me, and I love her. We didn't mean to take Gabriel. That was an accident. He was playing hide and seek. He was hiding in your submarine. We didn't know how to get him back to you without blowing our cover." Then he looked back at Michael. "For what it's worth, we love him. He was…is…our only son." Then he looked at Gabriel and his eyes overflowed with tears. He broke down completely and began to blubber like a baby. "I'm sorry Son. I'm so sorry. Please forgive us. Your mother loves you very much."

Michael said a silent prayer to Mene'ah and used his inner strength to cloak himself in an impenetrable shield of righteousness. He wanted to grab his son and hug him at that second, but he turned to Josi'ah instead. "Uncle Josi'ah, we hold this man's destiny in our hands. Shall we allow him to go unpunished for his sins? Shall we render him incapacitated, carry him home with us and imprison him for the rest of his life? Or shall we leave him here to live out the rest of his days in splendor on a tropical island with his beautiful wife?"

"You mean there is a chance you could just let me go?" James perked up to speak.

Michael, again speaking to Uncle Josia'h said, "You know he did fulfill one of his promises to me. He didn't tell anyone about New Mene'ah. It could have gone very badly for us if James had chosen to reveal what he knew about our colony."

"That's true," agreed Josi'ah.

"And I think he did take good care of my son." He looked over at Gabriel and asked, "Was James a good father to you?"

"He was a very good father." Gabriel gave a thumbs-up to James and then asked. "Will someone tell me what is going on. Who *are* you guys?"

Michael answered with another question. "And Luci'ah, was she a good mother?"

"Shit! You talk about her like she is dead! Yes, Goddammit she *IS* a great mother. She is Holy Mother Teresa! She's my mother. What do you want me to say?"

Michael received a nod from Josi'ah that told him, the decision about James's future was entirely up to him. Josi'ah knew Michael would honor Mene'ah in his decision. Michael knew the Mene'ahn council would not be charitable with James if Michael were to bring him back to the colony. Most likely they would finally succeed in exiling him as they had intended to do years ago. As much as Michael hated James he knew he could not allow that to happen. So he put aside his bitterness and cloaked himself with the teachings of Jesus and granted James the mercy he begged for.

"James, will you renew your promise to me, to keep your knowledge about New Mene'ah to yourself, as you have done for these past twelve years?"

"I will. I promise. I swear," said James rather desperately.

"I am here for my son and to retrieve the Elrey'ah wah Mene'ah that was stolen from me," said Michael. "I am not here for revenge."

"Wait a minute!" said Gabriel. "Don't I get any say in this at all?" Michael answered, " 'Fraid not son." Gabriel did not like that answer. Then Michael turned to James and said quite seriously. "Say goodbye to Gabriel and get on the elevator. Go back up to your hotel room. God willing, we will never see each other again."

"Thank you, thank you Michael," repeated James, over and over.

"Go, before I change my mind," said Michael.

After he gave Gabriel a quick but heartfelt hug, James hurried over to the elevator and pressed the button. As he waited for the elevator he quickly turned and shouted, "Michael, is Lune'ah OK?"

"They patched her up." Michael answered. "She's gonna be OK."

"Ah'men Mene'ah!" said James, relieved to know he had not killed his sister-in-law. The doors split open and he disappeared.

Then Michael looked at his newfound son, smiled and said, "Gabriel, how would you like to ride in a real flying saucer?"

Before returning to the safety and security of the secret city, the crew took a brief detour to the island of Sanctuary. Already knowing her answer, Michael wanted to encourage Luci'ah to come back with them to New Mene'ah. And Gabriel needed to say goodbye to Luci'ah, the only mother he had known since he was a toddler.

The hours in flight across the Pacific were spent in deep and steady conversation between Michael and his son. Michael told Gabriel about the amazing, excavated caverns and tunnels of New Mene'ah. Their home was a secret city of human citizens who came from a planet forty-three light-years away. He described the way Gabriel's mother and her sister saved both himself and James from the icy waters of the Antarctic ocean, and how he and his mother fell in love and got married. Michael was proud to see how bright and inquisitive his son had become. Gabriel told Michael about his life on the island of Sanctuary also. He looked deeply into Michael's eyes as they talked. Suddenly the boys blue eyes opened wide and he said, "I think I remember something. My dad...James, said something about a game of hide and seek. I think I remember that." They stopped talking for a while and just looked at each other smiling.

Gabriel thought it was pretty cool to be riding in a space ship. It didn't look like any space ship he had seen in the movies. He was fascinated with the advanced technology and wanted to know about everything. William was glad to give the inquisitive young man instructions and fill him in on the latest Mene'ahn technology.

Michael was right about Luci'ah. He could not convince her to go back to New Mene'ah. When they arrived safely on the island she told Gabriel how very sorry she was for everything, and he, of course, forgave her.

Gabriel gathered a few things from his room and asked if he could make a long distance call to Grace, who was in Paris studying art.

The strong feelings that he had always had for Grace now seemed to make more sense. She was *not* his sister. She was not even his half-sister. But she was his closest and dearest friend. He did not want to disappear, perhaps for many years, into a hidden city at the bottom of the earth, without saying goodbye to her.

Grace was sharing an eighteenth century apartment with three other young girls in a suburb of Paris, France. They were all students at La Parisianne, a prestigious school for gifted young artists. The phone rang at least eight times before Grace finally picked up the receiver, panting as if she had just run up a flight of stairs. "Bonjour" she huffed.

"Hey Gracie! It's me, Gabriel"

"Hi Babe! My goodness, I wasn't expecting a call from you today. Aren't you supposed to be in New York with your dad and Rahsheed?" Then she added breathlessly. "Gabe, I can't really talk right now. I'm running out the door with Cheryl. We're late for a class."

"I called to say goodbye, Gracie," said Gabriel.

"Goodbye? Where ya goin?" she asked.

"I can't really tell you, but I'm gonna be gone a long time."

"Hmmm, sounds mysterious. Well you be careful. Don't get into any trouble," Grace said lightheartedly. "I really gotta go now."

"There is something I just gotta tell you before I go," he said seriously.

"OK. What is it?" she said.

"I love you," said Gabriel, without hesitation.

"I love you too, you silly boy. I gotta run. I'll see you this Summer! Bye Babe!" and then she hung up.

Gabriel spoke privately, for a long time with Luci'ah. She had been a wonderful caring mother, almost to the point of obsession. The teenager was overwhelmed by the uncomfortable truth he had just learned. Together they cried and held hands. He embraced her affectionately and left her alone, sitting on her huge bed. He promised her that he would return some day.

All the men crammed back into the small colorful air craft and snapped and tightened their seat belts preparing for lift off. It was Ziggy that suggested a prayer before beginning that important journey home. They all lifted their hands and recited, *"Ah'men Mene'ah mon sa ha wah la she ha ' Mene'ah, Ah'men."* And then they were off!

When they arrived at the Southern-most part of the world, they hovered over the hidden city and watched through the monitors as a huge circular section of ice suddenly became a lake and instantly drained away to reveal the vehicle's landing pad, within the gaping hole. After the ship docked, the domed, ice ceiling was replaced as miraculously as it had disappeared.

Before long Michael was hurrying Gabriel through the catacombs of the hidden city to find Lune'ah. When they arrived at their apartment and sloshed open the doorway, she was there, alone, sitting in her floating chair. Michael had told his son about his mother's injuries. Still quite frail, she looked like an angel. She was not prepared to see her boy, looking more like a man, and happy tears began to stream down her flawless cheeks. Gabriel leaned down, and embraced her. Then she placed her delicate hands on each side of the boy's face and examined his features. "You look exactly like I pictured you in my mind." She turned to her husband, her face flushed, and said, "Thank you. Thank you, Michael, for bringing our son home."

"This place is amazing," Gabriel was bursting with excitement. "It's like a humongous ice cave, only it's not cold! And the ice, melts and freezes just like that," he said as he snapped his fingers. "It's very cool."

"You ain't seen nothin' yet, Son." Michael liked using the word "Son." "You know, Son, you have twin sisters you still need to meet."

"I know. Where are they?" he said as he pulled away from his mother's embrace to look around the apartment.

"Andre'ah and Indrah are at the lake. They are swimming. Just like Luci'ah and I, remember, Michael?" said Lune'ah. Then she reached up and held Michael's hand affectionately.

"Let's go and find them," Michael suggested. In the blink of an eye they were guiding Lune'ah in her hover chair through the curving hallways toward the lake. On their way they stopped for only a few seconds to admire the amazing water technology of the sparkling central elevator.

As Michael floated Lune'ah's chair down the hallways on the

second level of the colony, he remembered the first time he had seen the lake. It was a very long time ago. But he remembered like it was yesterday. He was pushing his friend James around in his anti-gravity chair and they were looking for their two beautiful nurses. That day they had watched as Lune'ah and Luci'ah dipped and swirled together, like mermaids dancing in the cool crystal clear waters of the lake, beautiful, graceful water-swans, synchronized below the surface. Michael's daughters shared their mother's love of the water and could often be found in the Great Salt Lake of New Mene'ah. And now his son Gabriel, was about to meet them for the very first time.

When they strolled up to the huge concave observation window and Gabriel saw the colorful formations and sea life below the surface, his jaw dropped. "Look over there" Michael said, as he pointed to the right where the girls were swimming deep beneath the surface of the water.

Andre'ah and Indrah were performing a water ballet under the rippling waves of the tropical lake. To Gabriel the whole framed scene looked like one of his video games. Schools of brightly colored tropical fish swam nearby apparently undisturbed by the girl's water dance. When the girls saw their father at the observation glass they swam right up to the window and waved. The twelve year old girls, in their skimpy, rippled teddies, and their small, perky little breasts, looked more mature than Gabriel was expecting. He thought his baby sisters would be "little" girls.

"Which one is which?" asked Gabriel.

"Impossible to tell from here, Son." Michael answered. "When they are dry, and talking to you, you can easily tell who's who, but now, look!" he pointed to the swimmers as they twirled together in a blur. "You can't even see where one ends and the other begins!" They all chuckled.

The light from the observation window outlined the finally reunited family in such a way that one could not be distinguished from the other. For a long time they watched the sisters and their exotic aquatic dance. As they watched, Lune'ah and Michael smiled and held on to each other tightly, with silent prayers of thanks to Mene'ah for the safe return of their son.

The story continues.
Watch for the sequel to

ICE *Angels*

coming soon.